NOBLE BRUNO

THE LONELY HEROES SERIES - BOOK 8

SAM E. KRAEMER

ALSO BY SAM E. KRAEMER

On The Rocks

(Forbidden Romance)

Whiskey Dreams

Ima-GIN-ation

Absinthe Minded

The Men of Memphis Blues

(Sports Romance)

Kim & Skip (Prequel)

Cash & Cary

Dori & Sonny

May/December Hearts Collection

(Age Gap Romance)

A Wise Heart

Heart of Stone

Weighting...

(Cowboy Romance)

Weighting For Love

Weighting For Laughter

Weighting For A Lifetime

Weighting... Complete Series Boxset

Elves After Dark & Dawn

(Urban Fantasy / Holiday Romance)

My Jingle Bell Heart (Christmas)

Georgie's Eggcellent Adventure (Easter)

Standalone Books

The Secrets We Whisper To The Bees

(Crime & Mystery)

Sinners' Redemption

(Priest & Ex-con Forbidden Romance)

Unbreak Him

(Dark Romance)

Holiday Gamble

(Christmas Romance)

This book is an original work of fiction. Names, characters, places, incidents, and events are either the product of the author's imagination or used fictitiously. Any resemblance to actual persons, living or dead, business establishments, events, or locales is entirely coincidental.

Copyright © 2022 by Sam E. Kraemer
Cover Design and Formatting: Arden O'Keefe, KSL Designs
Editor: Beau LeFebvre, Alphabitz Editing
Proofreader: Mildred Jordan, I Love Books Proofreading
Published by Kaye Klub Publishing 2022

These characters are the author's original creations, and the events herein are the author's sole property. All rights reserved. No part of this book may be reproduced, scanned, or distributed in any form, printed or electronic, without the express permission of the author. Please do not participate in or encourage piracy of copyrighted materials in violation of the author's rights. Purchase only authorized editions.

All products/brand names mentioned in this work of fiction are registered trademarks owned by their respective holders/corporations/owners. No trademark infringement intended.

THEIR STORY

What's more important to a man with noble intentions—the fate of innocents or the love of his life?

Bruno Garvin is in love with his husband. Trouble is, Dominic Mazzola was never supposed to be his husband. Their fake wedding was Dom's passive/aggressive way of showing his mother that denying Dom's sexuality didn't make it untrue.

Dom's less than thrilled to find himself legally married to Bruno Garvin—who has disappeared—when he receives an official marriage license from the Recorder's Office in Kentucky where they tied the fake knot with their friends on New Year's Eve. It was never supposed to be legalized, but with Bruno gone, Dom has no idea what to do about it.

During his undercover assignment in the enemy camp, Bruno resolves himself that he's going to try to find a way to win Dominic's heart, but when the traitor in their midst—the man he's seen meeting more than once with Francesco Mangello in Italy—is finally identified, Bruno is completely unsure of what to do with the information. Should he inform the Torrente family so they can bring the traitor to justice, hurting the man he loves in the process or will he keep the horrible secret in hopes of keeping Dominic for the rest of his life?

This work of fiction is approximately 86,000 words in length and ends with an H-E-A. It is book eight in "The Lonely Heroes" series. It is recommended that the series be read in the order released.

A FEW WORDS OF THANKS

I'd like to take a moment to thank my team—Arden, Beau, and Mildred. Without them, I would never be able to tell my stories and put them out for your entertainment. I appreciate all of the work that goes into these books, and I'm sure I don't tell you three enough, but I am indebted to you for your dedication and hard work on behalf of my stories.

I'd like to thank my patrons on Patreon for their interest in what I publish and "how the sausage gets made!" I offer future book ideas, exclusive excerpts, and first-look cover reveals. If you'd like to become a patron, go to Sam's Patreon and choose your level!

Finally, I'd like to thank my family for their support and listening ears. I can't tell you how much it means to me that I have you in my corner.

I truly hope you enjoy "Noble Bruno!"

BRUNO GARVIN
JANUARY 1, 2021

My wedding... I knew it wasn't real, but I wanted it to be. I wanted someone of my own to look at me like I was his hero.

Seeing everyone say "I do" had me believing it was a possibility... A dream come true. *It's okay to believe it's real,* I told myself. I believed Dominic and I were a real couple with plans for the future, and I was excited for it.

In my heart, though, I knew better than to think dreams could come true. They never had before, so why would they now? Like the dumb guy I'd been all my life, I still held out hope. I'd been so lonely for as long as I could remember...

Judge Caffrey had been a really nice man about everything involved with the midnight weddings. After the ceremony, Dominic had checked his phone to make sure he had the video footage he'd wanted to send to his mother of the two of us "getting married." I wasn't so sure it was the best idea, but I'd already fallen in love with Dominic, so I went along with what he wanted. I was pretty sure I always would.

Dom had then taken a picture of one of the signed wedding licenses before folding both of them up and shoving them into the pocket of his jeans. He'd explained to the judge that it was a practical joke he was playing on his mother—a family tradition for New Year's—and Judge Caffrey had only laughed.

After we'd all danced outside in the falling snow, me holding Dom for maybe the only time in my life, we'd gone inside and had had some of the dessert that Parker had made earlier that day. When Judge Caffrey, Justice, and Benny Jack had started to leave, I'd dragged Dominic with me to speak to them.

"Justice, thank you so much for letting me use your truck and stealing your Christmas lights. I'll return them in the morning and leave those tubs on your porch. Thanks for coming, by the way." We shook hands with them before Dominic stepped over to thank Justice and Benny Jack.

I turned to Judge Caffrey. "So, the copies of our marriage license—what would happen if one mistakenly got mailed to the State?"

Judge Caffrey had chuckled. "Well, then, you boys would be legally married. Are ya sure you just wanted to do this as a prank?" Everything inside me said no...

I ROLLED over to see Dominic sleeping like a baby in the other bed in our room at Smokey's lake house, so I slid out of mine and tip-toed over to his jeans that were tossed over the bench at the end of his bed, and I felt around in the pockets until I found the marriage licenses. I carried them into the bathroom and closed the door, taking a seat on the floor as I looked at the documents.

We'd both signed our names at the bottom of those papers. There were two copies each signed by Judge Caffrey and Raleigh and Ben as our witnesses. Shouldn't I have one for myself as a souvenir? I had a ring on my finger that matched the one on Willow's, as I'd always remember Dominic—graceful and beautiful. When we'd danced in the snow, I'd pretended it was our first dance as husbands, and I watched his every move. In my heart it would be that way forever.

I woke an hour after Willow had climbed on top of me in drunken confusion and passed out, me gently rolling him to the other side of my bed and holding him in my arms for a few hours. I woke to noises downstairs, so I got up and pulled on a pair of jeans to go check it out.

When I got down to the kitchen, I saw Mateo standing by the sink with a glass of water. I knew the front door had been left open for the couples staying in the campers to get inside if they needed anything, so I wasn't surprised.

"You okay, Mateo?" I asked. He'd told me not to call him *sir*, so I didn't. I called him what everyone else did, even though it didn't feel right to me.

"I thought about what you said when we went on our walk earlier—about the fact nobody in Italy knows who you are. We need to talk..." Mateo stated, so I followed him outside.

When I came back inside, mind made up, I grabbed a few things from the room I shared with Dom and watched him sleep for a minute. I stopped in Smokey's kitchen and went to the computer on the desk in the corner to look up the proper address and scribble it on the front of a piece of printer paper. I didn't second guess myself like I did about most everything I'd done in my life.

"Okay. I've texted the information to you. You'll be picked up at the airport in Rome, and Tommy will help you get some more clothes when you get there. Rafe will be coming over next week, so text me anything you need specifically from your place in New York, and I'll see that he brings it with him," Mateo instructed.

I nodded as I pulled on my coat. "I have a favor..."

I left the lake house an hour later with assurances from Mateo that he'd see Dom got back to New York in one piece, I had one goal... Protect those in Dom's family from any and all threats with my life.

June

1

BRUNO

"That way," I shouted as I pointed in the general direction opposite the way in which Duke Chambers had just run as we hid out beside the garden at Pietro Mangello's large estate in Venice. I even fired my gun in the air to scare the guard dogs from his scent as I pissed on the ground to try to mask it. I was only guessing if it would work. It was something my granddaddy back in Wyoming had told me when I was a boy to ward off wolves from the herd we ran on our thousand-fifty acres of Wyoming grassland.

Something must have worked because the German Shepherd trackers that Frankie had acquired then took off in the other direction with the German men who had trained them and brought them to Venice. That night, Duke would make it away from Pietro's compound without injury—except for the knot on his head where I'd knocked him out with my gun. His escape was a huge relief to me.

It was the weekend of Mateo and Shay's Italian wedding party, so everyone was at the family vineyard in Siena. Duke had come to check in with me because I'd lost my phone and couldn't remember the number I was supposed to use to check in with Tommy Torrente, my contact while I was undercover with Mangello.

I'd been hunting for my phone in the woods many times at

Pietro's large compound where we were all staying, but finally, I gave up and bought a cheap, disposable one in town a week earlier.

My time in Italy had been interesting—unlike anything I ever thought I'd experience in my life. To say I wasn't the same Bruno Garvin I'd been when Gabby had hired me after I quit my job at The Bone Yard wasn't strong enough.

Back then, I needed to leave my job as a bouncer at the gay club because the temptation to kill Jeffrey Oswald with my bare hands was nearly overwhelming when I watched the way he treated the dancers and the wait staff. I wasn't passed doing that yet, but I'd found a family with Gabby, Smokey, Nemo—especially Nemo and Ben—and all of the other people who worked at GEA-A, along with their families.

Protecting them was the reason why I'd asked Mateo to send me to Italy. I'd figured that if I could get into the Mangello organization, I could better insure the large Torrente family would be safe, and thankfully, Tommy Torrente had helped me set it up. A phony altercation with a Torrente guard got me an introduction to Frankie Man's head of security, Antonio Ricci.

After a background check confirmed for Tony that I was a former prospect for an outlaw motorcycle club, which was in my arrest record, along with my gun charges from Georgia, I was hired. It all seemed to be exactly what Tony wanted to see in a guard, and none of it was a lie. He'd decided I'd done things I really hadn't, but when he asked if I'd ever killed a man, I had an honest answer for him… yes.

I didn't like lying to anyone because a person had to remember their lies or they caught up to you and got you in trouble. That was why I'd requested that I was forced to lie as little as possible. Mateo had agreed with my terms, though he'd added a condition.

Giuseppe had insisted that the Torrente name be scrubbed from my police records as my place of employment, along with my place of birth in the event someone decided to go hunt down my family to investigate my story, and thanks to Casper and Mateo, I was a man without a home or parents. It didn't hurt my feelings, either.

Nowhere in the records did it mention that I was now a married man in the eyes of the law in Kentucky if not in the spirit of love. By now, Dominic knew what I'd done regarding our fake wedding on New Year's Eve. I was certain my husband hadn't been thrilled when he'd received the official marriage certificate from the Commonwealth of Kentucky. It had been a spur of the moment decision to ask Mateo to mail the application, and I would never regret it, but I had a feeling that if Dominic ever saw me again, he'd probably shoot me.

We hadn't consummated the marriage, unfortunately, so it would be easy to undo. I'd already talked to the lawyer from my gun case in Georgia, and he'd told me it was all a matter of paperwork.

I wasn't looking forward to that day, so until then, when I went to sleep in my apartment in Rome near GEA-I every night, I whispered *"Goodnight. I love you"* to the darkness in the hope that somehow, if there really were angels, one of them would whisper it into Willow's ear.

The next morning after Duke's unscheduled visit, the guards searched the grounds, and thankfully, the dogs picked up strange scents here and there, but nothing that could be traced through the woods. Once we could report the all-clear, we went back to the building where we slept on cots at Pietro's compound. It was like the cowboy bunkhouse on Rita and Yance Colson's ranch, but not nearly as nice.

The building where we were staying had been a machine shed during the time when the compound was a vineyard. The vines had long since died, or so I'd been told by Tony Ricci.

Now, Francesco was hiding out in the vintner's cottage at the back of the compound, having sent his wife, Rosa, to their apartment in Chiasso, Switzerland, just over the Italian border—and out of the reach of the Italian authorities if he were ever caught doing something less than legal. I really had to wonder at their definition of *legal*.

More weapons had arrived, along with men who looked like they knew how to use them. I wasn't sure what we were preparing for because I couldn't speak Italian, which was the only thing Giuseppe and his employees hadn't been able to hammer into my thick skull while I was with them.

As I worked with those people in Venice, I'd written down words I'd heard them say—words I could halfway spell but wouldn't remember. When I had a minute alone, I texted them to Tommy Torrente from the second cheap phone I'd picked up during a trip to the store with the cook—a phone that couldn't be traced to anyone as far as I knew because Tommy never texted me back. It was something Giuseppe had said was a smart thing to do, and I'd listened to everything he'd told me.

None of us were supposed to have phones, so I had to hide one in my dirty clothes bag—nobody was going near that stuff—and the other in a small hole in the wall where I'd seen a mouse come and go. One of the boards was loose, so I slid it into the hole when I didn't have it with me. The hole was under my cot, so I hoped nobody would go under there and look. If anyone got hurt because I'd acted stupid, I had no idea what I'd do.

I was assigned to walk the midnight watch, so I took my firearm and met for the debriefing, not that I understood what any of them said. One guy, Aldo Berlusconi, was one of the other guards I was usually partnered with, but the third guy was always a newbie.

We met up with the teams of guards we were relieving, and the team lead, a man everyone called Nardo, began rattling off something in Italian. *"Vigneto Torrente ospita il matrimonio di Mateo,"* the guy said. All I understood was Torrente and Mateo.

Aldo shrugged before he replied, *"Quando?" That* I understood. *When?*

"*Domani,*" the guy answered.

I looked at Aldo for instructions. "Be ready to move out in the morning," he explained.

"Where are we going?" I asked, feeling the hairs on the back of my neck stand up.

"Siena," Aldo answered.

That wouldn't be good at all.

July

2

DOMINIC MAZZOLA

The plane ride to Florence and then the subsequent limo ride to Siena with my mother and sister had been hell on earth. The news that my father was trying to reconcile with Mom had me pissed after everything that had come out during the divorce. He was a lying, cheating asshole, and during the proceedings, Mom had sworn she'd never take him back, but suddenly, he was the fucking love of her life? *Are you fucking kidding me!*

Mom had been having my father over for Sunday dinners and to spend the night, telling me that not only was I *not* gay, but I was to apologize to my father for all of the disrespectful things I'd said about him during the divorce—all the times I said he was nothing but a shithead douchebag who didn't give a goddamn about his family—and fix our father/son relationship.

At that point, I really wanted to jump out of the fucking plane over the Atlantic Ocean. Unfortunately, all of my coworkers were going to be at the wedding, and I was family, so I needed to be there, as well. I was determined to tough out the ride and get lost in the crowd when we arrived in Siena.

While there, I spent as much time isolated from the family as they'd allow, but the morning of the wedding, I couldn't hide out any longer. I got up early and went down to the swimming pool to put in a few laps in hopes of working off the tension that had caused my back to seize up like my spine was made of titanium.

"Dominic! Dominic!" I stopped in the middle of the pool and lifted my goggles, unhappy to see it was my mother.

"Why aren't you getting ready for breakfast?" Mom nagged.

"Why are you sleeping with Dad again?" I snapped back at her, no respect in my tone at all because Lucia Mazzola had used up all of my admiration.

I'd been born with a silver spoon in my mouth, and it was about to choke me. It was time I made my own way in the world, and I had the tools at my disposal to do so—looks, a career that would bring me as much ass as I wanted, and a family who loved me—not the one that was listed on my birth certificate, either. I didn't need the bullshit from my parents' mistake of a marriage to hold me back any longer.

I didn't realize that Nonna Grace was sitting under an arbor on the patio with her morning coffee. "*What?* What is this?" Nonna asked as she stood and walked over to where Mom was standing, hand on her hip like I remembered from a million other times. Nonna wasn't one to be trifled with, that was for sure.

"Mama, butt out of this. Giovanni is the kids' father, and he wants to have a relationship with his children—*all* of his children," Mom retorted before she glanced at me.

I laughed. "No thanks."

"What's wrong with you? You'd abandon your family over what? What's the problem you have with your father? The girls are happy to have him back in their lives, and if you'd stop this damn charade that you're gay like Gabriele, we could be a happy family again," Mom speculated.

"*Cazzate!*" Nonna protested. *Bullshit!*

"*Mama!*" Mom hissed at her.

I reached up around my neck and pulled the chain and ring down from where it was choking me. That was my other problem—based on the document I'd received from the Commonwealth of Kentucky; I was now a legally married man.

I'd met Bruno Garvin when we were sharing an apartment, and there was something about the man I liked. He was a simple guy—probably my exact opposite—but he was a man of integrity. I got the impression he'd grown up much differently than me, but he was kind and he was honest, so I knew he'd go along with the annulment. He had to agree that we weren't exactly marriage material—though, the man made me feel things I'd never felt before in my life with nothing more than a glance in my direction. It was very discomfiting.

My mother had ignored the photos and video I'd sent her on New Year's Day, and when I'd mentioned the marriage during the limo ride out to Siena, Mom had laughed at me and called me a drama queen, claiming I'd staged that, too, just to piss her off. That made my sister crack up.

"Dominic, I know you're taunting me with this wedding business. There is no way you'd shame the family by marrying a man. Now, stop being such a drama queen and behave yourself," Mom insisted.

Ava, my teenage sister, cracked up. "My god, Mom—listen to yourself! We are going to Cousin Mateo's wedding where he's marrying a man*! Geez, I'm beginning to wonder if any male in this whole damn family is straight!" Ava joked, which made me laugh. We did seem to have more than our share of queers in the Torrente bloodline.*

"I'll tell you who is straight—your father. He's straight and you are just like him, son. You need to call him, Dominic, and apologize for not taking his repeated calls. He loves you and wants our family to be whole, and for you to work at Mazzola Shipping as you were meant to do. None of that includes a husband for anyone except Ava and Gina," my mother stated, her hands flailing about in the limo. I knew it was useless to even try to make her understand.

"Does the fact Daddy doesn't leave until Monday morning mean the two of you are fucking again?" my sister blurted out, dodging my mother's hand as it reached out to slap her face. After that, we all went to neutral corners until we arrived at the vineyard.

I swam to the ladder at the other end of the pool and turned to see Mom storming up the stairs to the veranda. "What is wrong with her? Is your father sniffing around again?" Nonna asked.

I wrapped the towel around my waist and sat down at the black wrought-iron table with my grandmother, who poured me an espresso and placed an almond biscotti on my saucer.

"Corner Ava and ask her what's going on. She called me a few weeks ago and told me that Mom's been having Giovanni over for Sunday dinners to spend time with her, and he's not leaving until the next morning. I guess when Gina came home from Berkeley for the summer, she finally caved and joined them for dinner a few Sundays ago, so now she's on board with the grand Mazzola family plan that we all enjoy the fruits of the Mazzola Shipping Company and put on the show that Gio has a dedicated family. I, however, refuse to have the man in my life," I insisted as I sipped my drink.

"What's that ring around your neck, Dominic? Do you have an *amante*?" Nonna asked, her gentle smile reminding me there were people who actually loved me.

Hell, if I couldn't tell Nonna about what I'd done, I'd never be able to tell anyone. "Actually, I find myself with a *marito*," I responded in Italian, offering her a careful smile.

"*Che cosa?*" Nonna gasped. *What?*

Before I could explain further that it was only temporary because Bruno and I weren't meant to be together, my little sister Ava came flouncing down the stairs to the pool and dove in.

I held my finger to my lips for Nonna, who nodded and smiled as we continued to enjoy our morning together while Ava swam her laps. There would be plenty of time to talk to Nonna about Bruno, but I wasn't sure what to really say about him since I thought we weren't exactly marriage material—and damn that little voice in the back of my head that kept telling me I was being short sighted.

I also had no idea where the beautiful man had gone after he'd snuck off in the wee hours of the morning on New Year's Day, nor did I know if he was ever returning to New York. Hell, for all I knew, he wasn't planning to come back to me at all—though, that was probably for the best.

"You *are* coming back to San Francisco over the summer, aren't you? I'll tell Gabriele that I want you home, and he'll fire you," Mom threatened.

"No, you won't, but more importantly, Mom, no *he* won't. I'm a member of the team, and whether you believe it or not, I have obligations to keep," I insisted as I rose from my seat at the table we were sharing with Nonna and Nonno Tomas at breakfast later that morning.

I'd heard enough, so I politely excused myself and traversed the path to Tio Luigi's house where I was staying to avoid the family fray. I'd been helping Uncle Lu in the wine cellar, hauling the wine for the wedding over to the vineyard for him in the rickshaw delivery truck he'd used for decades around the property.

Luigi hand-picked the bottles from the family's private cellar, and I was only too happy to spend time with him while he did it, listening to his stories of when he worked with the vines as a boy, helping Bisnonno Lorenzo harvest the grapes. He explained that the sons were taught how to test the grapes for ripeness and how sweet the grapes should be when they were at their peak for fermentation. He also told me about puking after eating too many grapes, and we had a good laugh about it.

The time spent with Tio Lu reminded me of how simple life could be for some, though I'd never experienced it. I'd grown up in a family where it was important to present to the outside world that my parents had money and we—their offspring—were expected to look and behave a certain way. The impression of others was far more important that what we thought of each other. It was completely fucked up, and it seemed their disastrous relationship was back on, much to my dismay.

I wondered if I told Uncle Gabe or even Uncle Giuseppe about the bullshit my father used to spout about the family and how they were all weaklings... nothing but blowhard fags who liked to pretend they were important... would either of them do anything to make Giovanni shut his mouth? If given the chance, would I?

I decided to skip the wedding reception that night, having been at the first one which was much more enjoyable. I wondered if my fond memories had anything to do with Bruno being with me in Kentucky at the time and how incredibly mixed up I felt about him. I didn't let my mind wander too far down that path.

I turned on an action movie after bringing a bottle of Chianti and a glass to my room to drink the night away. Just as the super villain disrupted traffic on Fifth Avenue, I heard a clanging on my balcony before an intruder stepped into my room through the open French doors, scaring the fuck out of me. "Who the fuck is it?"

I didn't have a gun with me, of course, so I grabbed the lamp from the nightstand and hopped up from the bed, grateful I was wearing shorts and a t-shirt. When the intruder peeled off the face covering before I swung the lamp, I stopped in my tracks. It was the last person I expected to see in Siena—my accidentally legal husband.

I put the lamp on the bed and stomped over to him. "You've got a lot of fucking nerve. What the hell do you think—"

"*Shh!* I'm sorry to scare you," Bruno whispered as he placed the rifle he was carrying on the floor and stepped further inside, pulling the drapes closed so we weren't visible to anyone from the outside.

Oh, I'd waited for my chance to unload on him. "What the fuck are you doing here? Where did you go, goddammit! You left me in fucking *Kentucky*, Bruno. You didn't tell me anything, and then, the next fucking thing I know, I get a—"

Suddenly, I was swept into strong arms, and my mouth was crushed by Bruno's, shocking the hell out of me and taking my breath away at the same time. His kiss... His touch... His muscular chest made my mind fuzzy to the point I couldn't stop my tongue from swirling with his or my arms from circling his strong shoulders. His mouth tasted like cinnamon, and his short, soft beard brushed my chin in the most enticing way.

My mind was out of control, and when he softened the kiss and brushed his lips over mine a few times, I held onto him before he finally pulled back a few inches, looking deeply into my eyes. "I'm sorry, Willow. I'm sorry I left you, but there was something I needed to do, and it couldn't wait," he whispered as he released me to step back. In that moment, he sounded like a damn superhero.

"What couldn't wait, Bruno? Why couldn't you wait to talk to me the next morning? What the hell are you doing here in Italy? I hate to tell you this, but somehow the paperwork for our fake marriage license got sent in with everyone else's. I made Parker call the judge, and he said he had no idea what happened. We're married now. Like, for *real* married," I explained to him, looking at his face for any reaction—shock, fear, happiness... nothing.

"I... I don't know what to say," he answered, looking down at the floor before his hands began to open and close in a staccato beat.

"Wait a minute. You *do* know what happened, don't you? I worked with Gunter when I was training here, and he taught me all about deceptive body language. You're giving all the tells," I snapped at him as I made a gesture down his body with my hands.

He seemed to shift from foot to foot but no words came out of his mouth. I wanted him to panic like I'd been since I'd received that damn paper, but he didn't look flustered at all—maybe just a little uneasy about my next move.

"Bruno, we don't have those kind of feelings for each other, and you know it. Hell, we barely know each other, and now, we're fucking married," I growled, wanting to scream at him. It was the most absurd thing in the world that I found myself married to someone I barely knew—someone who I was nonetheless attracted to beyond reason. That pissed me off even more as I stood there staring at him.

I was a once-and-done kind of guy after an attempt at dating a pastry chef who dumped me flat after my first month in New York. I had a lot of hooking up in my future, and suddenly developing feelings for a kid—and that was exactly what Bruno was to me—was nowhere in my game plan. I was still trying like hell to get Uncle Gabe to take me seriously as an operative. I had no time for feelings.

Bruno hung his head before he looked at me again. He was a wall of a man, and he had the sorriest look on his face I'd ever seen in my life. "Yeah, it was stupid, and I'm sorry. I mailed in the marriage license myself without telling you. I guess I hoped—well, that doesn't really matter. I should be back in New York in a couple of months and then we can get an annulment. If you want to date someone while I'm gone, that's fine," he offered.

A gush of air left my lungs as I contemplated his words, and I began coughing. "Have you lost your fucking mind? I don't date and have no—"

A loud knock on the huge wooden door echoed through my room, so I pointed for Bruno to go behind the heavy blue velvet drapes. Once he was hidden, I walked over to the door and opened it, surprised to see Tio Lu's son, Tommy.

"Everything okay?" he asked, carefully scanning my room.

"Yeah, why?" I responded as he pinpointed his stare to the bottom of the drapes. I glanced behind me to see a pair of black high-top sneakers were visible before Bruno dramatically stepped from behind the curtains, his handsome face glowing like a neon light and making my chest tight. He had me so fucking hamstrung...

"Hey, Tommy," Bruno greeted sheepishly.

"You better get back down there. Frankie's men are leaving, and if they can't find you, your cover will be blown and you won't be safe, *amico mio*," Tommy insisted.

"What cover? What the fuck are you two talking about?" I demanded. Of course, both of them were ignoring my rants.

"You're getting the texts, right?" Bruno asked him quietly, a sense of urgency in his voice.

"*Sì*, but here. Take this one and destroy the other ones you have. This one I can trace if I don't hear from you. Just don't let them get ahold of it. Did your other phone ever turn up? If someone finds it, you'll need to get out of there *di fretta*. Nathaniel is able to track this one, and I don't want to take any chances that they have anyone on their payroll who's half as good a hacker," Tommy explained, handing Bruno a new cell phone before he looked at me.

"Everyone is leaving tomorrow. You'll need to pack and be ready to go early," Tommy commanded.

I stood my ground. "No! I'm not going anywhere until you two tell me what the fuck is going on! Where does he need to get out of in a hurry?" It was time I did a little commanding of my own.

We heard a few shots in the distance, and I saw Bruno freeze. "I gotta go. Like I said, I'll sign the papers and pay for the annulment when I get back to New York. I'm sorry," he stated.

Bruno stepped closer and leaned in as if he was going to kiss my lips—which I found myself wanting more than anything in the world. At the last minute, he leaned to the left and grazed his lips over my cheek.

"I won't kiss your lips again unless you ask me to. I'll see you in New York, Willow," Bruno whispered before he disappeared out the balcony doors, taking my heart with him, I feared. I turned to quiz Tommy, but he was gone, as well.

Bruno was in Italy on a job for Giuseppe that involved the enemy? What the fuck did they have Bruno doing, and how much danger was he in by doing it? I needed to talk to Uncle Gabe. I didn't like what was happening at all. It was my family, and it should have been me doing it.

I stuck around for two more days, searching everywhere for my cousin, Tommy, to find out what the hell was going on. Maurice Depew, one of Uncle Giuseppe's operatives I'd gotten to know from my time in Rome, had given me the highlights of what had happened at the reception.

Frankie Man had dropped by to pay his respects and likely try to kill my whole family, but for some reason, he'd left after a discussion with the older Torrente brothers, though nobody knew what was said. Frankie's appearance in Siena was why Bruno had shown up in my room unannounced and had scared the fuck out of me. I was still trying to reconcile why I'd been so damn glad to see him.

I was in the fermentation warehouse to say goodbye to Tio Lu when I saw Tommy behind one of the large silver tanks. He was with a woman in a red dress with a huge black hat blocking her face, and the two of them were in a heated discussion before Tommy pulled her into his arms and sealed her mouth with a kiss. *At least one of us is straight!*

I started to leave the warehouse through the door where I'd entered when the back door slammed and Tommy headed in the opposite direction. I rushed toward him and slid in front of him, stopping the man in his tracks. "Who was that?"

Tommy jumped at my sudden appearance, surprising me that he'd been so distracted. "*Bastardo! Mi hai spaventato a morte!*" I smirked at his protesting. *I was a bastard, and I'd scared the shit out of him. Ha!*

"Yeah, well, who the fuck was that? A kissing cousin?" I countered, pointing to the spot where I'd seen him kissing the woman.

"*That* was none of your business," Tommy growled.

"Wrong. I have a reason to be involved in whatever is going on, Tommy. Where's Bruno? Tell me what the fuck is happening," I insisted.

Tommy chuckled. "Why do you care about Bruno? Aren't you looking to get out of your sham of a marriage as soon as possible? Do you want him dead so you don't have to deal with him? I could make it happen."

"How do you know about my sham of a marriage?" I asked, not even addressing his veiled threat at killing a friend... who I'd married.

Tommy took my arm and led me out of the warehouse and down into the garden. "There are no secrets among comrades, *Cugino*. Tell me, you're not falling in love with Bruno, are you?" *Love?* I didn't think I'd call it love, though I was definitely attracted to the man. A lustful attraction, but not love.

"Don't divert, Tommy. You didn't answer my question regarding who that person was you were kissing in the fermentation room behind the tanks," I countered.

Tommy sighed. "That's our contact into Frankie Man's organization. Now, are you packed and ready to go? You definitely need to leave."

I wasn't exactly thrilled to leave Siena, but I had a feeling I'd get more answers in New York than I'd get in Italy. I needed to know what they had Bruno doing—obviously some sort of undercover bullshit. For reasons I didn't want to consider, I was suddenly very worried about his safety.

Everything I'd learned during my time in Italy while I was training with Uncle G's people and handling the tech work made me realize that the Mangello family was extremely dangerous. Bruno was still wet behind the ears and far from prepared to handle a group of mobsters. I should be the one fighting for my family, not the big teddy bear.

August

3

BRUNO

After the invasion at the Torrente vineyard the night of Mateo and Shay's wedding party the previous month, everyone from GEA-A left Italy, which gave me a bit of relief from worrying about Willow's safety. He was back in New York with Gabe and Duke, and he had people to turn to if someone tried to harm him.

Guns had been fired that night of the party, but I didn't know who had done the shooting. Thankfully, no one was injured, which was a miracle.

I'd received word from Tommy that Giuseppe wanted me to leave my position with the Mangellos, but I was determined to figure out when Frankie was going to go after Searcy and Dylan so I could warn everyone to ensure the family was ready. I couldn't let Frankie's people go in by surprise. I had to put a stop to it before anyone got hurt by mistake.

The last time I'd seen any of the Torrentes—Willow—Tony and the other guards who had accompanied Frankie on the trip had been at the reception. I'd been climbing the drainpipe outside of Dominic's room where Tommy had directed me when I'd found him outside the tasting room at the vineyard.

From what I'd heard through the retelling of events by members of the Mangello guard, Frankie and Giuseppe had had a discussion. What I hadn't heard was what they'd talked about, so I was hoping to find someone who'd been there in person to ask for more information. I was worried that too much interest on my part might tip off someone that I was there for other reasons besides protecting Frankie, so I hadn't pushed it—yet.

We had gone back to Venice for a week before returning to Frankie Man's home in Rome, and it seemed we were all in a holding pattern. I was walking the perimeter of the property as Tony Ricci had ordered, still trying to put things together in my mind about how Frankie's people found out about the wedding party in the first place. We were still on alert, but nobody had given me a reason why.

The radio on my hip sputtered to life. "Bruno? *Copia*?"

It was Tony, so I reached for it, sliding my rifle behind my back. "Copy--*copia*," I answered him.

"Report to the guard shack for the midnight shift. You'll be working with Dante," Tony ordered.

"Who's Dante?" I responded, not remembering having heard the name since I'd started working for the Mangello family months ago.

"Dante Barba is one of our guards. He's been away because of a family emergency. He's at the front gate guard station, so go there to meet him. Don't upset him, Bruno. He is quick to temper and quite dangerous when he's angry," Tony advised.

"*Copia*," I answered as I jogged across the property to the front security checkpoint.

A visitor had to be on the guest list generated by Frankie's assistant, Daniela. It was based on Frankie's calendar for the day, and if a person wasn't on the list, they weren't allowed onto the property, regardless of who they claimed to be.

I'd worked at the service gate at the back entrance to the estate once, and I'd hated it because it was so boring. I'd told Tony the same, and he'd laughed before he had said I wouldn't be asked to do it again. Maybe since it was the front gate, it wouldn't be such a dull assignment? I hoped not.

I arrived at the check point just as a fancy black sedan with tinted windows went through the open gate. I'd seen it on the property before, but I didn't know who owned it. "Dante Barba! It's me, Bruno Garvin," I greeted him a few feet from the guardhouse to keep from getting shot.

"Ah! My new partner for the evening," he greeted me. Having someone to talk to that night made the time go by much faster than it had when I'd worked the service gate alone, so I didn't mind at all.

The next few nights I worked with Dante had been quite enjoyable, and I'd liked getting to know him. He was about the same height as Willow, though Dante was more muscular where my husband was strong without the bulk. Dante had long brown hair, dark like mine, and he wore it in a bun like Ace Hampton did sometimes. He had brown eyes with nicely groomed eyebrows, and he moved like a dancer—much like Dexter.

We chatted about growing up. "My mother was an American. She married my father, a builder here in Italy. I'm sure she didn't know he was a mean drunk when she married him," Dante explained.

I didn't chuckle at his comment. "I know the feeling. My father was the same way," I answered.

"I trained with the *Carabiniere*—the Italian special police force—but I resigned after a few years because it seemed like dangerous work. A friend of mine set me up with a job, and I ended up working here. Much safer, I believe," Dante stated as we chatted away into the wee hours of the morning. I was coming to think maybe Tony didn't know Dante as well as he seemed to believe. The man appeared to be a gentle soul to me.

The next night, I walked up to the guard shack to see Dante texting on a smartphone, which was forbidden at the estate. The sound of my boots on the sidewalk seemed to catch his attention, and he quickly slid the phone into a pocket of his tactical pants.

"Bruno! It's so good to see you again, my friend. I understand we are to be paired permanently to work the guardhouse on the midnight shift. I just got here myself," Dante explained.

The LED lighting inside the little building was dim, but as I looked at Dante, I could swear I saw some sparkles on his eyelids. He sort of glowed in the light, which seemed odd. "How's your night been?" I asked him.

"It was great. I met a friend for dinner and it carried over a bit. I was almost late for work. How about you?" he asked me, the shimmer over his eyes catching my attention when he moved his head in a certain way. I noticed he seemed to be in a really good mood, and it made me glad for him. He'd been a little sad when I first met him, but I hoped maybe things were going better, whatever his problems might be.

"After I woke up, I listened to a lesson on an Italian-language app. I'm trying to learn the language, but I'm a slow learner," I admitted to him. I wasn't ashamed that I learned things slower than others, just as Ben had told me I shouldn't be. I wished he was around to help me like he'd done with my reading when we were in DC.

There was a concern about what my co-workers at GEA-A had been told about my absence? I hadn't spoken to any of them when they were in Italy—except my husband, and I couldn't say that had gone well. I truly missed having people—friends—to talk to about things I was familiar with, but I didn't really trust anyone who worked for Mangello, though maybe that was changing now since I'd met Dante?

"Slow compared to who? Don't judge yourself by other people. I learned that a long time ago. Something tells me you're a good guy. I think I can trust you with a secret. Wanna step outside?" Dante asked me as he pointed to the grass next to the guard shack.

I wasn't sure if it was a test or not, but something in his sparkly eyes told me that he wasn't going to hurt me. I hoped to heck I was right.

I stepped out of the shack, leaving my gun inside. Dante did the same. "Do you mind lifting your shirt? There are eyes and ears everywhere. Always remember that," he stated. It was good advice that Nemo had taught me when I was looking out for Ben.

I lifted my black t-shirt and spun slowly for him to see I wasn't wearing a listening device. "Now you," I demanded in return, which seemed prudent.

When Dante lifted his t-shirt, I was surprised to see a lacy tank top under it. It was a very light pink color and had pale green satin ribbons down the front. Dante slowly turned as well, and even though he was wearing the garment, I could see that he wasn't wearing a wire, either.

"So, now you know my secret," Dante stated, which confused me.

"I— I'm not sure what you mean," I answered him. When he dropped his tac pants to show me some pretty panties that matched his top, I was even more confused.

"I, uh, I'm sorry, Dante, but I'm married," I told him, worried he was interested in me. I'd told Dom to date if he wanted, but that didn't mean I would. I loved him, and he would always be the one for me.

Dante laughed. "Bruno, I'm ace—asexual. I'm just showing you the matching panties, not trying to seduce you."

"Oh! Sorry. That's really nice. Is it comfortable?" I asked him. The top looked okay, but those panties looked really confining.

Dante chuckled. "You really are a one-of-a-kind sort of guy, Bruno, just like I heard. I'm enby," Dante explained—or he thought he did, but I had no idea what he meant. Was it his ethnicity? He was handsome and probably thirty, but I didn't know where he was from.

"Where is Enby?" I asked him.

Dante laughed again. "Not a place, Bruno. It's my gender identity. I'm non-binary. It means I don't identify as male or female. My pronouns are 'they and them.' I had dinner with my sister and a good friend of hers today, and I didn't have time to take off my makeup before I had to be here. Luckily, I called the security office to clock in and didn't see Tony," he explained as he pointed to his eyes which I'd already noticed looked pretty. "Will you snitch?" Dante asked as we both redressed.

I smirked at him, glad he trusted me. "Snitches get stitches," I joked. Dante and I both cracked up at my comment.

Thankfully, Ben had been instrumental in helping me understand pronouns, though we hadn't talked in great detail about non-binary folks—mostly trans people because there was a trans woman in the House of Representatives that he respected. I was happy that Dante had explained their identity enough for me to understand it so I didn't offend them.

Back to business. "Who was in that car that drove through when I was coming on shift a few minutes ago?" I asked them.

"Uh, his name was Mr. Vanni. He's here to see Frankie, why?" Dante asked me as he glanced at a clipboard where people had to sign the sheet that was attached from the security office.

"The car looked familiar, but I guess there are probably thousands of black luxury sedans in town," I answered. Dante chuckled, which was a nice, pleasant sound.

The phone rang in the booth, so Dante hurried inside, ending our discussion. "Barba," they answered.

I stepped into the guard shack and sat down behind the desk. I logged into the laptop and pulled up the guest list to see if there was anything more to be found about Mr. Vanni. I found his name on the list along with his plate number, which I discreetly wrote down on a piece of paper and slipped into the pocket of my tac pants while Dante was preoccupied with his call. I'd send it to Tommy when I had access to my phone again.

My nerves started to increase as Dante silently listened to the caller, still holding the phone to their ear. They turned around to look at me and held a finger up to their lips. "Sure. He stepped out to use the restroom. I'll tell him when he gets back, Tony."

Dante hung up the receiver and turned to me with a big grin. "Tony said one of the groundskeepers found a phone in the woods in Venice. Did you lose a phone?"

My stomach clenched as I wondered how to answer them. Finally, Dante shook their head a bit. "The answer is always *no*. Never, ever let them think they have anything on you. Go to the house and put on your poker face. Deny, deny, and if they don't believe you, run like hell."

I nodded and headed toward the house at a slow jog. I reached into the small pocket by my waist and pulled out the cheap wedding ring I kept on me at all times. I slipped it on my left finger because if I was going to die, I wanted it there. My dying thought would be of Willow.

I'd had a shining moment in my life when I'd married a wonderful man and had been lucky enough to get to kiss his lips a few times. If that was all I was meant to have, then so be it.

4

DOMINIC

"Golden Elite Associates. Dominic speaking," I answered the ringing phone. Corby had left GEA-A to start his own garage, and Gabe hadn't hired anyone to take his place, which sucked for me as low man on the roster.

Corby hadn't really warmed up to the job at GEA-A, or so I understood, so he'd decided to do something he enjoyed—working on cars. Hell, it was something I could never do, so I admired the guy for his skills.

He seemed like good people, but I didn't know him all that well, even though we'd both spent the night in that fucking bunker downstairs. Those were memories I didn't want to relive. Maybe I could get Duke or Ace's permission to call him and go out for a beer? *Goddamn, I need some friends.*

"*Cugino!* It's Mateo," my cousin greeted. Thank god we'd dropped the premise of being a wedding photography and videography business. That was a fucking joke if ever there was one. Of course, that was all Gabby could come up with at the time to explain to Dr. Westphal—the previous owner of the Victorian—what our business was about when he was trying to rent the space. I definitely could have come up with something a hell of a lot more believable, no doubt.

Mateo and Shay were in the Seychelles for their honeymoon, and now that Duke was running GEA-A, I was back to square one regarding being sent out on cases—or so Uncle Gabe had said when I quizzed him about it.

"You'll have to convince Duke you're ready to go out on cases, Dom. Teo and I have put him in charge of scheduling, so state your case to him."

I could have spit nails in two. "You sent me to Italy to train to be a security operative, and I did. I came back here to do just that when I could have stayed in Italy and done the same work for Uncle G. I'm just as good as Nemo, Smokey... Hell, even you!" I snapped at him. Of course, he only laughed in my face and walked away.

I'd been fit to be tied after that and had to work hard not to hold a grudge for his smartass attitude. They sent Bruno, a kid, to do a man's job in Italy. What the fuck did he have that they seemed to think I didn't?

"Hey. How's the honeymoon?" I asked Mateo, not that I really gave a fuck after recent events.

"It's been fantastic, though I have sunburn on parts I never wanted to sunburn, if you know what I mean," Mateo joked. That almost brought a laugh from me, thinking about him sunburning his dick, but I wouldn't give him the satisfaction of thinking he was funny.

"Uncle Gabe is out. Duke and Mathis are on kid duty. They were taking Dylan and Searcy out to Long Island to Nonna's for the weekend. It's actually boring as hell around here," I complained to him because it seemed to be falling on deaf ears with Duke.

We weren't taking new cases, and most of the operatives were enjoying some time off, so it was just me in the office. Hell, I was tempted to just put the phones to voicemail and take time off myself because I'd been, once again, relegated to the reception desk, and it was driving me up the wall.

"Yes, well, everyone's staying in touch, right? School starts next week, so everyone will be back in the office. Enjoy the down time while you have it. We have a lot of things coming up this fall, so no worries. How's Duke doing at the helm?" Mateo asked me.

I'd heard secondhand how it was discovered that Duke Chambers was my mother's half-brother. Mom officially blew a gasket, which I was sure was fun to witness, though I was glad to have been spared the drama. Ava had called me to bitch about Mom's freak out the whole way across the ocean, and I was so fucking glad I'd dodged that bullet of going back with them.

"Not much to helm right now, but he seems to be settling in. Tonight's the re-opening of Blue Plate, so Ace and Smokey are at the restaurant helping Parker and Rafe with last minute stuff. How'd you get out of not being here for the event?" I asked him.

I wasn't looking forward to going to another family event alone. I always felt fucking pathetic as I sat with all of the happy couples. The good thing was my parents wouldn't be coming. Mom had said she was too traumatized from the night the restaurant blew up, and Jesus Christ himself couldn't get her to go back to that place. That, right there, should have been a good enough reason for me to be excited to attend the party.

"Trust me, my brother isn't happy with me at the moment for not attending. I'll make it up to Rafe when we return to the States. So, have you talked to your *marito*?" the fucker taunted me about Bruno —my husband.

"No, jackass. Have *you* spoken to him?" I questioned. Then something occurred to me—I hadn't told anyone we were actually married, though Tommy knew about it. How the fuck—

"How do you know Bruno and I are married? That thing we did at the lake was for fun. It was just a fucking *joke*!" I snapped at Mateo.

Mateo's low-pitched laugh tickled my ear. "*Sì*, it was a joke until I did Noble a favor—"

"Noble? Who the fuck is Noble?" I asked, wondering if Shay had literally fucked Mateo's brains out.

"Bruno—you're husband. He *is* a noble man, Dominic, and I'm surprised someone as intelligent as you hasn't noticed. Look, he's working for Frankie Man on behalf of the family. We know that Frankie is going to come after his brothers at some point over the vineyard property. Papa and Tio Lu agreed to have a meeting with

Frankie about a proper settlement, which is how Papa got them to leave the party. They haven't agreed on a date, and if Papa has his way they never will," Mateo informed me.

"You mean *that's* what Bruno's doing? He's *spying* on Francesco for Uncle Giuseppe—for the family? I should have been the one... How could you have sent him there? He's too innocent to be put in *that position!*" I snapped at Mateo.

"*I* didn't send him there, Dominic. Bruno *volunteered* to go. Since he's been there, we've confirmed that Frankie knows Dylan and Searcy are his grandchildren, and he plans to take them. That's why Duke is still on kid duty. Gabriele doesn't trust anyone but his brother with his children's lives, not even himself. Duke would take a bullet for those two, and Gabe knows it," Mateo further enlightened me.

"Why did Bruno volunteer to go on a suicide mission?" I asked as the probability of him dying if he were found out to be working for Uncle Giuseppe suddenly hit me like a baseball bat to the groin.

Mateo sighed. "He wanted to impress you, Dom. He cares about you, and he wants you to see that he'll do anything for you and your family. Like I said, he's a noble man. Think about that before you do anything about your marriage. I'm the one who put the license in the mail for him, so if you need someone to blame, blame me for not talking him out of it."

I didn't even answer him. I hung up the phone in anger and sat there, staring out the window until it was time to go home to the empty apartment I had shared with Bruno before he lost his mind and infiltrated the enemy camp.

After work, I showered before putting on a black suit and calling a rideshare to take me to Blue Plate for the grand re-opening. Thankfully, I was seated at the table with Duke, Ace, Corby, Nemo, and Ben, who I didn't know were flying in from D.C. for the party.

The restaurant, which was decorated in the fashion of a 1950s diner—the floor was black and white tile while the walls were painted robin's egg blue and covered in hundreds of decorative dinner plates. There were booths with blue vinyl seats and chrome edging, and it all fit together really well.

The restaurant had a more modern style before the explosion, but now that Parker was a partner in the place, Rafe had encouraged him to design the décor to his liking. According to Smokey, Parker had wanted a kitschier feel to it this time—one that reminded him of his mother's kitchen when he was a kid. It was a completely unique property in the Bianco Restaurant Group.

"Hey, congrats on finding a garage to work at. Duke mentioned you were doing really well there," I made small talk—which I despised. Corby was a nice guy, though, so I made the effort.

"Thanks. I hope Duke told you that if you need your car worked on, I'm giving a discount to friends and family," Corby offered.

I'd had to lean in because he spoke so softly—nothing like Shay. "I don't actually have a car, but after I sort some things out, I'd like to get one. Maybe you could help me find one?" I suggested.

"Sure, you'd help him, wouldn't you, Little Fox?" Ace stated, placing his hand across the back of the blue vinyl chair and hugging Corby to him. Corby's neck flushed and then the heat climbed up to his face, turning his cheeks a bright red, which reminded me too much of Bruno when his face flushed at being embarrassed. Fuck if I didn't miss the hell out of him and that had me pissed off immediately.

What the fuck was wrong with me? Bruno would make some guy a good husband someday, but I wasn't that guy. I had wild oats to sow, and a future to secure at GEA-A. I wasn't in the market for the fucking picket fence and a dog like the other operatives at GEA-A all seemed to crave. I needed to go out and find someone to take my mind off Bruno Garvin.

As the evening wore on, I was able to scoot over to Ben's empty chair while he went to the men's room. I pecked Nemo on the shoulder to get his attention from his discussion with Smokey. As Nemo turned to talk to me, a tall guy walked up to the table.

"What's up, Beaver?" Nemo asked me, a big grin on his face at using that stupid nickname. *Eager Beaver—I was a professional bodyguard, not some stupid "Jimmy Olson" wannabe!*

I pushed aside my anger at his comment and asked my question. "Have you heard from Bruno?"

"Yeah, where *is* Bruno? I have a hard time believing he'd miss this. He always thought you and Parker were the ideal couple," the stranger told Smokey.

I looked up to see a damn good-looking guy who was glancing around the restaurant, searching every face for one he wasn't going to find in the crowd. The man was slender like Parker, but he had shaggy, dirty-blond hair.

I didn't know who he was or why he was looking for Bruno, but I was about to find out as I slowly rose from my chair—that was, until Nemo jerked my arm hard enough to make my ass hit the chair.

Smokey chuckled. "Archer Huff, this is Dominic Mazzola. Dom, this is Archer, an old friend of Bruno and Parker's. Bruno stayed with him in Atlanta while he was on probation." Smokey voice had an air of sarcasm to it that I didn't understand.

He then looked at Archer with a smirk. "You had a little thing with the big guy, didn't ya?" Smokey seemed to tease the stranger. I felt the anger rise inside me like a volcano ready to explode.

Archer laughed and smacked Smokey on the shoulder. "Naw, but I wouldn't mind another shot at him. I'm single again, and Bruno is a hot young stud. No doubt he could get the job done," the guy commented like he was speaking of some whore who spent a lot of time on his back. *Bruno isn't a hunk of meat, you mother fucker!*

I started to get up again to kick the guy's ass, but Smokey stood between us and put his hand on Archer's back. "Let's go to the kitchen to see Parker. I don't think he knew for sure you were comin', did he?" Smokey quickly angled the guy toward the stainless doors leading into the kitchen.

Nemo put his big paw on my shoulder to get my attention. "I haven't talked to Bruno, but Tommy assured Gabby he's okay the last time they spoke. He's a gutsy guy to go into the... Well, I'm sure he'll be fine. Nothing to worry about," Nemo stated, definitely not making me feel any better.

In fact, my stomach began to roll at his comment that there was nothing to worry about. There was every fucking thing in the world to worry about, and as much as I continued to fight it, that world was beginning to revolve around Bruno Garvin.

LATER THAT NIGHT I returned home, let myself in, and headed toward Bruno's bedroom after arming the security system.

His door was closed but not locked, and I hadn't gone in there since he'd disappeared at New Year's. Was it crazy the room had been empty for eight months and I'd never bothered to look inside? The voice in my head said yes, but then it offered that if I'd gone in there and all of Bruno's things were gone as if he never intended to come back, my heart would shatter.

I'd brought his backpack home with me from Kentucky, stashing it in the coat closet in the entryway. I supposed I should have washed his things that were inside when I got back to New York, but I'd just tossed the bag inside and hadn't given it a second thought. I was such a selfish fucking prick sometimes. No, I was a fucking spoiled, self-entitled brat is what I was.

I'd grown up with money—my father's shipping business—and even though I had a job of my own that paid me well, I lived in an apartment that was paid for by my uncle. I'd never really had to worry about life's necessities because my parents always made sure I didn't have to. It was always right there for me without any effort on my part whatsoever, and that realization made my stomach turn. I wasn't a self-made man like Bruno was trying to be.

I was the product of a family who lived off the hard work of the generation before us. I'd never had to work hard a day in my life for anything. I'd gone to elite schools and graduated without much effort on my part. I was smart, and school came easy to me, but I knew it wasn't easy for everyone.

Bruno hadn't had it easy in school, and he didn't grow up the way I had. I knew about his dyslexia and a little bit about his childhood in

Wyoming because he'd sort of started to open up to me when we were in Kentucky. He'd been hesitant to share those private details with me, which was probably because he thought I was better than him and his life experiences would have me looking down my stuck-up nose at him. *Yeah, selfish prick covers it.*

I sat down on the side of his pristinely made bed, glancing at myself in the mirror of the dresser. I reached up to the neck of my dress shirt and pulled the chain from my undershirt and over my head. I looked at the cheap ring and wondered why in hell I'd kept it. To be honest, I was surprised it hadn't turned my finger green for the day and a half I'd worn it in Kentucky, but why I put it on a chain around my neck like it really meant something to me, I couldn't understand. Some things were beyond comprehension—but I'd never met a man like Bruno Garvin, and I couldn't get him out of my head.

5

BRUNO

I sat on a black padded bench outside of Frankie's office, waiting. My left leg was bouncing with nerves while my right hand drummed my fingers on my right thigh. I would have prayed if I believed in God, but I figured by then, all the bad things I'd done in my life would outweigh anything good, so I didn't bother. When the door opened and Tony stepped into the hall and motioned for me to enter, I whispered, "Goodbye, Willow. I love you," before I walked into the office, my thumb brushing over the wedding ring on my left hand.

Nardo had taken my rifle from me after a much too thorough pat down before I'd been allowed to enter the house. He'd probably figured out my boxer briefs were made with eight percent spandex by the time he was done.

Tony leaned toward my ear. "Be honest, and maybe you'll walk away with all your fingers, *idiota*." I probably was an idiot for volunteering for the assignment, but I wasn't sorry. If I died that night, I'd never be sorry for looking out for Willow's family.

I walked closer to the desk where Frankie Man was sitting, his hands resting flat on the desk in front of him. The man across from him was the same man I'd seen in Venice a few times. He was in his late forties, for sure, but he was a handsome man. He had dark hair with a few shimmers of gray at the sides by his ears, and his eyes were a nice brown that reminded me of someone, but I couldn't remember who.

"Bruno—what's your last name, *giovanotto*," Frankie asked like it was a trick question. *Young man? Not really.*

I turned to study the man with him to see he was smoking a skinny cigar and not really looking at me. He was dressed in a fancy black suit with a crisp white shirt and a red tie with a matching pocket square, as Maxi had taught me a fancy handkerchief in the front pocket of a suit jacket was called.

His legs were crossed at the knee and there was a sharp crease in his pant leg that pointed to the shiny black wingtips on his feet. His socks were red, too, which I found quite odd. The man was definitely handsome, and something about him tickled my brain, but I couldn't grab the thought to make it clearer in my mind. It was like a fly buzzing in front of my nose that I couldn't swat away.

Frankie cleared his throat, so I turned in his direction. "It's Garvin, sir," I answered Frankie.

Frankie nodded. "What were you doing here?" he asked. It was a test, so I answered as I had when Tony Ricci met me in that bar that night.

"*Parla italiano?*" *Tony asked. I shook my head. That was something that I'd learned from Giuseppe and Tommy—always say I didn't speak Italian. I didn't really, but I had picked up a little bit of the language, though I didn't admit it.*

"*Americano,*" *I answered. Tony scowled for a moment before he pulled out a stool for me to join him.*

I sat down and ordered when the bartender stepped forward, "*Peroni.*"

Tony held up two fingers before he turned to me. "*What brings you to Roma? You dropped that man like a sack of flour,*" *he commented, referring to the guy I'd just punched after he slapped the waitress.*

It was all a scheme to gain an introduction to Tony Ricci, which I owed Tommy Torrente for helping set up. There was no other way to casually meet the man who was the head of security for Francesco Mangello, so Tommy and I came up with the plan together.

"I didn't like being on probation, and he made me angry when he slapped the lady. As long as I stay under the radar over here, I can live my life without the cops looking over my shoulder every five minutes," I answered as I'd practiced with Tommy.

"Probation? You got into trouble in the States? What's your full name?" Tony asked.

"I'm Bruno Garvin. I'm on probation for possessing a gun without a license in Georgia. I got tired of being in Georgia so I came here to look for a job," I answered, feeling my hands begin to sweat. When the bartender placed the green bottles on the bar, I picked up mine to feel the coolness on my right palm as my left rubbed on the fabric of my jeans.

"Really? Did you fire that gun?" Tony asked. I nodded as I took another drink.

"Did you fire that gun at someone?" he pursued. I nodded again as I set the empty bottle on the bar. Tony motioned for the bartender again and signaled for two more beers.

I looked around the bar to see it was full and nobody was looking at me, which was a relief. "I did, sir, but why do you care about that? What's your name?" I asked, which I should have asked earlier even though I knew who he was. He was my target, but I wondered if I looked stupid for not asking his name sooner.

Tony chuckled. "I just might be your new boss. I'm Tony Ricci and my date stood me up. It was lucky I decided to wait a few more minutes for Daniela so I could see you in action. Tell me, Bruno Garvin, have you ever killed someone?"

I nodded.

"I was done with being on probation in the States, sir. I wanted a change of scenery," I answered, hoping I was holding up my end of the conversation like Ben and I had practiced when he was helping me with my reading. I generally tried to blend into the woodwork like I did as a kid, but everything was different now. I had to keep their attention on me. I didn't want to give them anything to be suspicious of so they'd start looking deeper into my history and find a connection to the Torrentes.

Tony stepped forward and held up my old cell phone. "Is this yours?"

I was never so relieved to see the screen was shattered. "I don't have a phone," I answered.

Tony snickered. "Really? Aldo said you mentioned losing a phone in the woods in Venice when the dogs were chasing you."

A chill went up my spine at his mention of those dogs, but if I ever wanted to see my Willow again, I had to keep myself together. "Those sweet dogs? They never chased me. I mean, I took them for a run in the forest when the trainer was taking a nap, but I got along with the dogs. I grew up with dogs back in Wyoming," I added, stretching the truth a bit.

We didn't have dogs on the ranch. My father hated dogs as much as he'd hated me, the *fag*—a word I despised—of the family.

"So that's not your phone, then?" Frankie asked as he pointed toward the device in Tony's hand.

"No, sir," I answered, standing with my hands behind my back so they couldn't see how much they were shaking. I'd been stupid enough to mention it to Aldo the night I lost it, but I hadn't thought he was paying attention to me. That was my mistake.

"Okay, Bruno," Frankie answered. He then looked at Tony and nodded his head. Tony went to a door I hadn't noticed and opened it, stepping inside. He returned, pushing a desk chair, and I was surprised to see Aldo was tied to it with silver tape over his mouth. I squeezed my hands into fists to keep from moving.

Tony ripped off the tape from Aldo's mouth and looked at him. "Try again. Is this your phone?"

"*No! È suo!*" Aldo answered as he motioned his head toward me before Tony pulled out a gun with a suppressor attached and shot him in the forehead.

I inhaled a deep breath, smelling the gunpowder in the air as Aldo's head fell forward and blood trickled down his nose from the hole the bullet had made while the back of his head—brain, skin, and bone—was splattered against the tan wall behind him, sliding down slowly while my stomach turned over ten times. Thankfully, I was able to stay still and calm.

"He said you were a spy for the Torrente scum, but I believe he was lying. He was the spy. If I was wrong, you'll meet the same fate, Bruno," Tony told me as he studied me carefully. I didn't flinch.

I swallowed down the minestrone soup I'd had for dinner to keep it from reappearing right there on Frankie's fancy rug. The mysterious man sitting in the burgundy leather chair to my right chuckled but didn't say anything to me, which fueled my nerves even more.

For some reason, I noticed the man was wearing bright red socks and had a golden ring on his pinky finger that had a fancy design engraved onto the flat top of it, but I couldn't make it out, so I stopped looking. I didn't want him to think I was paying extra attention to him. That behavior could get someone killed.

"Bruno, my friend, take the rest of the night off. Take *that* with you on your way out," Tony ordered as he pointed to the desk chair where Aldo was slumped over, blood still dripping onto his lap.

I walked over to the chair and placed my hands on the back of the disgusting cushion that was caked with blood and something gooey that must have been part of Aldo's brains, wishing I was wearing gloves so I didn't have to feel the debris as I pushed the chair toward the door without looking down again. I couldn't help being grateful it wasn't my brains splattered all over that room.

I was having a hard time breathing, but I knew I couldn't break down. When I'd shot Kyle Jeffries in the head, I'd done it because he was trying to hurt Parker Howzer and Archer Huff. As far as I knew, Aldo Berlusconi was just trying to survive like me. The guilt at his death would haunt me for a long time.

I pushed the chair out of Frankie's office, not sure what to do with it. I headed toward the front door where Nardo was standing, seeing his face turn as white as I was sure mine was. I nodded in the direction of the door, and he opened it for me so I could maneuver the desk chair down the stairs and the walkway, stopping at the guard house.

"Can you open the gate?" I asked Dante, who was still inside the guard shack. He looked up, shock and fear crossing his face as he stared at the dead man in the chair.

Finally, Dante pressed the button to open the automatic gate, and I pushed the chair down the driveway and onto the sidewalk outside the large black entrance, walking it about a mile away from the estate into a park with a duck pond. I took off my work shirt and put it over Aldo's head in case any kids showed up there and discovered him before the police, and I pushed his corpse into the bushes away from the pond and the playground.

I found some leaves and wiped off the back of the black chair in an attempt to erase my fingerprints. There wasn't anything I could really do for Aldo beyond that. I headed back to the estate, passing the gate and continuing down the road to my apartment a few miles away in my undershirt.

Climbing the stairs to my door slowly, I wasn't surprised to find it off the hinges. The place was a huge mess, so I decided my cover was probably blown. I truly wondered why Tony hadn't shot me, too, after I searched through my few belongings and discovered my burner phone was missing.

I grabbed a shirt from the floor and slipped it on before I walked out of my place and down the block to the *posteggio dei taxi*. When the black vehicle stopped, I got into it and directed the driver to Giuseppe's home in the garden district so I could pick up my passport.

My time in Italy was at an end. I hoped Dante survived there; I'd come to like them very much.

When I knocked on the door of Giuseppe's home in Rome, it was nearly two in the morning. There was no guard station or gate to keep out visitors, but there were cameras everywhere. When Maria, the housekeeper, opened the door, I wasn't surprised she knew it was me. "Signore Garvin," she greeted as she took my hand and led me inside.

During the taxi ride over to the beautiful house with the pretty gardens, I'd cried, but I wasn't really sure why. The cab driver seemed to freak out a little, but thankfully, I had some euros in my wallet, so I could pay the fare and then some to coax him to take me all the way.

"Hi, ma'am. Is Signore Torrente home?" I asked her.

She led me into the kitchen without a word, which made me wonder if she spoke any English, but when she picked up the phone on the desk in the corner, she rattled off a lot of Italian too quickly for me to begin to try to understand.

She hung up the phone and turned to me. "*Affamato?*" she asked as she made a motion with her hands as if she was holding food to her mouth.

"Oh, uh, no. No, thank you," I replied, sure she was asking if I was hungry.

She went about getting me a glass of water before she started to put a kettle on the stove. She turned on the gas burner and busied herself getting ingredients together for what I was assuming was espresso or cappuccino.

Suddenly, a man burst into the kitchen and startled me. I reached for the gun I'd been used to carrying, only to find it wasn't there. Thankfully, the man wasn't armed either.

"Bruno! *Stai bene?*" Rafael Bianco greeted me with a big grin. He walked over to the seat where I was sitting and pulled me up, hugging me as he kissed both of my cheeks, asking if I was okay.

I nodded. "I'm fine."

He gently pushed me away by my shoulders and held me there, a look of concern crossed his face. "What's wrong?"

"Is Mateo here?" I asked him.

"No. Shay and he are in the Seychelles for their honeymoon. Let me show you to a bedroom. We can talk there. Papa's not here right now," Rafael informed me before he turned to Maria, offering her instructions in Italian. She nodded, turning off the burner under the kettle.

"Come on, Bruno," Rafael invited, leading me up the back stairs outside the kitchen.

He took me to one of the bedrooms in the large home, opening the door and turning on the lights. The two of us went inside, and Rafael directed me to the bed where he gently pushed me to sit on the side.

He untied my boots and slipped them off my feet before he sat down next to me. "What happened tonight?" Rafael asked, his tone hinted that he wasn't going to deal with any nonsense or stalling I might try to offer.

"Tony Ricci killed a man tonight because of me. Aldo didn't have to die," I stated as I sat there, feeling completely worthless, a cold chill working its way through my body like I hadn't felt since I was a kid and my father had shown me that he was in charge, just like Tony Ricci had done earlier.

"Explain to me what happened. Leave nothing out," Rafael pressed, so I did.

I told him about Aldo and the not-great relationship we'd had while I worked for Frankie. I explained my mistake of losing my phone in the woods, and I gave him details about the mysterious man I'd seen at the compound in Venice.

Finally, I informed him about what had happened at Frankie's home earlier that night. I didn't mention Dante because I wasn't sure what to make of them. They'd been kind to me, and I didn't want to put them in harm's way for no reason.

"The man in Frankie's office, did he have anything unusual that you would recognize easily if you saw him again? Did he speak with an Italian accent? Did he have any scars or tattoos?" Rafael asked.

"He didn't speak at all, and I didn't look too closely at him, but I noticed he was wearing red socks that matched his tie and pocket square, and there was a gold ring on his pinky," I answered him as honestly as I could remember.

Rafael nodded. "Sleep. I'll still be here in the morning, and we can talk before I return to New York for the grand opening of Blue Plate next week."

"I don't think I can leave here yet because I haven't found out what Frankie is planning. How did he know everyone was coming to Italy for Mateo's wedding?" I insisted.

Rafael stepped forward and pushed me onto my back, swinging my legs up onto the bed. "We'll talk about it tomorrow. Sleep now, Bruno. Teo is right—you are a noble man," he whispered as my mind went blank and my eyes closed.

6

DOMINIC

I was sure the anger emanating from my body was palpable to anyone who walked in the kitchen at the Victorian as I stood there staring at Duke. *I was a Torrente!* Well, I was a Mazzola, but I had Torrente blood coursing through my veins just like the man in front of me. I was a trained professional, just like him, and what he'd just asked me to do had me seething. "I seriously don't want to work at the reception desk." It was said through gritted teeth that Monday morning after the grand opening party at Blue Plate on Friday night.

"Come on, Dom. This is a group effort. I'd do it if I didn't have other things that needed my attention." Duke lied so easily. He truly was a Torrente, the dick. I'd heard from my father my whole life that the Torrentes were nothing but liars. I was almost coming to believe he'd been telling the truth.

"A—no you wouldn't, and B—when will I get to start going out on cases? Mateo said he'd assign me to one, and I don't want you getting in my way on this, or I'll quit and go to work for another security service. I'll start looking on Monster.com right now," I threatened.

Duke stared at me for a moment before he invited me into the office that had been Mateo's and Uncle Gabe's before they'd handed over the reins to Duke. Hell, Uncle Gabe's pictures of Dex and the kids were still on the desk. They should have installed a revolving door on the damn thing as much as people vacated that office at the first opportunity.

Instead of sitting at the desk, Duke walked over to the couch and sat down, patting the spot next to him like we were going to have a heart-to-heart.

"Come on. Take a seat," he asked when I simply stood next to the black leather monstrosity that I was sure many, many people had had sex on. Instead of sitting on the couch, I took one of the nearby chairs.

"I'd be careful sitting on that thing—people have sex there, you know," I pointed out to aggravate him.

Duke's face broke into a huge grin. "I know."

"Oh, god! Not you, too," I complained.

Duke let out a warm, happy laugh and shrugged his shoulders, which surprised the fuck out of me. "What happened to the miserable bastard who liked to kick ass in the gym and seemed to despise anyone with the name Torrente?" I asked him.

Duke laughed again, which was sort of fucking scary. There was a knock on the door that caught both of our attention. "Come in," Duke announced.

Ace opened the door and stepped inside. When he saw me sitting there, I was worried for a minute that he'd kick my ass because it was just the two of us, but then I remembered Duke was my cousin, and I skeeved myself out.

"I just wondered if you wanted to go to lunch with Little Fox and me. He's delivering a car to Shay's salon that he finished servicing, and I volunteered to pick him up and take him to lunch. You wanna come along?" Ace asked his partner.

Duke reached into his pocket and pulled out a set of keys, tossing them to Ace. "Naw, but thanks. You guys go ahead without me. Give Corby a kiss for me, will ya?" Duke asked.

"I'm gonna puke," I mumbled, hearing Duke and Ace laugh at me.

"Bitter, party of one," Ace announced as he blew Duke a kiss and stepped out of the room.

I glanced at my phone to see it was eleven in the morning. "They're going to lunch kinda early? Is that what you old guys do after you get into a relationship? Early bird specials?" I teased.

Duke smirked. "Corby is only a couple of years older than you, remember? They'll probably fu—have sex in the back of my SUV and then go eat. Ace had a headache last night. He has a very high sex drive, but he just wasn't up to it, so Corby and I—"

I held up my hand. "*Stop!* Don't need to hear it," I demanded.

"Fine. Let's talk. You don't want to be behind the reception desk, so help me find someone who does. You were Nemo's right hand, so help me find another receptionist—someone we can trust—and I'll reassign you," Duke assured.

I nodded. At least I had something to do instead of staring out the window and worrying about a man who had wedged himself into my heart with only one kiss.

I GOT HOME from work later that afternoon, leaving after Ace and Duke headed out. I stopped by the store to hit up the deli for a little premade food, and I settled in at the island with my laptop and dinner, perusing resumes on an employment agency's website that I'd signed us up for earlier in the afternoon.

I was eating my chef's salad when my phone rang. I picked it up to see an unknown number, so I sent it to voicemail and continued eating as I scrolled through the resumes of those who had been listed under the receptionist/greeter/office assistant category.

The boring task of reading everyone's accumulated skill set boiled down into bullet points nearly had me falling asleep as I chewed. Duke had mentioned finding someone who could type when I'd told him what I wanted to do, and then he smiled and got a weird look on his face, so I left him alone until he and Ace walked out holding hands about four o'clock.

I truly hated being the only single person in the office—though, Mathis Sinclair didn't seem to have a love life, just a life's mission, though I had no idea what it was.

My phone rang again, so I looked, seeing it was the same number. I started to push it to voicemail when a thought occurred to me—*what if it's Bruno?*

I quickly picked up the line. "Hello?" There was silence for a moment before a throat cleared.

"Dom? It's your dad," Gio answered.

Fuck! "What do *you* want?" I asked him, figuratively kicking myself for taking the call.

"I want to know why you won't talk to me. I've been racking my brain, trying to figure out what I did wrong *to you* that makes you hate me so much. Son, we used to get along so well, you and me. What's going on with you? You've changed so much since you moved to New York," Gio commented, the lying bastard.

I wanted to just tell him I was gay and get it over with, but I was such a chickenshit. After at least twenty seconds of silence, I settled on a response. "I grew up, Dad, and you and Mom seem to have trouble accepting it, plus, you didn't just cheat on Mom—you cheated on our whole family. If the girls can forgive you, good for them, but I'm not like the girls," I answered him honestly.

An all too familiar sigh echoed in my ear. "Is Mom there with you?" I questioned, thinking she'd been the one to put him up to the call in the first place.

"No. I'm actually not in San Francisco this week. I just wish you would talk to me. I love you, Dom. You're my son. I'm willing to accept that you're a grown man. I know I made mistakes with you, and I'd like the chance to make up for them," Dad explained.

No way was he ready for what I had to tell him. "Dad, I hate doing this over the phone, but you'll change your mind about wanting to make things up to me, so let's just get it over with right now—I'm gay," I admitted, preparing to hear the dial tone when he hung up on me.

There was silence for a moment, which told me mom had already told him my news. "I understand that, but you're still my son, Dominic. Your mama, she thinks she knows how I feel about such things, and I'll admit I haven't been open minded in the past, but if you tell me you're gay, then I'm willing to talk it out and listen to you. I'll do my best not to be a pig-headed asshole about it, okay? I want to understand, Dom. I want my son back in my life, and I want you to come work in my family's business, not the Torrentes." I actually heard a sniffle. *Did that come from Gio Mazzola?*

"Can I think about it? I'm not saying no, but I need to really think things through," I finally decided.

I'd rushed into something recently that definitely hadn't gone in my favor, so I was turning over a new leaf to think before I acted. The situation with my father was definitely one of those things to give a lot of consideration.

I WOKE THE NEXT MORNING, and I had a game plan. I would open a dialogue with my father through email. I didn't want to see him because I had a hard time getting my point across with my parents in person because they made me feel like I was still twelve when I was in their presence.

Putting things down in black and white would allow me time to organize my thoughts and make sure there was no way they could twist my words to suit their agenda as my mother was so great at doing.

When I arrived at the Victorian early that morning, I let myself in through the front door, hearing loud noises from the gym in the basement. I made my way to the stairs, rushing down to see Duke and Ace laughing as they worked out.

"Hey, Beaver! You wanna join us?" Ace asked, using that fucking nickname I hated. It made me think of Bruno and what *he'd* called me... Willow. I wanted to hear him whisper it into my ear again.

"When's Garvin coming back?" I asked Duke.

He stopped lifting the barbell he'd loaded with a lot of weight, securing it on the stand before he sat up. Ace tossed him a clean towel before he took a seat behind him.

"I'm not sure. He's currently out of touch. Is something wrong?" Duke asked me.

"No. We're roommates, and I just wanted to know if he was coming back or if I should get someone to share expenses and pack up his shit for storage. Nothing more, nothing less," I excused before I stormed back upstairs.

I sat down at the front desk and fired up the computer, beginning to type out the email I wanted to send to my father, ignoring the pain in my chest at the idea of putting Bruno's few possessions into a box as though he meant nothing to me. That wasn't really the case any longer.

From: Mazzola, Dominic dominic.mazzola@gea.a.com
To: GioMaz@MazShip.com
Date: 31.Aug.2022 07:12:32 AM
Subject: Father/Son relationship

Dad –

I decided to reach out this way to discuss things with you. I realize we've been out of communication for a while now, but Mom's a big part of that. She refuses to accept I'm gay and some other stuff, and I'm trying to keep negative energy out of my life right now.

I didn't just become gay when I got to New York and started living with Uncle Gabe. He's bisexual—FYI, even though he's married to Dexter. Anyway, unlike Mom believes, he didn't "turn" me gay. I'm able to finally live my life the way I want, and I'm not going back in the closet for anyone.

I started dating guys here, and I became more comfortable in my own skin. I'm not sure if you'll like hearing that, but that's the way it is.

If you're willing to try to get to know me as I am now, then I'd be willing to have a meal with you the next time you're in New York. I'm not coming back to San Francisco like Mom demanded—my home is here now, and someday, I hope to have a wonderful guy in my life to share it with me.

I do love you, but if you can't agree with my terms, then maybe we'll just have to let our relationship go. I'm not saying that to provoke you, but it's what would be better for both of us. Life is too short to live it in misery.

Your gay son,
Dom

September

7

BRUNO

"So, are you anxious to go home?" Gunter Schell asked me as he changed lanes. He was taking me to the airport where I was going to board a commercial flight back to New York. I hadn't been able to find any trace of the man I'd seen at Frankie's home in Rome the night Aldo was shot and I left the compound.

The license plate number I'd managed to get to Tommy came back as registered to a rental car agency, and while Nathaniel was nice and smart, all he was able to find out was that the driver's license used to rent the car had been a fake. That news had been very frustrating for me.

"I'm anxious to get home, but I feel as if I've failed Giuseppe. I didn't accomplish what I came here to do, and I wish I had more time," I answered, not going into detail with Gunter. He was a nice man and had been great with helping me refine my fighting skills while I was in Italy before I went into Frankie's organization, but what had been told to him about my assignment, I didn't know.

"Sometimes, my friend, it's better to step away and re-evaluate things. Giuseppe knows what he's doing. Don't worry," Gunter stated as he pulled up to the departures platform at the airport.

He shook my hand and popped the trunk, and I retrieved my duffel, waving to him from the curb before I went into the terminal to maneuver security and find my gate. I stopped at a kiosk and bought a magnet with the Colosseum on it. I had only driven by it a time or two, but if I ever got to come back to Italy, I wanted to take a tour. It was pretty cool from what I'd seen. Maybe Willow could… I really needed to stop thinking those things.

Another reason I wasn't in a hurry to get back to America was because it would be time for the two of us to get the marriage annulled. I wasn't looking forward to that part of going home at all.

I had time before my flight, so I sat down at a café outside of security and ordered an espresso. I'd gotten used to drinking it while I'd been in Italy, and I was sure it wouldn't taste the same when I got back to New York. It was one more memory to tuck away.

After my drink and biscotti were delivered, I placed the cookie in the cup and held onto it as I glanced around. I was sort of hypnotized by the number of people coming and going through the large airport. I wondered where they had come from and where they were going. Would there be people waiting for them at their destinations who had missed them, or were they leaving those people behind?

The sun was shining through the large windows near me, and as I continued to watch the people rushing around, I noticed a man and a woman kissing. He was holding her in his arms like she was precious to him, and it reminded me of the kiss I'd shared with Willow when I'd seen him in Siena. I wondered what he'd say to me when I showed up at our apartment. *Should I go to the apartment or to the Victorian?* Suddenly, my stomach was filled with nerves.

As I thought about what to do, the kissing couple stepped away, and I saw their faces, shocking me. It was Tommy Torrente and Daniela—I didn't know her last name, but I knew she was Frankie Man's assistant.

I tossed a few euros on the table for a tip and grabbed my duffel, following Tommy to the security line. I noticed Daniela hurry out the doors to the taxi line, and since I didn't want to alert her to where I was in case she reported that back to Frankie and Tony, I decided to follow Tommy.

I allowed a few people to go ahead of me, and I kept my sunglasses on, not that Tommy wouldn't recognize me. Thankfully, he was busy on his phone, so he wasn't looking around. I couldn't get my mind to slow down enough to consider the impossible—was Tommy the rat? Had he been feeding information to Daniela for her to tell Frankie? Was that how the Mangello organization knew the Torrentes were in Siena for Mateo's wedding party?

I watched him as he went through the body scanner and then when he collected his carryon bag and shoes from the conveyor belt before he went to a bench to sit down. Once I was through, I collected my things and after sliding my feet into my sneakers, I stood behind a post to watch Tommy as he leaned forward, resting his elbows on his knees. He was typing something into his phone before he looked around and stood, heading toward the departure gates.

I waited a few seconds and followed him, curious where he was going. Suddenly, I felt a strong hand on my bicep, squeezing hard. "Where do you think you're going? Don't turn around, just keep walking."

I was steered to a family bathroom and the door was opened before I was shoved inside. I fell on the floor, tripping over a foot, and when I scanned the coverall encased body in front of me, I was surprised to see my friend, Dante Barba.

"Dante," I greeted him. I didn't expect the gun he pulled from his pocket, but I had no idea what he planned to do to me. Maybe our friendship was only important to me?

I judged the distance between us and figured out I couldn't get to him before he shot me—especially with the suppressor on the end of the Glock in his hand.

"What are you going to do to me?" I finally asked. Seemed it was better to know my fate than be surprised.

"Who are you following?" Dante asked me.

My mind raced with the right answer. "I'm not following anyone.

I'm heading back to America," I finally answered. The white tiled bathroom echoed the sound of both of our heavy breathing.

"I thought you didn't want to go back to America," Dante challenged.

I started to get up from the floor, trying not to think about how dirty it might be, when Dante tutted at me. "Who were you following? I like you, Bruno. I don't want to do you harm."

"What are you doing here dressed like that?" I asked him instead.

"Looking out for a friend," Dante answered. He reached into the pocket of his coveralls and pulled out a syringe. "We can do this the hard way," he threatened.

"What are you gonna do, poison me?" I questioned him.

He looked at the syringe and chuckled. "No, I wouldn't poison you. I'll knock you out and take you somewhere I can question you. So why were you following my friend?" he asked.

"What friend?" I pushed him.

"If I tell you, I'll have no choice but to kill you. Do you really wanna know?" he asked.

"Look, I saw someone I thought I knew. He was kissing Daniela who works for Frankie, and I wanted to know where he was going," I finally answered. We could have been in that bathroom all dang day if one of us didn't give in.

"Why are you worried about who my sister is kissing?" Dante asked as he put the syringe back in his pocket, which was promising.

"Daniela is your sister?" I asked as I slowly stood. He kept the gun on me, so I didn't make any sudden moves.

"Yes. She is. That man she was kissing is her fiancé," Dante admitted.

I held up my hands and stepped a little closer to him. "Your sister is marrying Tommy Torrente? What does Frankie Man think about that?"

"Are you going to tell him?" Dante asked, raising the gun higher to take aim at my forehead.

"No. I left them. I thought you were sent here to kill me," I finally admitted.

Dante lowered the gun, thankfully, and pushed it inside his coveralls. "We need to talk. Let's get out of here. We need somewhere more private," he insisted.

He quickly took off his coveralls and shoved them into the large trash can in the bathroom before he opened the door. There was a janitor's cart in the way with a sign about the floor being slippery, so Dante scooted them out of the way and motioned for me to follow him out. I had no idea what was going to happen, but it felt too big not to go along with him.

We left the airport and Dante flagged a taxi, rattling off an address to the driver. He sped into traffic, and I felt a little better knowing Dante had left the gun in the bathroom at the airport. I didn't know if he had another, but I was willing to take that chance.

Fifteen minutes later, we pulled into a rough looking neighborhood. The street was covered in garbage and many of the buildings looked to be in disrepair. We got out of the taxi, which wasn't exactly what I wanted to do, and walked up the front steps to one of the worst looking buildings on the block.

"Whose place is this?" I asked Dante as he let us into the door of an apartment building that reminded me too much of the awful place where I lived when I first went to work at The Bone Yard.

The metal door was battered and rusty, and the lock appeared as if someone had tried to bust it more than once. The hallway had flickering fluorescent lights and smelled like rotting garbage, and I heard the squeaky sound that was solely made by rats.

"It's my safehouse. Not much to look at, but nobody from Mangello will come here looking for me," he stated as he unlocked the deadbolt and pushed open the door.

Dante stepped inside... "*Whoa!* It's me!" Dante announced as he lifted his hands into the air.

I shoved on the door and someone behind it hit the wall, making Dante laugh. I stepped inside and saw Daniela holding a gun by her side as she rubbed her shoulder with her left hand.

"Oh, sorry. I hope I didn't hurt you," I apologized to the woman.

She smiled at me. "Glad to know you're on our side, Bruno. Come on in and let's talk," Daniela insisted.

If she was engaged to Tommy and said she was on the same side as me, I hoped maybe the two of them could help me figure out who was going against us. I wasn't ready to throw in the towel just yet.

8

DOMINIC

"First day of school, huh? Are you excited?" I asked Dylan as I sat at Uncle Gabe's kitchen counter waiting for Duke to pick us up. I'd walked over to Gabe's that morning, unable to sleep well with everything I had crowded into my mind.

I was taking over for Sinclair on kid duty, and Dexter's apprentice yoga teacher was going to handle the phones when she wasn't teaching yoga classes. Dex had worked out Sabrina's schedule such that she didn't have classes until three in the afternoon, which was convenient. Gabe and he trusted Sabrina, who'd said she needed the extra money and had happily agreed to watch the phones. Myself, I was grateful to finally have a new assignment.

"Yeah. Did you like fifth grade?" Dyl asked as he got the milk from the fridge while Dexter made them pancakes.

I chuckled. "From what I remember about fifth grade, I wasn't a fan, but that's because my best friend had moved away over the summer, and I was going to a new middle school by myself," I explained. I had to wonder what Kyle Summers was doing these days. We'd been thick as thieves back in the day. Unfortunately, I'd never seen him again after his family moved to Seattle from San Francisco.

"Eat. Where's your sister?" Dex asked as he dumped four silver-dollar-sized pancakes on Dylan's plate.

I pushed the butter and syrup to the kid and looked at my cousin's husband. "You sure you're okay with me taking over for Sinclair?" I asked before taking a sip of my coffee.

"Are you..." Dex held up his thumb and finger and pointed toward me like a pistol.

I nodded, touching the shoulder holster on my left side through my suit jacket. I had finally received my private investigator's license from the State of New York, along with my concealed carry license, and I was part of the security detail to guard two of my favorite people in the world. I was looking forward to it.

My firearm of choice was a Ruger LCP II. It was lightweight, even with a full mag, and while it wasn't as powerful as the Sig Sauer that Nemo carried, I had no doubt it would be effective in stopping a threat. I had pretty damn good aim, as Duke had pointed out when he took me to the range to see how well I could shoot. I'd learned to safely handle a gun when I was a kid, and while I didn't hunt game, I enjoyed skeet and target shooting with Nonno Tomas on Long Island.

"Good. Don't spare the hardware if necessary," Dexter directed.

"What hardware?" Uncle Gabe asked as he brought Searcy downstairs with him.

Her hair was combed, and she was wearing a cute barrette that she kept pointing to as she stared at me. "That's very nice. Is it new?" I asked her.

"It is. Daddy got it for me as a surprise because I folded my own clothes from the laundry basket and put them away," Searcy bragged.

"Yes, and as long as you continue to help him with things around the house, you'll get nice treats on occasion, but not every day," Uncle Gabe reminded before he kissed her cheek and put her on the floor.

"I just want cash," Dylan announced, which made me chuckle.

"Are you saving for something special?" I asked him.

"A minibike," Dylan whispered to me.

"Shh," Gabe hissed at Dylan before he made funny eyes in Dex's direction, which had me laughing. If those two thought Dex didn't know everything that happened in his house, they were nuts.

The bell rang for the front door before it opened. There was no sound on the hardwood, so I stood and headed through the kitchen door toward the hallway, reaching under my shoulder for my Ruger when Magic ran by me, nearly knocking me on my ass.

"Hey, ya stupid mutt," Duke greeted the big black dog as he leaned forward and scratched it behind the ears while I struggled to regain my footing.

Duke glanced up to see me with my hand still under my arm. "You'll wanna be a little quicker next time, Beaver. Also, I doubt the bad guy would have a key to the house. Anyway, is everybody ready for the first day of school?" Duke's booming voice echoed off the walls of the entryway. His enthusiasm was unsettling because I'd never seen the guy as happy as he'd been lately.

I walked back into the kitchen, resisting the urge to put a muzzle on Magic out of spite because he made me look like a clumsy dumbass. I had the feeling Duke was scrutinizing every move I made since I was his new partner for the kids' protection detail. Hell, even *I* knew being slow on the draw wasn't a good reflection of my abilities to react under pressure. Of course, shooting him by mistake would have probably been worse.

After the kids had backpacks and lunches in their hands, we left to take them to school. I followed the protocol Smokey had taught me over the weekend—I went outside first and scrutinized the neighborhood, searching for any vehicles that didn't belong or any unfamiliar joggers or dog walkers. Apparently, there had been an issue with Maxi regarding a dog walker a couple of years back that taught them all a lesson in surveillance. Who knew?

When I was certain it was okay for the kids to come out, I waved to Duke, and he brought out Dylan and Searcy while I opened the doors to the backseat. Duke helped Searcy into her safety seat, and I covered Dylan while he got in on his side and buckled his seatbelt before I shut the door and stood outside the vehicle, continuing to observe the surroundings.

Once Duke was in the SUV and the motor was running, I hopped inside, and we were off to their private school, Mosby Academy, about a mile from Gabby and Dex's home. Everything went off without a hitch, and I was very proud of myself. I owed Smokey a steak dinner for running me through the paces.

"So, after school plan. You'll drive separately to the school—get Gabe's SUV because it has a safety seat for Searcy. You're taking her to Nana Irene's to make cookies, and I'm taking Dylan to football practice after I pick Gabe up at the Victorian," Duke instructed before he glanced in the rearview and continued.

"Make sure Irene sets the security alarm after Searcy gets there. She doesn't like to arm it because she forgets it's on and sets it off when she opens the door, but we're on orange alert as far as their safety is concerned," Duke stated quietly as he motioned to the back seat with his head. Thankfully, he'd directed the sound for the Radio Disney to the back of the vehicle so the kids couldn't hear us talking.

I was well aware of why we were on orange alert—it was because of the threat the Mangello family posed, which had me worrying about Bruno even more. I wanted him out of that mess as quickly as possible.

"Copy," I answered. I heard Duke chuckling next to me, so I gave him the finger where the kids couldn't see me. I was a professional investigator, and I'd paid attention to the other operatives to learn the ropes. I would follow the rules because if I didn't, someone could be injured or killed. That was the most important thing Uncle Gabe, Smokey, and Nemo had hammered into my hard head since I'd started working at GEA-A, and Uncle Giuseppe had emphasized it when I was in Rome, too. I wasn't stupid. Unclear instructions led to confusion, which led to shit I didn't want to think about.

Duke parked down the street from the school, and we both got out. I opened Dylan's door and took his backpack and lunch box so he could get out before the two of us went around to where Duke was freeing Searcy from her booster. Duke walked them inside while I waited outside, watching all of the parents bringing their kids for the first day of school with big smiles that the summer vacation was over and the kids were someone else's problem for seven hours a day.

Once Dyl and Searcy were safely settled, Duke returned, and the two of us hopped back inside the vehicle to go back to the office, or so I thought. Instead, Duke drove us to a coffee shop down the street. "Come on. I didn't have time to get anything this morning before I worked out and I'm starved." I never turned down food, so I followed him inside.

"I don't like this place all that much, but Sinclair loves it. It's close to school, so that's why we stopped today, but I like the place where Smokey goes much better. Tomorrow, I expect you to be at the Victorian to work out before we have kid duty," Duke insisted. I nodded. We ordered some muffins and coffee and took our seats to be served.

"So, have you heard from Bruno?" I asked as I checked my phone, feigning disinterest in his answer.

I had a text from my father that I decided I'd read later. He hadn't answered my email yet, so I would take my time getting back to him, still wary of his intentions.

"Gunter Schell took him to the airport yesterday, but he didn't make the flight. Right now, he's off the grid. We're not sure what's happening with him right now. What's the deal with you and Bruno?" Duke asked. *I wasn't answering that!*

As far as I knew, Mateo was the only one who really knew what happened with the marriage license because he'd been the dick to put it in the mail. I wondered if I could trust Duke with the information because I desperately needed to talk to someone about how I felt. My head was like a fucking spinning teacup at Disneyland.

Then, I had a better idea. "So, would you care if I called Corby sometime to get together for a beer?"

Duke sort of cocked his head as he studied me, and suddenly, I got it. "Not to date him. I mean, he's a good-looking guy, but I know he's with you and Ace. I just meant maybe to have a beer or shoot some pool or something," I backtracked. The man could break me like a toothpick.

"What's wrong with me?" Duke asked.

"Nothing... Wait, *what?*"

"What's wrong with going for a beer with me?" he asked me.

That was a loaded question if I ever heard one. "You're—it'd be like going out with Uncle Gabe for a beer. I'd rather not. He's ol— busy," I corrected.

Duke arched his eyebrow at me before he broke out into a deep chuckle. "I'm not that much older than you, and you didn't grow up around me like you did Gabe and Mateo, so I think we could maybe be friends, but to answer your question, I'd love it if you'd call Corby for a beer sometime."

The woman dropped off our food and coffee, so Duke was quiet for a minute until she left us. He had a smile on his face the whole time, which was a new thing for him that others had noticed, as well. His less uptight-and-angry demeanor had to be because he was in love.

He thanked the lady and took a muffin from the plate before he continued. "The guys he works with at Herbst are real motor heads, you know. They've figured out he's gay, so they don't talk to him, even when he offers to help them with something, they ignore him. We try to drop by and see him during the day, but I'm getting the impression it makes things worse for him. With Shay on his honeymoon still, I don't know that Corby has anyone to talk to about things going on in his life. Ace and I try to make sure he knows we love his company, but it's different because we're his boyfriends. I think he'd like to have a friend who he can bitch about us to and do things with that don't include us," Duke suggested.

That surprised me. "You won't get jealous and try to throttle me if I call him?"

Duke had just bitten into a poppyseed muffin, which came flying out at me as he coughed at my comment. I handed him napkins from the table next to us since our dispenser was empty.

He held a bunch of them up to his mouth as he continued to cough. The waitress brought him a glass of water, and he nodded in thanks. After a few gulps, he wiped his mouth and the front of his shirt where there were crumbs, and he cleared his throat.

"I guess I'm owed that reputation, but I hope I can prove to you and everyone else that I'm not like that, really. I let all that shit go after I finally let my guard down and got to know the family. Grace keeps calling me to bring Ace and Corby out for Sunday dinner, but I'm not sure Corby's ready for the full family onslaught. If you're there, I think he'd be grateful and could relax around everyone," Duke explained.

"Really? Great. I can ask Nonna to keep the guest list down to just a few. She likes to get carried away sometimes when she's inviting the family over, but eventually, you'll have to meet the rest of them who weren't at the wedding—my cousins, uncles, and crazy aunts. They're not all like my mother, I promise you." I hoped I was offering him some assurance that it wouldn't be too bad. My mother was no brand ambassador for the Torrente family, that was for damn sure.

"I'll talk to Corby and Ace about it. That might be easier for them, I think. Ace doesn't really give a damn about meeting new people, but Corby is pretty shy, and I know he'll worry himself into a stupor. So, nephew, tell me why you and Bruno Garvin don't just speak to each other? He asks about you, and you ask about him. Why don't you get his number from Giuseppe? You were working over in Italy for a while and training with the guys over there, right? Is there a rule against you talking directly to Bruno that I don't know about?" Duke suggested. Of course, any logical person would think the same thing, wouldn't they?

It wasn't like I hadn't thought about it or anything, but there were so many things we needed to discuss that my mind just wouldn't let me take the step. The longer I put off the discussion, the longer I didn't have to decide what to do next. I was truly a coward.

"Do you think he's in danger?" I asked. I knew Duke had gone looking for Bruno at one point when we were all over there because everyone was worried about him. When Bruno got back to New York, I was planning for us to have a serious conversation—or ten.

Unfortunately for me, Duke only shrugged. That didn't give me a feeling of tranquility.

Once we were back at the Victorian, I checked the text from my father.

I got your email. Thank you. I'll be in New York this weekend and would like to talk to you about some things in person. Are you available to have lunch on Saturday or brunch on Sunday? I really want to see you. Love, Dad

I thought it was best to sleep on it, so after a shower, I went to bed—snagging one of Bruno's t-shirts that I'd laundered from the things he'd taken to Kentucky. I'd already been married for eight months, and I'd only seen my groom for about an hour since we'd said, "I do." How pathetic could I get?

I thought about the kiss Bruno had given me when he found me at Tio Lu's place. His body had transformed even more since he'd been in Italy. I had to be honest with myself that if I'd met Bruno in a bar, I'd make a play for him. I wondered if he was a top or bottom. I was vers, so it really wouldn't matter to me. Would it matter to him?

I groped around in the drawer of my nightstand and grabbed the lube as my dick came to life just fantasizing about the man fucking me. I'd pleasured myself while watching porn a lot recently, but hell, I was married to a beautiful man. I'd once thought him not my type—he was actually the complete opposite of me—but now, I knew that was stupid logic. He was exactly what I wanted in a guy, and if I couldn't have him in person, I could have him in my mind.

"Take my shirt off, Willow." I slowly slid it over my body, his groans as I revealed my suntanned stomach and chest would only add more heat to my blood that was already searing in my veins. I'd pulled the green t-shirt over my head, revealing my black bikini briefs. I had long legs, so the look of appreciation in Bruno's eyes would be warranted, and I couldn't wait to wrap them around his waist as he pounded into me.

I pulled his shirt open, sending buttons flying across the bedroom to finally see what I already thought was there—his body was sexy and strong with a little extra thickness over his abs that I absolutely love on a man. His chest was covered in wiry hair with a little soft fur on his belly that trailed into the hidden land of his jeans. I couldn't help but want to rub myself all over his sexy body.

I reached for the button on his pants before he stilled my hand. "I've missed you, Willow. I want to watch you touch yourself. Will you?"

I slipped off my briefs and took my hard cock in hand, stroking myself once... twice... "I'd love it if you'd touch me," I whispered as Bruno reached for the lube and took hold of my hand, squeezing some lube into it.

"Show me how you like it," Bruno urged, his voice low and rumbly, before he leaned forward and kissed my lips, only to sit back and touch my hand to move over my shaft.

"I wish you'd touch me," I whispered to him again.

Bruno placed his hand over mine and we both stroked my cock. I never wanted the feeling to end. I began fucking up into our hands as Bruno kissed my chest while guiding my hand before I moved it and put his in its place, overcome with the feeling of his touch... finally... on my body.

Five pumps of his strong fist gliding over my cock, and I spilled over his hand and my stomach. It felt more incredible than anything I'd ever experienced in my life...

9

BRUNO

I made my way through security at the airport on Monday evening, having spent the weekend with Dante and his sister, Daniela, since I couldn't get another flight until after the weekend. Finding out Daniela was engaged to Tommy Torrente was a surprise, but learning the brother and sister were working on Giuseppe's payroll was a massive relief.

I was returning home to New York. It was time for me to see Dominic and finally say goodbye. I didn't want to do it, but I had to allow Willow his choice. For nearly nine months, I'd been living the fantasy of having a husband I knew I'd love forever, and if it was time for it to come to a sad end, I would accept the consequences for my actions without protesting and let him move on.

I walked out of the Newark airport and headed to the taxi line before a whistle I recognized sliced through the night air and crowd noise. I scanned the people in front of the arrivals pickup area, amazed to see Gabe Torrente standing by a large, black SUV I recognized, motioning me over. I was stunned to see him there waiting for me, so I rushed to where he was parked.

"Hi, Gabby," I greeted him.

"Holy fuck! Look at you, *amico mio!*" He called me his friend as he wrapped his arms around me and hugged me. When we parted, he offered a friendly smile that made me really glad to be back home.

"I didn't expect you to pick me up," I stated as he opened the tailgate of the vehicle and I tossed my bag inside.

Gabby laughed. "I'm here because I wanted to make sure you got back to Brooklyn safely. How were your flights?" he asked.

"They were fine. How's Do—how's your family?" I asked, catching myself.

"Come on. Let's talk." He pointed to the front of the vehicle, so I walked up the passenger side and hopped in.

I buckled my seatbelt as he got inside. "What would you like to discuss?"

The ride back to Brooklyn was filled with small talk—"Did you get to do any sightseeing?" "Did Uncle G give you any idea what's next with Frankie Man?" "I can't thank you enough for what you did, Bruno."

I answered him that I'd seen a few sights, but not nearly enough. Mr. Torrente, Senior, hadn't given me any information regarding what was going to happen with Frankie Man, just that he had eyes on the man—which I didn't say were Dante and Daniela. I also didn't mention Tommy's engagement to the woman, either.

Those weren't things that were my place to tell anyone, and as far as his appreciation, in my mind, we were even. He'd been the person to give me a chance when I didn't think anyone else would by hiring me to work for GEA-A.

We arrived at the Victorian, and since it was late in the evening, the place was dark and the parking lot was empty. "I'll get a cab home from here," I offered as I unbuckled my seatbelt.

"Come inside, first. I'll drop you off at the apartment when we're done talking, but I have an assignment for you that I want to keep between us," Gabby informed me. I hopped out of the large SUV and followed him to the backdoor of the building.

He placed his hand on the scanner and the door opened, the lights flashing inside as expected. We stopped and listened for a moment before he flipped some switches and closed the door. "Just checking to see nobody's going to scare the piss out of us. My cousins have a habit of showing up when I least expect them," Gabe explained to me.

I nodded and followed him up the two flights of stairs to the offices. It was good to see the place again after being gone for so long, but I was really anxious to get home. Of course, I didn't tell him that—it would have been disrespectful.

We stopped by the kitchen, and Gabby opened the fridge, handing me a bottle of water before he took one for himself. We then made our way to his office. "Excuse the mess in here. I'm moving my shit out so Duke can have more room for his stuff. He's doing all the case scheduling these days, and he needs the space."

I nodded and watched as Gabby went to the desk, unlocking the bottom drawer. I saw a box on the couch with some things in it—pictures of Dexter, Dylan, and Searcy, and a trophy with a small football player on it, which I picked up.

"That's from Dyl's last game of the season. His team came in third in their league. He said I could have it here at work with me so I remembered..." Suddenly, Gabby's words cut off, and I turned to see him leaning both hands on the desk, his head down as his body shook.

I hurried over to him. "Are you okay? What's the matter?"

He sniffled and opened the desk drawer, pulling out an envelope and tossing it on the desk before he reached into his pocket to retrieve a handkerchief to dry his cheeks. "This is between us, *capiche*?"

I knew enough Italian now that I nodded in understanding. He turned over the envelope to show me a note—

You took something that belonged to me, and I want it back or a million bucks in exchange unless you want this to happen to your prize. I'll be in touch.

Gabe then opened the envelope and slid out pictures of Dexter—or rather, what had been made to look like Dexter's dead body.

The photos had obviously been created to make it look like Dexter had been murdered—in one, he was hanging by his neck from a rope in a dark space that was only lit up by a glowing light from beneath him. There appeared to be slash marks on Dexter's body, and he was naked.

I reached for the photos, shuffling through them to see more of the same, which made my stomach turn in disgust at the sight of them. "Where'd these come from?" I asked the obvious question.

"I don't know. They were taped to the windshield of my Escalade in the parking lot where Dylan had football practice the other night. Nobody knows about them but Casper, who was able to confirm they're photoshopped images, but that is my husband's naked body. I know every mole, dimple, and scar on that man, and that's my Dexter," Gabby stated.

"Do you think Dexter's... He loves his family. He didn't do this of his free will," I assured him.

Gabby looked up at me and offered a sort of broken smile. "I know. These pictures were taken before Dexter and I got together, and I want to know who took them; where they were taken; and why. Whoever it is will die; I just need to make sure I get the right person," Gabby confirmed what I'd already thought.

"Anybody come to mind?" I asked him.

"No. That's what I want you to find out. I can keep an eye on Dex when he's here, but he's been doing some charity work with senior citizens, and he won't let me come with him. I want to assign you as his escort. He'll get pissed, but I don't care. You only report to me, okay? I have enough over my head with Frankie Man coming for my babies. I can't have anyone after my husband, too." The man looked like he was at the edge of his sanity, so I gathered the pictures and put them in the envelope, closing it and handing it to him.

Gabby walked over to the box with his things and tossed the pictures inside before he exhaled loudly and took a drink from the water bottle in his other hand. "What do you need? You still have that concealed carry issue, right?" my boss asked.

"I don't need a gun," I assured him.

Gabe nodded and grabbed his box before we headed toward the stairs. "Be back in the office next Monday. Take some time off. I'll watch Dexter until then. You'll probably want to crash for a couple of days, anyway," Gabby offered.

I nodded and followed him downstairs. He stopped in front of the wall in the hallway and pushed on a portion of it, a panel popping open that I didn't know was there. It revealed a steel door with a palm scanner on the front. Gabe placed his hand on it and the door began to rumble to life, opening to reveal a whole room I never knew was there.

"Wow! Is this new?" I asked him as I glanced around. There was a cot in the corner, and a table and chairs, along with a small kitchenette area.

"No—well, sort of. It's a need-to-know situation. Anyway, when you find out who is threatening my husband, I want you to bring them here and call me," he insisted. Then he walked over to a wall and pressed in a code. There were a couple of beeps that had me looking around the room before a panel slid to the side revealing an arsenal of fire power that rivaled what I'd seen at Frankie Man's estate in Italy.

Gabby walked to a shelf and retrieved a small revolver and an ankle strap. He opened a drawer and pulled out a box of bullets, stacking it on top of the holster before he handed it to me. "This is between us. Put your hand there," he insisted, pointing to a palm reader on the right side of the weapon shelves.

He punched in a code and motioned for me to put my hand on the device. After a quick scan of my right hand, the box beeped twice and then Gabe motioned me out of the way.

Another code was punched into another security keypad. "Put in a code known only to you," he instructed, so I did, and then he hit a button and the box beeped again.

We stepped out of the room, and Gabe held his palm over the reader. The door slid into place, and the locks engaged. I turned to the man for an explanation.

Gabe smirked. "You're now authorized to come and go from there with your code and to secure any weapons we have that you might need. Mateo and I can override your code in an emergency, but if you put someone in there, you have to let them out. We'll work on getting your record cleaned up so we can get you an investigator's license and a concealed carry permit. Any questions?"

I shook my head. We weren't so formal in Italy with obtaining official paperwork, but I knew U.S. laws were different, having been on the wrong side of them more than once. Without another word, I shoved the holster and revolver in one pocket of my tactical pants and the shells in another before we left the building.

Whatever was going on with Dexter, I was determined to get to the bottom of it. For however long it took for Willow and me to get our annulment, they were my family.

I STOOD on the sidewalk with my duffel, staring up at the building where I shared an apartment with Dominic. Fear had taken over after the adrenaline rush of talking to Gabby about his issue, and I was tempted to just sleep outside on a bench in the nearby park until I saw Dominic leave the next morning.

I wasn't generally a coward, but I was afraid to go inside and face the man. The future was completely uncertain, and it made me feel like the eighteen-year-old kid who left the family ranch in Wyoming to get away from a drunk who liked to pound on him and a mother who didn't really seem to care.

After a couple of deep breaths, I went up the stairs and pressed the entrance code, relieved when the door buzzed and opened when I pulled it. Thankfully, Dominic hadn't changed it while I'd been away.

I took the stairs up to our floor, anxious to get a shower and remind myself what a bed felt like again. I hadn't slept well at Dante's place because of the disgusting mess it had been. The stench was still in my nose, it seemed, and the image of cockroaches skittering over my skin when I laid back on the horrible bed had me scratching like a deranged man the whole plane ride back to New York.

I'd rather camp in the woods than stay at a place like that, which reminded me—I'd need to find a new spot to live. There was no way Willow and I could continue to share a place after everything that had and would happen between us. I didn't believe my heart could take breaking every day when I saw him.

I found my key and let myself inside as quietly as possible. I slid off my sneakers and put them in the tray next to Dom's trainers and a pair of loafers. A messenger bag was on the floor by the coat closet, and the place was dark except for the glow of the moon through the windows of the living room.

I made my way around the kitchen and into my room, seeing everything looked exactly as it had when I'd left. The door was open and the room smelled fresh. I knew I'd closed it when we'd left to go to Kentucky—I always closed my bedroom door. I had to wonder what Dom had been doing in here.

I decided to take a shower, so I grabbed some fresh clothes from my dresser and went to the hall bathroom. I glanced toward Dom's room to see the door was open and the bed was empty, which explained why he hadn't come to check on the noise when I'd come inside. My stomach clenched at the thought of him being out with someone. Would he bring a guy home? I had to fight hard to keep from becoming ill at the idea.

After I cleaned up, I went to bed, closing the door to my room in hopes that I didn't hear Dominic's voice talking to someone who wasn't me.

10

DOMINIC

"Thanks for the ride, Corby. I'm glad we got together," I offered to my companion as we rode up in the elevator together. I'd come home after work and changed into jeans and a t-shirt, happy to rid myself of the suit I'd worn to work that day.

Corbin Barr and I had met at a sports bar not far from the apartment building where we lived—him with Duke and Ace, and me—well, at the moment, alone.

"Yeah, thanks Dom. Maybe next time we can go to that sushi place you mentioned—I mean, if you wanna get together again sometime," Corby suggested. The guy was really shy, which made me wonder how their three-way worked. Maybe it was true that you had to look out for the quiet ones. Maybe Corby was a real tiger between the sheets. The idea of it made me chuckle.

After I unlocked the door and stepped inside, the hairs on the back of my neck stood at attention. Everything looked exactly the same, but there was a smell in the air that was unusual. *Vanilla mint?*

I slipped off my flip flops and started to put them in the tray when I saw a pair of black sneakers that I would know out of a room full of identical ones. *Bruno!*

The shoes were worn down on the outsides because of the way he walked. I hadn't realized I'd studied him so closely to know his gait, but apparently I had.

I slowly strolled into the living room and looked to my right to see his door was closed. *Now what?* Should I pound on it with indignation that he showed up without warning, or should I leave the man be? Hell! Was I even ready to talk to him?

Glancing at my watch, I saw it was midnight and I had to be up in about five hours, so I decided to go to bed and deal with things in the morning. I tiptoed over to the door and put my ear against it, but I heard nothing. Slowly turning the knob, I glanced inside, seeing the brute in the middle of the king-sized bed. He was on his right side with both of his hands under his left cheek like a sleeping baby.

All the fight left me as I stared at him. I sensed he'd changed since his time in Italy, based on the few moments I'd seen him while I was staying at Tio Lu's. I wondered what that meant for us—I meant *me*, there was no us. What the hell were we going to do about our situation? Our accidental marriage that wasn't really an accident? *Ugh!*

My alarm startled me. I picked up my phone to stop the blaring of the horn I'd chosen to blast me out of bed in the mornings, and once it was silenced, I listened for any sounds to indicate Bruno was really there. It was absolutely dead quiet.

I got up and did my bathroom business before I walked into the kitchen to see the coffee maker was pulled out and a mug was sitting next to it along with two pods of my favorite coffee. Bruno's door was open and his bed was made, so I walked over, passing the hall bathroom where the minty smell of his toothpaste struck my nose, along with the residual scent of vanilla that I'd noticed the previous night.

Stepping into the bathroom felt like I was invading his space, but I couldn't help myself. I opened the shower door and picked up the bottle of shampoo on the ledge next to a bottle of conditioner and body wash. "Spiced vanilla," I read out loud.

I opened it and sniffed, finding it smelled damn good. I returned it to its perch and looked at the few things on the bathroom vanity—a nail kit, face wash, and a bottle that matched the things in the shower. "Spiced vanilla beard serum."

These were the things of a man I didn't know well. I remembered touching his beard when we were in Kentucky almost ten months ago. Now, here I was, faced with—and having sex dreams about—a man who was more or less a stranger.

The man I'd first met when we started sharing the apartment while Bruno was in D.C. was nothing like the man I saw in Italy. Bruno was now confident and surer of the man he wanted to be, and I was becoming less and less sure about the man I'd become. My arrogance toward others was truly ugly, and I was coming to feel shame for how I'd treated others in the past. It was as if someone finally stuck a mirror up to my face to show me what a horrible person I'd been, and I didn't like the reflection at all.

I hurried back to my room and gathered my clothes to take to work before I dressed in workout gear. I zipped a garment bag around my suit and slid on my sneakers as I summoned a ride share. I thought about going upstairs to knock on Duke's door, but I was sure he was already gone, so I ran down the stairs and proceeded to pace the sidewalk as I waited anxiously for my ride.

Fifteen minutes later—*"your ride is one minute away"* my ass—I walked up to the porch of the Victorian and let myself in through the front door. I heard the beep of the alarm, so I reset it and took my things downstairs to the locker room.

The gym was busy. Ace gave me a wave from where he was on the treadmill running like he was in a race. Smokey was next to him, likely cooling down from his run, and Uncle Gabe was on a rowing machine in the back of the gym, surprising me.

I hurried to the locker room and shoved open the door. *"Whoa!"*

I came face to face with the handsome man who made my heart

pound in my chest—my husband. He had a towel around his neck, and his face was red—redder than when he blushed.

"What time did you leave this morning?" I snapped at him. It was the only thing that my mind could conjure to say.

"I left a four-thirty and ran here. I just got out of the ring with—" Just then, Duke walked out of the bathroom.

"You're late, Beaver." For a moment, he was the same grump I remembered from a few months back, but then his face morphed into a big, happy grin.

"Thanks for taking Corby out last night. He was in a really good mood when he got home, so I won't bust your chops about being late. Anyway, come out and let's spar. Your roommate here nearly kicked my ass." He then looked at Bruno and winked. "Next time, warn me that you've been learning MMA tricks. I'll put you in the ring with Ace," Duke seemed to compliment.

Bruno chuckled and nodded, his face heating again. My insides melted right there.

"So, when did you get home?" I asked him, my voice sounding a little bitchier than I'd have liked.

Bruno looked down. "Last night. You weren't home yet. I'll try to be out in a week, okay? I have a new assignment, but I'll look for a place when I have time." He then walked toward the lockers without another word, and I was too stunned to speak.

I went out into the gym and proceeded to warm up on the stationary bike. Duke came over and punched up the tension—like I wasn't already tense enough.

"What's Bruno's new assignment?" I asked my recently-discovered uncle, keeping my voice low.

"Beats me. Got it directly from Gabe," Duke answered.

I nodded and got busy, trying to work off some of the nervous tension in my muscles. Contemplating the idea of Bruno moving out had struck something inside me that I really needed to think about long and hard. There was no denying that I was attracted to the guy even more after seeing him in my room at Tio Lu's. The feelings I had for him were a bit harder to sort through.

I'd really started to like him when we were hanging out in Kentucky. He was respectful and friendly, but not clingy, a trait I'd come to dislike in some of the guys I hooked up with. What was it that was so different about Bruno? That was something I needed to figure out. I wasn't looking for a relationship, was I?

Seeing him in the locker room all sweaty and gorgeous had my cock starting to swell in my thin shorts. The thoughts I'd once had about him being a clueless goth kid because he didn't wear brand names like I did made me feel like a superficial douchebag. I knew everyone loved him at the office, but I'd formed a shallow opinion based on his appearance back then, and I'd immediately banished him to the friend zone. Now, I was hating myself for it. Thinking he might leave me had brought a low-grade panic into the mix that I wasn't comfortable with at all.

DEXTER WENT with us for the ride to school and then the return to the Victorian that morning. "Why are you riding with us?" I asked as I turned in my seat of Duke's SUV. He and Uncle Gabe usually rode to work together in the mornings.

"Gabe wanted to go in early to work out, and I have a doctor's appointment this morning that's not far from the Victorian. You'll probably have to man the phones, Dom, because Sabrina is taking my early classes. I'm praying to God it doesn't take more than an hour," Dexter explained to both of us.

Duke looked up into the rearview. "You okay?" he asked.

Dexter's face turned a little red before he grinned. "Yeah. I, uh, I have to give a sample. I had an issue with my last donation toward the baby soup, so I've been on some meds to help out. If things are okay, then Gabriele and I can go later in the week to do our part. Our egg donor has already done their part, and the surrogate has been taking hormones, so she's almost ready. Just the dads who are the hold up," Dexter stated, a look of sadness crossing his face.

I knew next to nothing about what it took to make babies the way they were going about it, but I honestly knew they were fantastic parents. Any baby would be lucky to have them for dads.

"I have a feeling things will be fine," I told him when Duke pulled into the parking lot of the Victorian where I saw Bruno was dressed in a pair of dress slacks and a white dress shirt. He had on a pair of black dress shoes and a nice gray jacket.

Duke and I got out of the SUV, and Bruno hurried over to open Dex's door. "Good morning. Gabby told me you were headed my way, so I thought we could walk together," Bruno announced.

Dex looked at me with a smirk, but I looked away, guessing every-fucking-body knew about our stupid fake marriage debacle. "Okay, Bruno. Where are you headed?" Dexter asked. I didn't wait for the answer. I hurried inside and upstairs to the bathroom, locking myself inside to catch my breath. "Goddammit!"

I splashed some water on my face, trying to clear my head. The knock on the door wasn't at all what I wanted to hear. "*Yeah? Out in a minute!*" I yelled through the door. It wasn't like we only had one fucking bathroom!

"It's me," Uncle Gabe announced, his tone tense.

I opened the door, and without permission, he pushed himself inside and closed the door. "What's up?" I asked him, trying not to sound irritated.

"I want you to leave Bruno alone. I've got him on an assignment, so don't get in his goddamn head. He needs to be on alert, and it seems like you always distract him," Uncle Gabe ordered. If Dex knew about the marriage, then I was pretty sure Uncle Gabe knew as well.

I was immediately pissed at him. "It's none of your fucking business what I do or don't do with Bruno, Gabby." It was the first time I addressed him as an equal and not as my uncle. If we were working together, he needed to treat me as such, or I'd fucking leave and convince Bruno to come with me.

Uncle Gabe raised his eyebrows before he growled at me. "Listen to me, Dom, I'm not here to judge you for the colossally stupid thing you did by marrying Bruno in Kentucky to piss off your mother. She called me and asked if it was bullshit, and I had to tell her I didn't give a good goddamn and to keep me out of it. To you, I say don't fuck with Bruno's head because I have him on a special assignment and that's all you need to know. I'm going to have him come stay at the house for a while. Case closed."

My heart seized in my chest at the idea of Bruno leaving the apartment, but until I got my shit straight, maybe it was for the best. Besides, I needed to focus on Dyl and Searcy as well.

"What's he doing? I could have done it," I protested. It was damn time I got taken seriously.

St. Michael came in just as Uncle Gabe was leaving. "Hey, Beaver. What's up?" he asked, pissing me off at the use of the nickname.

"Fuck off," I snapped at him before I left the room, leaving St. Michael in my dust. I wasn't in the mood to deal with anyone.

11

BRUNO

"So, tell me, Bruno, why are you escorting me to the doctor's building?" Dex asked me, as I accompanied him to his doctor's appointment. Gabe told me to stick to him like white on rice, and that was exactly what I intended to do.

"I'm going to the pharmacy on the ground floor to pick up a prescription for my eczema," I repeated what Gabe had suggested to me as an excuse Dexter would accept. At first he'd said jock itch, but then he laughed and said eczema, which made me feel a lot better. It wasn't much of a lie, really. I could remember it easily.

"Oh. Is it bad?" he asked me.

I thought for a moment—would he ask to see it? Without thinking, I blurted out, "It's on my butt."

Dexter stared at me for a moment before he began cackling, stopping to rest his hands on his thighs to keep himself from falling down. Heat spread up my neck and settled in my cheeks, which was just embarrassing.

Once Dexter calmed down, we continued walking. It was a comfortable silence for me, but I needed to figure out how to ask him if he had any idea who was threatening him without him knowing he was being threatened. Finally... "So, do you have any friends other than the people who work at GEA-A or their partners?" I asked. I definitely doubted it was anyone who worked with us, but I wasn't sure if I knew all of his friends.

Dex zipped up his jacket and pulled the hood over his head as a chilly, late-September breeze kicked up, the smell of rain on the wind. I grabbed his tote bag to carry for him so he could shove his hands into his pockets.

"Uh, let's see. Sweet Pea—Paul Ogden—takes my Saturday morning class, and we've gone for coffee a few times to catch up. He's an understudy for one of the leads, along with having a spot in the chorus of that Broadway play about a student who commits suicide at a high school. I haven't seen the play because it seems pretty depressing to me, but he's enjoying being a part of it. Do you remember him? He was just starting at The Bone Yard before Gabe... Well, *you* know what Gabe did by carrying me out of there that night," Dex reminded me, which made me smile. It seemed like it was love at first sight for my boss and his husband.

Paul Ogden, as I remembered him, was a nice young guy who I knew had lied about his age to get a job at that awful dance club—just thinking about the place made my skin crawl. He'd only been sixteen when he came to look for a job that I was sure he wouldn't get if Jeff Oswald had any hint of decency inside him. Unfortunately, he didn't.

I knew how old Paul was because I'd been working the door the night before when he'd tried to get into the club with a really rotten fake ID. I made him tell me how old he really was, but I didn't let him inside. I could see the kid was gay and likely on the streets, so I didn't mention he was underage when I saw him putting beer in the coolers the next afternoon when I showed up for work. I promised myself to look out for him as much as I could, and kept my mouth shut about the secret we shared about his birthdate. We were all just trying to survive back then.

Over that week, I'd gotten to know Paul a little as part of looking out for him. He was really sweet. I'd been the one to start calling him Sweet Pea to tease him, and then everyone picked up on it. I was right that the kid had been kicked out of his house in Nebraska because he was gay when he was fifteen and had hitchhiked his way across the country to New York to become a dancer.

I could tell it had been hard on him, so I took pity on his situation and invited Paul to sleep on the floor of the apartment I'd shared with a guy I'd met when I'd worked as a dishwasher at a small Mexican restaurant in Hell's Kitchen. It was before I got the job working for Jeff Oswald when he was opening The Bone Yard.

I decided it was time to track down Sweet Pea to see if he had any ideas about who might want to harm Dexter. At least it seemed like I had a place to start.

I WAS STANDING at the stage door of the Walter Kerr Theater on West 48th Street, waiting for Paul Ogden to come out after the performance that Tuesday night. The theaters were dark on Mondays, and since I had no idea where Paul was staying, I'd waited until Tuesday evening when I knew Dexter was safely at home with his family.

I'd seen Dom that rainy fall afternoon when he and Duke had dropped off Dylan and Searcy after school—I was now staying at Gabe and Dex's house. Dom hadn't said anything to me—just stared at me the whole time he was there while Duke was giving Dexter the backpacks. I had no idea what to say to him.

Just then, Paul came out of the stage door with another dancer, both laughing together in a friendly way as they opened umbrellas and walked to the end of the block. They hugged before they went their separate ways, the other dancer crossing the street. I was observing them from the shadows but decided to go after Paul.

"*Paul?*" I called to him as I walked faster to catch up as the rain tapered to a drizzle, but he didn't stop. "*Sweet Pea!*" I called again. The young man stopped in his tracks and slowly turned around, keeping the umbrella over his shoulder.

For a moment, he didn't say anything. Finally, he answered, "Yes, I used to be called Sweet Pea."

"It's me, Bruno—Bruno Garvin," I re-introduced myself. I knew I'd changed over time, but I hadn't realized I'd become unrecognizable.

Sweet Pea snapped his fingers and his face bloomed into a big grin as he dropped his umbrella and threw himself into my body and hugged me. "I wondered where you went after you left The Bone Yard. Where are you now?"

It made sense that Dexter wouldn't have said anything about Gabe's business when he and Paul were talking, and I wondered if I shouldn't either, finally deciding not to mention my employer. "I just got back from a job in Italy, so I'm taking some time off. You have time for a beer?" I asked him.

Paul looked down with a shy smile. "I'm in recovery. I don't drink anymore," he responded, and I wondered what had happened to him while I wasn't around.

"Oh, then coffee?" I suggested. Paul nodded and took my leather-clad arm as the two of us walked down 8th Street to a little all-night coffee shop. We seated ourselves at a four-top near the windows and ordered coffees.

"How've you been? What were you doing in Italy," Paul asked. I definitely had to get better at asking and answering questions if I was going to make investigations my career.

"I was working as a security professional for a while. There are some bad people interested in harming someone I care about, and I'm trying to see to it that it doesn't happen. I'm back here for a while to clean up some personal business, and then I'm not sure what I'll do after. Look at you.... On Broadway," I replied. It wasn't really a lie, my current plans, so I was okay saying it. As Ben Hoffman said a time or two when he was in Congress, it was truth-adjacent.

Paul giggled. "Yeah, and they actually know I'm only twenty. Thank you, Bruno, for not ratting me out to Jeff back then. Though, as I think about it, maybe I'd have been better off if you had."

That caught my attention. "Why? What happened?" I asked him, trying not to jump to a conclusion on my own.

His face seemed to fall a little as he shook his head for a second. "It wasn't good, but I'm working through it with the help of AA and a counselor at the Brooklyn LGBTQ Youth Center," Paul explained. My stomach dropped at his comment.

"Who did it?" I knew in my gut what "it" was, but I didn't really want to be right.

Paul glanced up with a look of surprise. "You mean you weren't forced to take naked pictures when you went to work at The Bone Yard? I was told everyone had to," Paul answered.

I took a second to figure out what to say. I'd never had to take naked pictures of myself—even my old mugshots had me dressed in those ugly jumpsuits. "I— When did he make you take naked photos?"

Paul took a sip of his coffee before he placed the cup on the little plate, looking down at the scratched wooden tabletop. "Before he'd give me the job," he replied.

That was disturbing. "Did you talk to the other guys at The Bone Yard? Was it the same for all of you?" I tried not to interrogate him, but I couldn't help myself.

"I know he showed the pictures to some of his friends because they tried to date me, but I said no—well, to most of them. One night, he didn't listen when I said no," Paul admitted, not looking at me.

"Who was *he*?" I pushed him.

"I better not say. I still have friends who work there," Paul responded.

I had a damn good idea of who it was, but I couldn't act without proof, so I walked Paul to the corner of 8th and 46th where he lived in a walkup with five other dancers, and I hugged him before I reached into the pocket of my leather jacket and pulled out the napkin I'd written my number on when he went to the restroom at the deli.

"If you need anything at all, call me, please," I advised him. He finally nodded before he went down the block.

I hurried to the subway station to get back to Gabe and Dexter's home where I was staying. As I was walking toward their home, I heard footsteps behind me, so I walked faster. The footsteps followed quicker, but when I slowed down so did my stalker.

I made the next right in front of a large brick home and ducked into a bush in front until the person walked by. When I looked out between the branches of the spent azalea, I saw familiar black shoes, so I popped up. "Willow?" The man spun around, a surprised look on his handsome face.

"What a coincidence," he quickly commented as he slid his hands into the pockets of his blue rain jacket.

I tried not to laugh at his attempt at playing it off like he wasn't following me. "Where are you headed?" I asked him.

"I'm going... I was on my way to—who was that cute little blond you were with earlier?" Willow asked me. He looked pretty mad, too. I honestly had no idea what to tell him that wasn't a lie. I had a feeling I was in trouble.

12

DOMINIC

I returned home from work to find most of Bruno's things were missing. I'd seen him at Uncle Gabe's house when we dropped off the kids from school, but he hadn't said a damn word about moving out, the bastard. Uncle Gabe had mentioned Bruno was going to be staying with them until his mystery assignment was over, but he hadn't said immediately.

After fifteen minutes of searching the house for any kind of note from Bruno—and I was pissed that there wasn't one—I picked up the phone to call my *favorite* uncle for an explanation. Unfortunately, it rang through to voicemail, so I ran upstairs to Duke's place.

"Hey, Beaver. What can we do for you?" Ace greeted when he opened the door in his boxer shorts and no shirt. Ace, Duke, and Corby shared Mateo and Shay's former apartment in Uncle Gabe's building a few floors above us.

Mateo and Shay had moved to Maxi's brownstone when he and Lawry moved into their new place in the neighborhood where Smokey and Parker bought their house. I wasn't looking forward to the constant reminder of all of the happy couples who had cycled through that apartment building if I was going to be stuck there living alone. While I'd cherished my privacy before Bruno moved in with me, I suddenly found it unbearable to be there without him.

"Is Bruno here?" I asked, certain he wasn't.

"Nope. I saw him leave the Victorian with Gabe earlier, so maybe he's over at their house," Ace suggested.

I nodded, swallowing the lump in my throat, and ran back downstairs without a goodbye. When I got back to my apartment, I changed into jeans and a sweater as I paced the living room, unsure of my next moves until Casper popped into my head. Well, Casper's skills anyway.

I called him, glad he answered. "Beaver?" Well, I wasn't thrilled he answered like *that*, but at least he picked up.

"Hey. Bruno isn't answering his phone, and he's late meeting me for dinner. He's so late that I'm worried about him. Can you check the tracker on his cell?" I asked, hating the pang in my chest at invading his privacy. *It's justified—you're desperate!*

"You have big plans with Noble?" Casper asked, which surprised me.

"Is that really a thing? Everyone's just calling him *Noble*?" I asked him, disbelief evident in my voice, though they were sort of a lemming kind of group, weren't they? They did all follow each other's leads, which I supposed made them a great team.

Casper chuckled. "Look, kid, I know all about the marriage license debacle, which is the only reason I'm doing this for you." I heard his fingers skitter over a keyboard, for which I was grateful.

Casper then continued. "I'd say what Bruno did for the family, going undercover to infiltrate the Mangellos without any thought to his own safety, is one of the noblest things I've ever heard. When Mateo called him that, I jumped on board immediately," Casper continued.

He definitely had a point. What the fuck was my hang up with it? "Thanks, Casper. I won't mention you helped me," I confirmed in case he was worried I'd rat him out.

Two clicks of the mouse... "He's at 8th and 48th, outside the Walter Kerr Theater," Casper told me.

"Thanks," I answered before disconnecting the call. I grabbed my navy rain jacket and slid on my black loafers, running downstairs and out the front door toward the subway station because it was quicker, and after far too long for my tastes, I arrived at the 49th Street subway platform and headed up and out, running the block to the theater just in time to see my husband hugging a cute blond guy with long legs and a dazzling smile.

The two of them went into a deli down the street, so I stationed myself across from it in the alcove entrance of a closed shoe store to watch them through the window. They chatted and drank coffee, spending about forty-five minutes with each other—forty-five minutes in which I stood in the cold drizzle and froze my ass off, growing angrier by the second—and finally, Bruno paid and the two of them left.

Once they were halfway down the block, I hurried across the street and followed them from a safe distance, relieved to see they weren't holding hands or walking close together. Thankfully, the young guy turned at the corner, but I stayed on Bruno to see where he was headed.

He went down to the 49th Street subway platform with me following him but taking the train car behind him, and we both got off at the stop near Uncle Gabe's neighborhood. I followed him down the tree-lined street where he turned right.

Unfortunately, when I got to the turn, Bruno had disappeared. I was completely dazed until he popped up from behind a goddamn bush and scared the living shit out of me. "Willow?"

At that point, I had nothing to lose. Playing it off as a coincidence didn't work, so I went with the jealousy—"Who was that cute little blond?" *There.* It was out there for the world to see and hear. I cared about the guy a lot, and if he was seeing someone else, I might just tear out their sunny blond hair, strand by strand.

Bruno tried really hard not to laugh, I could tell, but finally, he offered a little smile. "That was an old friend from before I knew you. He was a dancer at a club where I used to be a bouncer—that place Dex worked a few years ago when Gabe met him. I was just checking on him. He's only a kid," Bruno responded as he walked out of the bushes.

I chuckled. "Oh, because *you're* so old." He was a few years younger than me, but he seemed so much more mature, it kind of freaked me out.

"He's a friend of Dexter's, and I—"

"You moved out?" I interrupted.

Bruno sighed. "Walk with me?"

I nodded, so we headed beyond Uncle Gabe's street and slowly walked together. "Gabe swore me to secrecy, but I owe you an explanation for moving in with them. There's possibly a threat, and I'm looking into it," Bruno finally admitted.

I rolled my eyes. "I know—the Mangellos. I was there, remember?"

Bruno smirked. "Oh, I remember, Willow. I can't tell you much about it, and I'm praying it's not related. That guy I was with—Paul Ogden—he offered me a direction to go so I can get to the bottom of it. Now, I'm sorry I moved out without talking to you first, but Gabe wants me at the house to help keep all of them safe, so that's where I'll be staying for the time being. It's not because I wanted to leave you," he offered quietly.

My heart pounded in my chest. "What are we going to do about... Hell, I'll say it. What are we going to do about *us*?" I asked, surprising myself.

I'd been avoiding the subject of our marriage, but it seemed as if it was a huge looming monster right in the middle between us, and I was sick of it being there. I wanted it dealt with so we could each move on.

Bruno stopped and touched my forearm, pulling my hand free of my pocket before he slid his hand into it. "That's the part that's up to you, Willow. I told you I'll give you the annulment if you want it, but I can't make that decision for you."

He was right. He'd been upfront about his willingness to get an annulment when I'd seen him in Italy, and now he'd returned and was keeping his word that he'd do whatever I wanted. Why the fuck was I so damn undecided about the two of us? Finally, I struck on an idea. "How about I take you for dinner tomorrow night? You know, like a date?" I suggested.

Bruno looked at me, his eyes studying me closely. "I thought you don't date?" Clearly, he remembered my stupid fucking comment on not dating, and he was throwing it back at me—though there was no smartass look on his face.

I had to believe he was trying to figure out my mixed messages, so I sighed. "Well, that was me being an immature imbecile. Now, dating dating—or dating you, doesn't scare me."

Bruno's smile was as bright as the moon in the sky. "Okay, if you're sure. Think about where you want to go, and we'll go. Let me get you home. It's late, and you'll catch a cold if you stay out in the rain any longer," he pointed out as he retrieved his phone from the pocket of a really sexy leather jacket that looked like it was made to highlight every muscle in his handsome torso.

"Where'd you get this nice jacket?" I asked him as I watched him type our location into the rideshare app.

"I got it in Italy before I came home. Your car will be here in two minutes. Tell me what's going on with the kids and the new school year," Bruno questioned as we stood together on the sidewalk. I so wanted to kiss him, but I knew it would send even more mixed signals to the man, and I'd already done enough to confuse the guy for a fucking lifetime. Until I could get my head straight, I needed to be careful with him. He didn't deserve the selfish bastard I'd become.

THE NEXT MORNING as I was having my coffee, my phone rang. I glanced down to see it was my father's number, so I answered it, determined to figure things out with the man one way or the other with him as well. "Hey, Dad."

"Hi, son. How are you?" he asked. It had been a while since I'd spoken to him, but I wanted to get to the bottom of whether he was sincere about wanting to try to rebuild our father/son relationship—and if he'd accepted what my mother had found impossible to even consider. I was a gay man, and I wouldn't be bringing home a nice girl… ever.

"I'm well. Busy at work, but that's no surprise. How about you? How are things at Mazzola Shipping?" I asked. My father ran a smallish freight-moving business that transported cargo up and down the West Coast. He had five freighters that moved anything from plastic dog poop to BMWs from the intake port in San Francisco to points north and south.

It was mostly cheap crap from China as I understood it—I had no interest in my father's business—but I knew he traveled to China a few times a year to meet with clients. Why they'd partner with my dad's dinky ass operation was a mystery to me, but then again, my grandfather, Carmine, had started the business as a young man and had left it to my dad when he died. I much preferred the exciting world of the Torrente family to the shipping of novelty plastic kazoos up and down the West Coast.

"Things are going quite well, son. Are you too busy to meet me for lunch? I'm here in Manhattan for a meeting, so maybe you can take a little time and we get together?" Dad offered.

I decided I'd never know the truth of his intentions unless I bit the bullet and met the man, face-to-face. "Sure," I agreed. I'd been looking for a reason to stop by a restaurant in Manhattan where my old boyfriend, Corey, was working as a pastry chef to say hi. We'd parted somewhat amicably after seeing each other—read that, hooking up—for a few months the first year I moved to New York, but we were still in touch on social media. He was part of a soul-searching project I had undertaken, and I believed his input could be helpful in me sorting through my fucked-up commitment issues, as I was coming to think might be part of my problem.

I wanted to ask him why he dumped me. It wasn't in the name of rekindling our relationship—which it really wasn't—but trying to understand what he thought he couldn't live with when it came to me. The trip could serve double duty.

"How about we meet at Amsterdam Seafood Grill at Amsterdam and 88th? It's on the Upper West Side. Let's say one-thirty? I'll make a reservation," I suggested.

"Sounds good. You still on kid duty with Dylan and Searcy? Your mom mentioned it to me last Sunday that she thought you were wasting your time babysitting those two. How long does Gabriele think he can keep their true parentage a secret?" Dad questioned. My heart began beating a mile a minute at his words. That information was supposed to be kept in the family.

"What do you mean?" I asked him. I only knew about Dino Mangello being their father because I'd worked for Giuseppe in Italy as his IT geek after Lotta left. I had access to tons of information on that network, some of which gave me insights I doubted I'd have gotten had I not been in the position. It was also where I learned their parentage wasn't common knowledge.

"You know what I mean, Dom. Mom told me about it when Dexter came into the family. It's a well-known secret that those kids aren't really Dexter's or Gabriele's," Dad explained.

Shit! I had no idea Mom had told him anything about the kids. *What the fuck should I do?* Uncle Gabe would kill my father if he knew.

"Yeah, well, it's a hell of a lot more than that, but we can discuss it at lunch. See you later," I signed off. *How damn far had that important secret been shared?*

I GOT to the Victorian after dropping the kids at school with Duke just as Bruno and Dexter were arriving at Dex's studio. I'd confirmed as I watched the two of them that Bruno's primary was Dexter, even though Bruno didn't say it to me, specifically. He didn't get more than a few feet from the man as I watched them.

It didn't take a genius to see the pattern or that it was sanctioned by my uncle because if it wasn't, Gabby would've beaten the life out of Bruno—or tried to, anyway. I had my doubts he'd win on that front.

Dex went to the studio and Bruno went to the reception desk, taking a seat, which was odd. Usually, Sabrina manned the phones. I walked over to the hall tree in the foyer, taking off my jacket to hang it before I approached the man.

"Good morning," I greeted.

Bruno looked absolutely incredible, and when that minty vanilla scent entered my nose, my cock started to plump in my slacks at a most inconvenient time and place. I quickly shoved my hands in my pockets before it became apparent, and I cursed myself under my breath. Something was going to have to give before I combusted.

"Good morning. How'd you sleep?" Bruno asked, his voice deep and sexy—or maybe it was my imagination just hearing it that way. I was sure my sanity had taken enough of a beating of late that most of what was happening was actually in some warped alternative universe where my mind spent most of its time.

"I, uh, I slept okay—I hate being there alone," I admitted before I could turn on the filter.

A look of concern crossed Bruno's face. "Why don't you come stay with me at Gabe and Dexter's, too?"

Was that the simple answer to the problem? I was watching out for Dylan and Searcy, so staying at my uncle's large house made sense. Maybe it was the best way to finally get my head together.

I'd finally realized I wasn't *the shit* like I'd always believed I was, and I knew I needed to think about someone other than myself for once. I had no problem making Bruno the object of my affections.

"I'll talk to Gabby about it. So, you're Dex's body man?" I whispered after I looked around to see no one was in the lobby. Bruno's face shifted to worry before he appeared to question me.

"Don't freak out. I only noticed you were spending a lot of time in his vicinity. I'm sure nobody else noticed or even gives a shit about it. Does that guy last night have anything to do with it?" I asked him.

Bruno glanced around as well. "Yeah. Maybe I'm not very good at this job?" he offered, which made me chuckle.

"Don't think like that. It's not the case at all; you're good at the job, Bruno. Anything I can help you with?" I offered.

"Let me think about it, okay? I guess you called Casper to find me last night?"

I nodded. There was no use in denying it. "But only because I wanted to talk to you about your moving out. I don't make a habit of spying on people," I defended myself, then I added, "Besides, he only helped me because he knows about the marriage license thing."

"Got it," Bruno responded, his look unreadable.

"I'm sorry if it was—"

"It's okay. I'm not mad," Bruno answered me before the phone rang.

I went upstairs to see who was around, happy to find Smokey at his desk in the office he'd used since he'd started working at GEA-A. At the moment, he was sharing it with Mathis, who was out with Ace on a security appraisal at a soon-to-open boutique in DUMBO. "Morning," I greeted as I went inside to take a seat. He had papers spread on the desk, but I didn't look to see what they were.

"Beaver, my friend, what the fuck is going on with you? You've had the shittiest attitude these last few months, and I can't figure out why. Is it kid duty that's got you down, or are you really turning into that much of a prick? I know about the damn marriage license, and I don't like the way you're dragging my friend Bruno around by the short ones. Be married to the man or divorce him, but don't keep treatin' him like he's dogshit on your fancy shoes. What's the problem?" Smokey asked as he sorted through all the loose pages in front of him, seeming to organize them. I knew his assessment of my behavior of late was spot on. The man was a frickin' genius.

"The kids are really the least of my worries, but I am trying to get things straightened out with Bruno, I promise. Do you know what's going on with Dex? Why does Gabby have Bruno acting as his body man?" I inquired. Since Nemo had moved to DC, Smokey was generally Uncle Gabe's confidante. I was certain he had to have some idea of what was going on.

"Huh?"

"Surely you've noticed that Bruno is with Dexter every time he leaves the Victorian," I pointed out what I felt was perfectly obvious.

Smokey closed his eyes for a minute before nodding his head. "As a matter of fact, I have noticed Noble as Dex's shadow these last few days. I don't know what it's about, though," the cowboy answered without looking up at me.

"Gabby didn't say anything to you?" I asked him again.

"Nope, but maybe it's a fidelity issue. I don't get in between a couple, and Gabby knows it," he responded, offering a perspective I hadn't considered. Would Bruno be okay spying on Dex for Uncle Gabe to see if Dex was being faithful? I couldn't see either Dex or my uncle cheating on the other, especially since they were in the midst of making a baby together.

I let that issue go in favor of one I was sure Smokey knew more about. "How many people really know who Dylan and Searcy's parents are?" I asked.

Smokey chuckled in his own inimitable way. "Too fuckin' many, why?"

"I found out last night that my mom told my dad," I responded, feeling weird about talking about my parents with the cowboy.

"Well, she told Sal—she did, huh?" Smokey answered, seeming to change his track in the middle of a thought.

"Who else did she tell?" I asked. *Who knew my mother was the goddamn town crier!*

"Look, Dominic, I'm not lookin' to stir up trouble. I seriously doubt Gabby thinks Dexter is cheatin', so there's another reason why he's got Bruno paired up with him. I also don't give a good god damn what happens in people's bedrooms—somethin' you oughta think about—so I only give a shit about what you and Bruno are doin' because I don't believe the guy deserves to be strung along. As far as Dyl and Searcy go, I'd say your family is the worst secret keepers on the planet, but that doesn't change the fact I'd give my life to protect the whole fuckin' lot of ya. It's my job, but they're also my family, so it's easy to do," Smokey answered, causing me to have more questions than answers.

"What about my bedroom?" I asked, seeming to pick that issue to press for reasons unknown to my feeble mind at the time.

"Son, instead of worryin' about all this other shit, you need to figure out if you're gonna keep that big kid down there danglin' from a string or are you gonna cut him loose. What you're doin' to him ain't right, and that's all I have to say." With that, Smokey stood from his desk and opened the door, sweeping his hand for me to leave. I walked out and jumped when the door abruptly slammed behind me.

Am I doing that? Fuck!

13

BRUNO

I was surprised when the front door opened and Mateo walked into the Victorian. His skin was tanned, and his features were relaxed. He looked like a man who was well-rested, and I was happy for him.

"Welcome back," I greeted.

"*Grazie!*" he responded as he stepped behind the large wooden reception desk and pulled me up into a bear hug, surprising me a bit.

"What's the word around the office?" Mateo asked as he stepped back and took off the driving gloves he was wearing, tossing them on the desk before taking the chair next to me.

"Not sure, really. As far as I know, nothing much is going on. How was your honeymoon?" I asked.

"*Perfetto!*" You should try it, my friend. Where's your groom, by the way?" Mateo asked me.

"Upstairs. He and Duke just returned from dropping the kids at school," I answered.

"You shouldn't be sitting here, my friend. We still have a few issues with the Mangellos, and here, you're an easy target for a walk by, much less a drive by. I thought Dom was going to hire someone?" Mateo questioned.

I chuckled. "Above my pay grade," I answered as I left the desk and walked over to the door of the yoga studio to see Dexter was holding a class. With him safely in the Victorian, I had time to do a little more digging and leave the phones to Mateo to answer, so I went downstairs to the gym, glad to find it empty.

I went to my locker and pulled out my gym bag, opening it to find the loaded Ruger LCR and ankle holster where I'd stored it that morning. We didn't carry firearms in the office, so I'd stored it in my locker, but I had a feeling I'd be better off to take it with me. I strapped it to my ankle and headed out the back door to see if I could find a cab.

I ended up walking to Franklin Avenue, enjoying the brisk fall air. Halloween was at the end of the next month, and I knew it wouldn't be long before the rest of the holidays rolled around. That meant our one-year anniversary was coming soon, which had me worried. Was there a time clock on getting an annulment?

I quickly called Blue Plate, remembering our date that night. "Blue Plate." I recognized Parker's voice immediately.

"Hi, Parker. It's Bruno," I greeted.

"Bruno, my friend! How are you?" Parker replied, a happy smile in his voice.

"I'm great. How are you? Smokey tells me things are very busy at the restaurant," I offered, feeling a bit guilty for asking him for a reservation for that night when I hadn't called him in a while.

"Thankfully, yes, they are. So, are you just calling to chat, which is totally okay, but since you called the restaurant, I'm guessing that's not the case. When would you like to come for dinner?" Parker asked, saving me from having to put my friend on the spot.

"I, uh—Is there any way you can fit us in tonight?" I hesitantly asked Parker.

Parker giggled, which was one of my favorite things about him when I was with him in Atlanta, though that wasn't a time I liked to remember—having shot that soldier and all.

"Yes. I'll set the two of you up in my kitchen. I have this nice little alcove I had built for Shep and I to have dinner in, so you and

Dominic can be my guest tonight. It's private," Parker assured, which I appreciated very much.

"Thank you so much. What time is convenient for you?" I asked him.

"Why don't you come in at seven and have a drink in the bar. I'll have you seated at eight, if that's okay," he offered. It was exactly the perfect thing that might impress my Willow.

After I hung up from talking to Parker, I messaged Dominic.

I'll pick you up at the apartment at six-thirty for our date. Have a great day. Bruno

I read it about three more times before I finally hit send because I was relatively new to texting, and Ben had mentioned that context could be lost in a text message. I wasn't one to usually question myself, but with Dominic, I questioned everything. I was coming to think I wasn't very good at dating.

As I made my way down the street, I saw a beer truck parked in front of The Bone Yard, so I walked up to the man with the dolly and offered a friendly smile. "You need some help? I'm on my way in, and I can carry a few cases for you," I offered. It wasn't a lie, but thankfully, the man took it to mean I worked there and pointed to three cases of Bud on the back of the truck.

I picked them up and followed him inside where a new bartender was busy checking the inventory as the truckdriver unloaded them. I placed the three cases on the bar near the cooler where they were stocked. "Hey, man, I'm gonna use the john," I called out to no one in particular as I headed toward the bathrooms, which were next to Jeff Oswald's office.

It was only just after ten in the morning, so I was sure Oswald wasn't there yet. The slimeball usually came in early in the afternoon to do the bank deposit from the previous night, so I had a little time to look around without anyone getting suspicious.

The safe was behind the large oak desk which was covered in loose purchase orders and receipts. I moved the chair and knelt down, sliding the door on the piece of furniture behind the desk where there were drawers and a few shelves. The safe was there and locked, but as I stared at it, I wondered if Oswald would be so stupid as to hide naked pictures of the dancers in it when the bartenders had the combination to be able to put the nights receipts in it before they left at three in the morning.

I didn't think the awful man was that dumb, so I started looking around for locked drawers or another safe where he'd hide something of the sort. There were curtains along the wall behind the long piece of furniture behind the desk, so I found the split and checked to see if there was something hidden back there.

Unsurprisingly, there was a window in the middle that looked into the dancer's dressing room and staff locker room. It would be easy enough for Oswald to take pictures of the dancers while they changed without their knowledge, which made me mad.

I adjusted the curtains and looked around for cameras, seeing the security cameras in two corners of the room, both strategically pointed away from the hidden window and the large couch in the room.

Once I was sure those were the only two cameras in the room, I went to Jeff's desk and sat down after pulling out my phone to call Casper. "Hey, Noble. Where are you?" he answered.

"I'm working a case, and I need to know how to erase a security tape. Can you help me?" I asked him as I continued to look around the office for hidden drawers, my frustration mounting as I kept coming up empty.

"Sure. I need the ISP address so I can take over the computer. I can triangulate where you are based on your phone. Gimme a second," Casper informed me.

A few minutes later, he was inside Jeff Oswald's computer. I sat in front of the large monitor watching files pop up and disappear as Casper searched the computer for the security system while I continued to check the desk for any secret drawers. I was probably looking for something that didn't exist. "Whoa! Holy porn stash, Batman," Casper stated as a bunch of folders popped up on the screen of the computer.

I watched the door in case anyone tried to come inside while

Casper continued to search the computer. I'd engaged the lock on the door after using my driver's license to slip the lock to get inside, but I had to be ready in case someone heard me rifling around in there and decided to come check it out.

The naked pictures that were flashing before my eyes made my stomach turn sour. "Slow down. How are they filed?" I asked, not trusting myself to read the labeled folders quickly enough with my dyslexia.

"Okay, they're divided by year. Are you looking for someone in particular?" Casper asked. Yes, I was, but I couldn't tell him that.

I remembered Dex worked there in 2017, so I moved the mouse to take control of the screen. "Oh, okay, you're taking over. Go ahead."

"Shut your eyes," I instructed Casper. I had to trust him because I wasn't there with him to be sure.

"Okay. Eyes are shut," he answered me.

I clicked on the folder marked 2017 and began scrolling through the pictures that popped up until there, in the middle, were the five pictures of Dexter as he seemed to be putting on lotion and preparing for his time on the box—that was when it occurred to me that the white light from under Dex's supposedly dead body were the lighted cubes in the main room where the dancers performed.

It was as I suspected when Paul mentioned the naked pictures. Jeff Oswald was the person threatening Dexter. "Casper, can you copy a file without looking at it?" I asked my friend.

"Sure. The one where the pointer is hovering?" he responded.

"Yes, but please don't look inside. Download it and send it to Gabe, then delete it and all of these pictures from this computer," I suggested before Casper spoke up.

"You know, if we're going after this guy for child porn or trafficking, we need to leave these images on the hard drive and call the cops," Casper pointed out. That was one option, but that wasn't what Gabe had told me to do.

"No—delete them. Actually, copy everything on the computer and put it somewhere safe before you delete everything on this one, please. Fry the heck out of it," I instructed, hearing his laugh over the phone. I quickly put my hand over the mic to muffle the noise just as there was a knock on the door.

"You got it?" I asked Casper.

"Consider it done. Be careful," he told me before I ended the call, putting my phone in my pocket before I went over and opened the door to see the bartender with papers in hand.

"What are you doin' in here?" the guy asked. He was about the size of Dom—tall and slender—though he wasn't nearly as handsome as my husband.

"I thought this was the john, man. Sorry about the mess. Tell Jeff he needs to have better security around here," I told him before I darted around him and out the door. The beer man was gone when I got to the curb, but that was fine. Jeff would probably know who I was when his bartender described me, but that would make it easier for me to catch him. I'd lock him in that room at the Victorian as Gabby had told me to do, and I'd find out what he was trying to do with those pictures. I'd just given Jeff Oswald something to worry about that wasn't Dexter. It was going to be a good day.

I KNOCKED on the door of the apartment I shared with Dom, wiping my hands on the sports jacket that Gabe had loaned me when I told him I had a date with Dominic that night. I didn't mention anything about Jeff Oswald, just that I was close to getting to the bottom of things, and he'd told me he would be fine with Dex and the kids at home alone that night.

Dom opened the door, and a big smile spread over his pretty mouth. "You have a key, you know."

I chuckled. "It's not mine to use right now. You ready? I have a car waiting for us downstairs," I informed.

Dom hurried to grab a sports jacket of his own, and we were off. I held the car door for him and once we merged into traffic for the short ride, I finally exhaled the nerves.

I turned to Dominic, seeing he appeared to be as nervous as me, so I opened my fist, resting my open hand on my thigh. Thankfully, Dom put his hand in mine. The warmth from it surged through my insides like fire. "How was your day?" I asked him.

By the time I'd made it back to the Victorian earlier in the day, Dom was gone to pick up the kids, and I'd left with Dexter at four that afternoon to beat them home. Dom hadn't come inside when Duke brought the kids home from school, so we hadn't talked.

"It was good, I guess. I had lunch with my father, today," he responded. I couldn't tell what he thought about that because his face was a little blank, which didn't make me happy. I always wanted to see his beautiful smile.

"Do you not get along with your father?" I asked him. We didn't know things of the sort about each other, but I was hoping to change that.

The driver stopped in front of Blue Plate, and Dom looked out the window before he turned to me. "Called in a favor?" he asked with a slow grin lighting up his face, finally.

I felt my cheeks heat a little. "I did save his life once in Georgia," I joked as I hopped out and offered my hand for Dom to slide across the seat. I quickly pulled up the rideshare app and tipped the guy before we went inside.

I took Willow's hand and walked us into the restaurant and toward the bar where two seats had reserved signs in front of them. A pleasant looking lady stepped up to us. "Are you Bruno? Chef said these were for two handsome men, and I'd say you fit the bill, perfectly."

My face heated again, but I nodded. She removed the signs, and I pulled out a stool for Dom before I took a seat next to him. The lady put napkins in front of us, which was when I noticed her name was Emily. "Welcome to Blue Plate. What can I get you gentlemen to drink?" she asked.

Dominic picked up the small drink menu from the bar and looked at it, finally chuckling. "I'll have a glass of the Torrente pinot grigio, please." He then passed it to me, but I didn't look at it.

"Peroni, please," I responded to the lady before she hurried away. I swiveled my stool to face him.

"So, was the lunch good?" I asked, picking up our conversation from the car.

Dom turned toward me as well. "It was weird. Growing up, Dad and I had nothing in common, and now, he's trying to get me to come back to San Francisco to work at Mazzola Shipping with him. He said I should bring my boyfriend with me, which means either Mom didn't tell him about the wedding, or he doesn't believe it either," Dominic explained.

The idea of him leaving town had my head spinning.

14

DOMINIC

The look on Bruno's handsome face was one of sheer terror. I quickly touched his forearm that rested on the bar. "I'm not going. I want nothing to do with the business, okay? Shipping finger traps and rubber dog turds up and down the West Coast isn't my thing," I assured him.

Bruno chuckled through a sigh as he picked up his beer bottle. "Is that what it really is?" he asked me.

"I think so, but hell, I'm not really sure. I never paid attention when he talked about it. I know he's moved luxury cars down to San Diego before. It's just a weird business, you know, and it doesn't really sound exciting to me. Most of the stuff he hauls comes from China, I think, but he picks up other contracts on the side. He has five medium-sized freighters that are always full, so he must be doing something right," I answered before taking a sip of the delicious family fortune. It tasted crisp and fruity, reminding me of my time in Siena and how much I wanted to go back with Bruno.

"Did you like your time in... Oh, wait, you weren't there for fun, were you? Italy, I mean. How'd that work out?" I questioned. It was something we needed to dig into, I believed.

Bruno looked down and ran his thumbnail against a seam in the bar top. "I failed," he whispered. I reached over and touched his hand again, finding myself unable to keep from touching him somewhere.

"I doubt that, but what were you supposed to do?" I asked him. I could see the self-disappointment on his handsome face, and I didn't like it at all.

"I was supposed to find out who is feeding Frankie Man information about the Torrentes so we can be ready when he comes for Dylan and Searcy. We know he knows they're his grandchildren. We just don't know when he's going to come after them," Bruno explained very quietly.

"Well, I'm on alert, and so is Duke, so if they come for the kids, we'll protect them," I boldly affirmed. Nobody was getting passed us.

We chatted about his childhood—well, what he was willing to share. "It's not anything good that I want to taint you with. I'm sure you had a great childhood growing up with so many cousins and family around all the time," he assumed.

I sighed. "I'm the oldest. All of the cousins are younger, and most are a pain in the ass. My sisters are great, but my oldest is too much like my mom. Right now, she's in school, so she doesn't really have time for me, but she accepted my dad back into the family in a hot minute," I admitted. It bugged the shit out of me that Gina was so quick to let him back in. Ava had always been Daddy's Little Girl, but I thought Gina was more independent than to just follow Mom's lead. I guessed I was wrong.

"Gentlemen, welcome," Parker greeted us from the spot between us, his happy smile on display as expected. He hugged us both as he spoke. "You ready for dinner? I have some appetizers I prepared just for the two of you," he invited. Bruno chugged the last of his beer as I downed the rest of my wine. Bruno threw some cash on the bar and placed his hand on the small of my back, guiding me along behind Parker as we made our way to the kitchen.

Bruno pulled out a chair for me and scooted it under when I was seated before taking his own seat. The table was round, situated in the corner of the kitchen. It was made of maple—which I only knew because Nonno liked to make things from wood. The chairs were made of the same maple with robin's egg blue and white checkered cushions on the seat and over the back. The walls that surrounded three sides of the area were covered in white shiplap, and it was closed off a bit from the full view of the kitchen. It felt a lot like I was sitting in my nonny's kitchen, and I loved it.

"We'll get you some more drinks and then I'll serve your apps. Can I get you some water? Still or sparkling?" Parker asked us.

I glanced at Bruno to see a sweet smile on his face as he stared at me. He nodded, so I turned to Parker. "We'll both have still, please. Thanks."

The chef left us, and I looked back at Bruno. "So, have you been making headway in your secret mission?" I joked.

Bruno grinned. "I think I'm about to wrap it up. How are—" He was going to continue the inane small talk, I was sure, but we had more serious issues to discuss.

"Does that mean that you'll be moving back home with me?" I challenged.

Bruno's eyes nearly doubled in size for a moment. "I, uh, I think if you want the annulment, we have to live apart," he stated.

There was that word again! "Who told you about an annulment?" I asked.

Our appetizers were served, Oysters Rockefeller. They looked delicious, but when I turned to Bruno, I saw his nose was scrunched up. "You don't like oysters?" I asked him as I put one on each of our plates from the platter where they were nestled in rock salt.

"I've never had them. What are they?" he asked as he poked them with the tiny seafood forks that accompanied the platter.

"They're oysters topped with spinach, cheese, butter, garlic, and other herbs. Nonna Grace makes the best I've ever had, but let's try these," I suggested, squeezing lemon on his then mine before I topped them with a little cocktail sauce and picked up my own small fork. I showed him how to eat it, and I watched as he lifted the hot shell, almost dropping it. He leaned forward and sniffed, making a face that wasn't unpleasant.

"It smells good," Bruno offered before he used his fork to pick up the oyster and pop it into his mouth. He chewed slowly, his face showing no expression and then he swallowed.

For a moment, he stared down at the empty shell before he looked up at me and grinned. "If Mrs. Torrente's are better than these, I'd like to taste them. Anyway, my lawyer in Georgia told me that we could get an annulment in New York. There have to be grounds for the judge to issue the order to annul the marriage, but we would qualify under more than one reason if you want the marriage voided," Bruno explained to me what I'm sure was a quote from his lawyer.

"Like what grounds?" I asked as we each ate a couple more oysters.

Bruno retrieved his phone from his pocket and scrolled for a few seconds before he handed it to me. It was a Google entry entitled, "On what grounds can you get a marriage annulled in New York State?"

I glanced through the list—an undissolved previous marriage; underage spouse at the time of marriage; one spouse is physically incapable of sexual relations; forced consent to marriage; fraudulent consent; or incapability to legally consent to marriage. "None of these fit us," I protested before handing back his phone.

"I'm willing to allow you to charge me with fraudulent consent or forced consent. Or you can say I'm physically incapable of sexual relations. I'll pay for you to get an attorney to draft the petition, and I'll sign whatever you choose," Bruno suggested.

"Are you incapable of having sexual relations?" I pried. I sincerely doubted that was the case, but I wanted to see how he'd answer.

Bruno's stare was unwavering. "If that's what you want me to say, then yes."

"That's not an answer. Are you a virgin?" I quizzed.

"I've had sex a few times," he answered. I saw his beer was empty, so I motioned for the nearest waitress to bring us two more drinks. Thankfully, she nodded.

"With whom?" I asked as if I had a right. I reached up and

touched the chain under my t-shirt where my ring was resting. I saw Bruno was wearing his, and I wondered what it meant for him.

"Two different guys. Nobody you know," he answered, and I was certain he was being honest with me. I didn't think the guy had it in him to lie.

"Okay, so you can have sex. Nothing wrong with the plumbing," I commented and then saw the look on his face. "Wait, I'm sorry. That was totally rude. I never thought there was anything wrong with… Damn! I'm making a mess of this. So, you *are* gay?"

Not exactly the smoothest thing to say considering he'd kissed me twice so well that I barely remembered my damn name after, but somewhere in my jumbled mind, I had a point to make.

"Yes. I figured out I'm gay. Do I not act gay enough?" Bruno asked me, seeming to bristle a bit as he sank back in the chair. There was a little bite in his voice that told me I'd struck a nerve.

"I didn't say that at all. I don't know how one acts gay enough. I've had sex with guys and I've even married one, but still my mother doesn't believe I'm gay," I responded with a laugh, trying to sooth his ego that I'd apparently chafed a bit.

Bruno smiled a little and took a sip of his beer before he spoke. "When I lived on the ranch with my parents and a few ranch hands, they used to call me names because of the way I was back then," he explained to me.

"How were you—if you want to tell me?" I asked, trying to be respectful to his situation.

"I used to like colorful clothes, and I kept my appearance tidy, unlike that bunch of slobs at the ranch. My learning disability made me a target for everybody already, but one day during my sophomore year of high school, I got caught walking home alone after school. The football team drove by me, and they all jumped out of the back of the quarterback's pickup truck. They called me names and beat the hell out of me, leaving me on that gravel road by myself. Turned out my father paid them to do it. 'Beat the man into ya,' he'd said when I got home. I had a bloody nose, black eyes, busted lips, loose teeth. I was a mess, and it was because I wasn't man enough for my father," Bruno admitted as he looked down at the table.

I was speechless. My father was truly a jackass, but to have someone intentionally beat up your son—that was unfathomable.

"What did your mom say?" I asked him, seeing him picking at the napkin under his bottle of beer, the frosted mug untouched.

Bruno offered a humorless chuckle before he looked up at me. "That was the thing—it was her idea to do it in the first place. She was friends with the quarterback's mother and apparently suggested to my father that Walt and his friends might scare me into acting more like a man. After that, Dad punched around on me to make me a man, and Mom did nothing to stop it. That was why I left home at eighteen."

"That must have been hard, being on your own," I remarked.

He looked up and shrugged. "I survived. Along the way, I changed everything about myself to try to look like the man everyone thought I should be. I worked at a few cattle ranches as a travelling cowboy, and then I made my way to Bakersfield where I learned more about working on engines—I knew some from working on the ranch—and I became a prospect for a motorcycle club. I thought I'd found my home until they asked me to run dope for them. That was when I left and worked my way across the country," Bruno outlined.

I had questions, of course, but Parker stepped over and cleared the plate of empty oyster shells away, putting it on the tray the friendly waitress was holding. "So, any special requests for dinner?" he asked, his bright smile and sparkling eyes seeming to cheer Bruno up immediately. A pang of jealousy surged through my body at the sight.

"Willow," Bruno urged me to order first—just like the perfect gentleman.

"I'll have the blue plate special," I ordered, tempering the acid in my voice for Parker, who was only being his normally sweet self.

"Ah! Good choice. Barbecue pork dumplings. Rafe taught me how to make the wonton wrappers. He learned from a lady during his travels around the world, and they're really great. What would you like as a side?" Parker asked.

"I'll have the veggie fried rice and the sauteed sugar snap peas. Oh, and an order of the fried wontons, please," I ordered. That was the thing that was so great about the place—every day they had a new special from around the world. Parker's barbecue pork was incredible on its own, but in a dumpling, it was amazing.

"I'd like the chicken fried steak, please. Mashed potatoes and green beans if you don't mind, Parker," Bruno ordered.

Parker nodded. "Gravy on the side, right?"

My companion nodded, and Parker mentioned something to the waitress before he took the tray from her. She scampered off, returning a minute later with a bottle of Torrente wine and another beer for Bruno, along with a glass of iced tea. Bruno chuckled.

"I should have known Parker would remember I liked tea to drink with my meal. Anyway, I told you my sad tale. I don't want that to make a difference, Wil—Dominic. Get a lawyer and send me the papers to annul the marriage, and I'll leave you alone. I'm looking for an apartment right now," he announced, surprising me.

It was apparent to me that the man was one of a kind, and I'd seen how much he'd changed since he'd first come to work at GEA-A. He was a polite, sweet man who had never, or so it seemed, had anyone to care about him. His smile made my heart pound, and his deep laugh did funny things to my insides.

I was twenty-six, soon to be twenty-seven, and I'd never been in love. I'd grown up with lots of family and lots of love around me, but I'd taken it for granted. Seeing Bruno describe his childhood made my chest ache for him. No way could I let him just walk away without seeing if there could be something more between us.

We ate in relative silence, though at one point, Bruno cut a bite of his steak, dipped it in the pepper gravy, and put it on my bread plate. "This is really good. I don't use much of the gravy, but that's because I watch what I eat, not because it's not good."

I took the morsel and popped it into my mouth, tasting the simple deliciousness of it. I'd have to remember it for the next time I was at the restaurant. It was damn good.

"Here, try this," I replied as I cut one of the four large dumplings in half and placed it on his bread plate. He cut it in half and took a bite, smiling at the sweet and smokey taste of the sauce and the succulent pork inside the delicate dumpling.

"Wow, that's good," Bruno responded. After that, we ate off each other's plates until we were stuffed.

Bruno drained his tea with the meal and then poured me another glass of wine. "How's it working with Duke?" he asked as he placed the bottle back into the bucket of ice.

The waitress cleared our empty dishes and left us. Bruno was staring at me so intently that gooseflesh popped up on my arms. "Uh, it's not bad. He's a really great guy, but you probably figured that out already," I commented with a smirk.

Bruno offered a sheepish smile. "He's always been nice to me. When he came looking for me in Italy because I hadn't checked in, I knew he would be a good friend to anyone who needed one."

I laughed. "When he first came around, I doubt anyone would have agreed."

Parker appeared. "Dessert, guys?" It was incredible that the guy was giving us so much attention, what with the fact the restaurant was packed.

"Yes, please. We'll have the flourless lava cake and two spoons. Oh, and the whipped cream, please," Bruno ordered, which surprised me.

"Coming right up," Parker announced as he poured the last of the wine in my glass before he took the ice bucket and left us.

During the time Bruno had been away from New York—after I found out we were really married—I'd tried to decide how to handle things when he returned. But I didn't really have a clear answer until I tracked him in Manhattan and saw that blond man with him. In that moment, I realized that I'd fallen in love with Bruno Garvin, and I'd be a damn fool not to give us a chance. I just hoped to hell he felt the same way.

"So, let's get down to it. I think we shelve that annulment idea. If we don't work out as a couple, then I'm fine with getting a divorce," I stated. I wasn't exactly sure if we'd work out but throwing in the towel without really giving the two of us a shot didn't feel right all the way down to my core.

"You mean... Tell me what you mean, please," Bruno whispered.

"I mean I think we owe it to each other to get better acquainted and see if our impulsive actions were being guided by the universe," I answered.

Bruno looked at me, turning his head a bit before he smiled. "Like I told you in Italy, I won't kiss you again until you ask me."

"Don't worry. If this goes right, I'll be the one kissing *you*." I meant every word.

15

BRUNO

The morning after my date with Dominic, I woke at four-thirty, my body humming with a new energy. I had to get my current case wrapped up so I could move back to the apartment with Willow. Our goodbye the previous night had replayed through my mind all night long on a loop.

The chocolate lava cake was shaped like a heart, which made me laugh. I hadn't said it, but Parker had picked up on how much I wanted things to work out with Dominic. The little boost to my cause didn't go unnoticed, so I gave Parker a kiss on the cheek for his thoughtfulness before the two of us left the restaurant that night.

When I turned to look at Willow, his eyebrow was cocked at me in disapproval—I'd seen it before—and I had a warm feeling in my chest. "I'll see that you get home okay," I informed him as I led us out of the restaurant to the sidewalk where I flagged down a taxi and gave the driver the address for the apartment building.

We pulled to the curb outside the white stone building. "I'll be right back," I told the driver as I got out and held my hand out to assist Willow as I'd seen Nemo and Smokey do for their husbands on more than one occasion.

I walked him to the building door and put in the code, opening it when it buzzed. We went to the elevator and I pushed the button. "You really don't have to ride up with me," Willow protested.

"Door to door," I responded. It was what Nemo had told me when I was looking out for Ben. "Always door to door," Nemo used to say. I followed that rule without fail.

Once we were inside the elevator car, Willow slid next to me, his pinky finger gently touching mine. "I had fun," he commented.

"Even with me spilling my guts about my family?" I found it hard to believe he found that part fun.

He nudged my arm. "I like getting to know more about you."

The doors opened and I put my hand in front of the sensor so we could step out. I walked him to the door of our apartment and used my key to unlock it. "I guess I'll see you tomorrow," I told him as I took his hand and pulled him into my arms, hugging him so I could resist the urge to kiss him. I meant what I'd said about not kissing him until he asked me to. Thankfully, he hugged me in return. My heart danced during the whole cab ride back to Gabe and Dexter's home.

I quickly gathered my things for work and carefully put them in my backpack before I dressed in running clothes to head to the Victorian. I couldn't wait to see Dominic at the office. I truly wanted to look my best.

The whole run to the Victorian, I kept thinking about the hug Willow had given me at the apartment door. I'd wished I could go in behind him, but I wasn't about to rush him when it came to our relationship. If it took ten years for him to invite me inside because he wanted me there, then I'd wait.

I happened to notice a car sitting across from the Victorian that I didn't recognize, so instead of going inside through the front door, I went behind the large house next door and cut through the yards, letting myself into the Victorian through the back door.

Once I was inside, I dug into my backpack to find the small Ruger and checked to see it was still loaded. I was wearing running shoes and shorts, so I secured the revolver in the pocket of my hooded sweatshirt and went upstairs, glancing out the window to see the car was still parked at the curb.

I went back downstairs and outside and ran through two yards so I could get behind the vehicle and use the element of surprise. I kicked myself that I didn't stop in the bunker to grab some night vision goggles from the weapon vault so I could see what the driver was doing, but I hadn't thought of it, and I wasn't about to take the chance of going back for them.

Thankfully, I had my phone in the pocket of my sweatshirt, so I pulled it out and took a snap of the license plate for Casper to check. I returned the phone and fitted my fist around the small pistol, pulling it from my pocket and holding it low as I made my way toward the car.

I snuck up on the passenger side to get a clear view of the driver, seeing it was the bouncer I used to work with at The Bone Yard, Cletus—or Clete as everyone called him. Apparently, Jeff Oswald had gotten my message. I put my gun back in my pocket and knocked on the window of the passenger side with my middle knuckle.

Clete turned toward me, a crooked smile crossing his face before he reached across the bench seat and lifted the small lock on the door. I opened it and hopped in, pulling out the pistol again to point it at him.

The guy laughed. "Dude, I'm only the messenger. You ready to go to the club to talk to him now, or you wanna come by later tonight. The boss is really pissed and wants to see you. He was bitchin' about the computer system. Did you do somethin' to it?" Clete asked.

"*I* didn't do anything to it, but I'm pretty sure I'm not the only person who hates his guts. Why are you still working for him?" I asked, holding the gun steady.

Clete had been as quiet as me when we worked together. I knew nothing about him and he knew nothing about me. He was the guy who had replaced Smitty, the guy who quit right after I took the job at the club. Gabe had punched Clete in the nose the night he'd rescued Dexter from the club. I had to wonder how he'd gotten the better of Clete that night because the man was massive.

"I'm workin' for Oswald 'cause it's a job, same reason you did before you hit the big time. What do you do in that big house?" Clete asked me.

"Security—same as you, but for the *right* people, not people like Jeffrey Oswald. My bosses are always looking for new people. I could ask about a job for you if you're interested. How bad is your criminal record?" I asked the guy.

Clete and I had discussed our criminal pasts one night when things were slow at the club, so I knew he had a couple of controlled substance charges along with a battery charge for beating the hell out of a guy at a gas station who had cut him off in traffic, which was probably why Oswald hired him in the first place.

"What's it pay?" Clete asked, not surprising me at all. Money was his main interest in every situation, which reminded me that Clete really didn't have a heart, so working for GEA-A was out. Then, I had another idea...

"How about you come inside with me while I, uh, wait for my boss," I suggested to Clete.

"You got coffee?" Clete asked me as he pulled the key from the ignition of his classic '69 Mustang.

"The best in the city. We have an Italian coffee maker and freshly ground beans. Espresso, cappuccino, latte—you name it, and I can make it," I tempted the big idiot.

Clete stepped out of his car and quietly closed the door. He was wearing sweatpants and flipflops along with a dirty white t-shirt, which wasn't a surprise to me at all. I'd dressed as bad or worse back when I worked at The Bone Yard. *He'll never make it at GEA,* I thought as I crossed the street with him.

I looked at his size and decided I'd never be able to drag him into the bunker alone, so hitting him with that little revolver would be like swatting a buzzard with a cotton swab. I'd need to lead him into the bunker and somehow immobilize him. I placed my hand on the reader for the back door, and when the door opened and the lights flashed, I had Clete follow me inside.

I closed the entrance and locked it, stepping over to the panel in the hallway and pressing it to open. I put my hand on the palm reader there and allowed it to run the necessary scan. It beeped twice, and I entered my personal code as Gabe had shown me to do. Once the door opened, I turned to Clete and offered a fake smile.

"Come on into the conference room. Let me get the lights," I lied, which wasn't something I liked to do as a rule. Unfortunately, it was my only choice because Clete was simply too big for me to handle alone.

He stepped into the bunker behind me and looked around while I went to the kitchen area and opened the small refrigerator. I'd explored the place enough to know there was a vial of GHB—the date-rape drug—but the problem was I didn't know the correct dosage to give someone. I couldn't trust myself that I wouldn't overdose the guy, so I grabbed two bottles of water, offering one to Clete.

"Let me run upstairs and turn on the coffee machine. Make yourself comfortable," I suggested, certain the man wasn't dumb enough just to sit down and stay in the bunker while I locked him inside.

"Got anything to eat in here? Is this where you work?" Clete asked me as he took a seat at the table, eyeing the gurney in the corner carefully.

I went to one of the drawers in the built-in bookcase and opened it to see all kinds of snacks inside. "Snacks in here. Help yourself. I'll be right back," I told him as I stepped out of the bunker and put in my code before I put my hand on the reader. The door slid shut, and the locks engaged without effort.

"I guess he *was* that dumb," I commented as I closed the panel and rushed up the stairs. Nobody was in the office yet, so I called Gabby.

"Hello?" he answered on the second ring.

"Sorry to call so early. I have a problem at the Victorian that I don't think you and I can handle alone," I answered.

"On my way. I'll bring help," he answered, not asking another question. That was definitely blind faith that I would be grateful to have for the rest of my life.

I went to the upstairs kitchen and turned on the big copper coffee machine, listening to hear if any noise could be heard from the bunker. Not one sound was I able to detect, which was a relief.

I paced nervously, unsure how I was going to explain Clete's presence to Gabby. He'd told me to lock the culprit into the bunker, but I didn't think Clete had been the one to alter the pictures of Dexter. He just didn't seem to be that smart.

A few minutes later, the lights flickered. I walked to the head of the stairs in time to hear, "C'è qualcuno qui?" *Is anybody here?* I was grateful to know that much Italian.

"*Sì!*" I yelled back.

I heard three sets of feet on the stairs, so I walked halfway down from the second floor to see Gabby, Mateo, and Rafe stroll into the lobby, all looking up the stairs to the third step that squeaked when I landed on it.

"Hey," I greeted. It was early—just after five—and I knew I needed to talk fast.

"I'm sorry to have you bring backup, Gabby, but by now, he's probably mad, and I don't think the two of us are strong enough to subdue him. I was going to dose him, but I was afraid I'd kill him. I'm not familiar with dosages for a man of his size," I explained to them.

Mateo stepped forward, extending his hand for me to take to help me down the stairs. I didn't need it, but I took it, anyway. "What vermin have you caught in our trap, Noble?" he asked me.

"That's the problem. I'm not sure yet if he's involved at all, but he was sitting in that Mustang across the street when I arrived here at four-thirty this morning. I was able to surprise him and get him to come inside with me without a fight, and he even went into the bunker without me asking twice. He just sat down at the table," I confessed.

"Wait, so he just went in and sat down and allowed you to lock him inside without a fight at all?" Gabby asked me. I nodded as he began chuckling.

"Well, Noble, don't keep us in suspense. What kind of rabbit is in your snare, *amico mio?*" Rafael questioned.

I looked at Gabby. "Remember when you came to The Bone Yard

that night and carried Dexter out of there? Clete and I were trying to stop you from taking him, and you punched Clete in the nose and flattened him before you came after me. You threatened to dislocate my shoulder but you were nice and told me if I didn't fight back, you'd let me go. It's Clete, the guy whose nose you broke, remember?"

Gabby sighed. "Barely. Is he an enemy combatant?"

I looked at Mateo, who offered a smirk. "Pardon him. His years in the Army Rangers still surface from time to time."

Gabe nodded and looked at me again. "Do you believe he'll be difficult to handle? I remember he's a pretty big boy."

Rafe stepped forward, flipping a knife into the air and catching it by the handle instead of the blade. "One flick of the wrist and I can make certain he can't move," the chef suggested. I didn't want to think about what he meant with his comment.

Gabby looked at his cousin and rolled his eyes. "Let's save that as a last resort. Is everyone ready?"

Mateo and Gabe pulled their weapons and Rafe crossed his arms over his chest, holding throwing knives in both hands. "Open it up, Bruno," Gabe insisted, so I put my hand on the reader and input my code.

I stepped away and pulled my revolver from the pocket of my sweatshirt, prepared for anything—except what we all saw. That was nothing I ever expected to see.

October

16

DOMINIC

"Good morning," I greeted Bruno when he opened the door at Uncle Gabe's house. The man had been out of town for a few days—according to the voicemail he left on my phone the morning after our date. I was relieved to know he was back.

"How are you? I'm sorry I left town without warning, but I had to help a friend move. Everything okay with kid duty?" Bruno asked me. I stepped into his body and wrapped my arms around his neck, offering a tight hug that he returned.

Before we pulled away, I kissed his cheek, inhaling his intoxicating scent, which made my blood heat in a way that had never happened to me before. "The kids are fine. Nothing unusual has come up with their security since I started working with Duke, so I have to wonder if Frankie Man was bluffing," I responded.

Bruno didn't answer, changing the subject. "How're things with your dad?"

My dad. That was a curious situation. We'd had lunch the day Bruno and I had our first official date, but I hadn't heard from Gio Mazzola since he'd given me an extended marketing pitch about the wonders of working for Mazzola Shipping. I wanted to jab a fork in my eye as I sat there trying to block it out. I had to wonder if it was just bullshit, my father reaching out like he wanted to establish a relationship with me for real. Something in the back of my mind made me wonder about his real motivation for the hard sell.

"Not sure. Haven't talked to him since we had lunch a week ago," I answered Bruno honestly.

"Do you need to go to San Francisco to talk to him and your mother face-to-face?" Bruno asked, his expression showing a sincerity that was truly rare, though I was sure it wasn't for him.

My features quickly formed into a scowl. "Oh, *hell* no. If they want to talk to me, they know where to find me."

Bruno flinched at the tone of my voice, and I was immediately sorry for raising it. I definitely wasn't mad at him. "Trust me, I'm not upset with you. It's just my parents are—they're real pieces of work. I still don't trust my father because I don't see why, all of a sudden, he's interested in my life. He had twenty-six fucking years to get interested in my life, and he didn't bother," I stated, curbing the venom to keep from worrying Bruno too much. He couldn't help it my parents were assholes.

I took a deep breath and continued. "Anyway, on to something much more pleasant—I had a good time the other night. Will you come over to the apartment for dinner Friday or Saturday night? I'll make Nonna's baked ziti and braciole," I offered, holding my breath for his answer.

Well, I'd try to make the food, and if all else failed, I'd go to Long Island, have Nonna help me make it, and then I'd bring it home and bake it at the apartment as if I'd made it myself. My sweet nonny would vouch that I'd been the chef if push came to shove.

The funny thing was that before I met Bruno, I'd never taken an interest in cooking—though Mom never tried to teach me. "Cooking is woman's work," she'd say when I tried to help in the kitchen. I couldn't imagine what she thought of Rafe—four very successful restaurants in New York and a new one underway in Las Vegas. And then there was Parker Howzer, another fantastic chef. I was coming to think my mother was as misogynistic as my father!

"I'd love to. I'll bring dessert, okay?" Bruno suggested before we heard running feet and Dexter's shout of, "Slow down before you break your neck." Bruno pecked me on the cheek before he let me inside.

"Gabe's on the way down, Bruno. Good morning, Dominic. How are things?" Dex asked, shifting his gaze between us as if he were waiting for some sort of revelation into our personal life.

I smirked. "Moving right along," I responded as I glanced at Bruno to see his cheeks had a slight pink tint to them. I patted his shoulder a couple of times before I made my way into the kitchen for coffee.

Dylan was filling Magic's water bowl when I walked into the room. "Where's that maniac dog of yours?" I asked as Dylan put the water bowl down in the laundry room where the pets ate. He quickly filled the food dish and turned to me, pushing up his glasses.

"He's in the back yard. I woke up too late to take him for his walk. I'm gonna ask Bruno if he'll take him for me. Dad says I'll have to give him some of my allowance," Dylan moped.

"Why did you get up late?" I asked him.

"I kept hearing noises in the yard last night, and I couldn't sleep," Dylan responded.

"You stayed up after you were told to go to bed and watched a scary movie on your phone, which reminds me," Dexter announced from his spot next to the kitchen door, his hand extended.

Much to my surprise, Bruno shot out of the house like he was on fire. I stood and walked to the back windows in the family room, seeing him purposely striding along the back fence and pushing against the boards before heading toward the house where Dyl's room was on the second floor and checking out the grounds. My heart pounded in my chest as I finally figured out he was trying to see if there was any trace of an intruder.

The guy had keen instincts, and I wanted to hug him close to me for them. I felt warmth surge up my spine and into my chest as I watched him do a thorough inspection of the property. He cared about my family very much. Did that mean he could care about a selfish asshole like me? God, I prayed he could because I had the feeling he just might be exactly what I needed in my life... for however long I still had on the planet.

Bruno glanced toward the window and smiled at me, offering a wink and a thumb's up that everything was okay before he picked up a tennis ball from the grass and tossed it for Magic, the two of them playing for a few minutes while the drama continued to unfolded in the kitchen.

I walked back in just in time to hear Dylan whine, "Dad, come on, *pleeeease!*" Dex shook his hand again, and the kid pulled his phone from his pocket and slapped it into Dex's palm, glaring at his dad. I could see how pissed the boy was, but I understood Dex's point. He was ten, soon to be eleven, and while he was being a typical boy, his actions had consequences.

"Where's your necklace?" Dexter asked him.

"I hate that thing," Dylan complained before he stomped through the kitchen and up the stairs.

"What necklace?" I asked. I'd never seen Dylan wearing a necklace, though something tickled the back of my mind as I thought about it.

"Dyl and Searcy have GPS chips in their necklaces that Gabe gave them when we got married. I have one in mine, as well," Dex stated as he pulled the necklace with the heart pendant from under his shirt to show me. He then continued, "Dylan was allowed to not wear his because he got a phone that is trackable, but I get to keep his phone through the weekend, so he has to wear the necklace," Dexter explained to me.

It hit home with me in that moment how protective Gabe was of his family. It was a shining example of how one cared for those they loved. I had no doubt my father had never felt the same about me.

"I'm sorry, but you know the rule about your phone. It's a privilege, not a right. If you hate wearing the necklace, put it in your pocket," Gabe explained to his son in the hallway before they entered the kitchen.

When Dylan slowly trudged in it was confirmed that he'd tried to plead his case to a higher court, or so he thought. If he didn't know who really wore the pants in that household, it wasn't my place to tell him. He'd figure it out sooner or later.

After Searcy joined us, Dex made them breakfast, and I took Dylan aside. "I'll come back after we take you to school and take Magic for his walk. You can owe me a favor. I won't take your allowance. I know you're saving for the minibike," I whispered to him.

Dylan slapped his hands together as if in prayer. "Thank you, thank you, thank you. I'll owe you a favor forever," he whispered.

"I'll cash it in right now. My favor is that you wear that necklace under your shirt, *not* carry it in your pocket," I emphasized. Knowing —or rather, not knowing—what was going on with Mangello made me feel as if it was imperative he wear the necklace. It was there for a reason.

As if to emphasize that there was nothing wrong with wearing a necklace, I pulled out the chain I wore with the silver ring attached and showed it to him before I dropped it back down my shirt and adjusted my collar and tie. "It means a lot to me, so I want to keep it close to my heart. That necklace should mean a lot to you, so you should keep it near your heart, too," I told him, suddenly meaning the words with everything inside my body. The design had something to do with Dex's mother, Shirley, but I couldn't remember what. The necklace was intended to save the boy's life if someone took him, so Dyl needed to be glad someone gave a shit about him.

I RETURNED from walking Magic to find my father sitting on the front porch of Gabe's home, which didn't set well with me at all. He hated Uncle Gabe, so why was he at the man's home?

"I was in the area and decided to check out the neighborhood where Gabe bought his house. I saw you head out with the dog earlier and decided to wait for you to return. You wanna get some lunch? Kids are at school already, right?" Dad asked.

Of course, my mother would have told him where Uncle Gabe lived. There was nothing suspicious about him showing up unannounced, right? Magic growled, low and rumbly, before he began barking angrily and lunging at my father, tugging hard on the leash.

"*Magic!*" I yelled, reeling him back toward me. "Sorry, Dad. He's not usually like that," I defended the stupid dog.

I was a little embarrassed at the mutt's reaction to my father, so I agreed to lunch. "Let me put him inside. You can take me by the Victorian so I can check in and then we'll get lunch somewhere." His request reminded me of our last lunch and the quick conversation I'd had with Corey, a guy I used to fuck when I'd first arrived in New York.

"Dominic! How are you?" Corey greeted me where I was standing outside the kitchen doors, having asked a server to bring him out. He was still a handsome guy, but he couldn't hold a candle to Bruno.

"I'm great. I was in the neighborhood with my dad for lunch, and I wanted to say hi," I offered my lame excuse.

"I haven't run into you around town. Are you still living in Brooklyn?" Corey asked.

"Yeah, but I'm busy with my job, so I don't go out like I used to. How've you been? Still living with your cousin?" I asked, beating around the bush until I could figure out how to ask the question that was burning in my mind.

"Naw. She went back to Michigan and got married. Her first kid is due at Christmas. How's your family? Hot Uncle Gabe?" Corey asked, offering a wink for emphasis, I supposed. He'd always had a thing for Uncle Gabe since the time Mom, Gabe, and I had gone to the restaurant where he used to work.

"Hot Uncle Gabe is married, has two kids, and getting ready to try for another one. The rest of the family is just as crazy as always, which brings me to a question. Did you dump me because I was afraid to come out to my family?" I asked hm.

Corey laughed, crossing his arms over his chest in a defensive manner.

"To be honest, I'm still not out to my family, but that has nothing to do with why I broke it off with you. To you, we were just fuckbuddies and I got tired of wondering if I was one in a long line of guys you were fucking. It seemed to me that we ran our course, and it was time for both of us to move on. I knew you weren't ready to settle down because you were just out of the closet back then. Hell, I bet you're still not ready to be with only one guy, are you?"

I'd been thinking about that conversation a lot more than necessary, and I was still trying to figure out the answer to his question about me settling down with one guy. I had the feeling I knew the answer, though I had a hard time believing it as true. However, the more time I spent with Bruno, the clearer things were becoming to me. Somewhere along the way I'd started falling hard for the guy. Maybe it had been happening without me noticing, but I knew it now. I just had to hope he'd forgive me for being such an asshole to him early on and give me the chance to prove to him that I was a better man now and that we could be good together.

I turned to my father. "I'll be right back."

"Mind if I come inside and use the bathroom?" Dad asked. I nodded as I unlocked the door and took Magic through the house to the laundry room where Sparkles was bathing herself on the large window seat in the sun.

I checked their water bowls, knowing they'd both been fed, and then I closed the door to the room where the two of them spent their days. I went to the kitchen and loaded the dishwasher while I waited for my father, and when he appeared in the doorway to the kitchen, I dried my hands and set the dishwasher to run.

"Ready?" I asked him.

"Sure. This is a nice place Gabe's got here. It's amazing what Giuseppe's money can buy," Dad commented, innuendo ripe in his voice.

"Uncle Gabe runs GEA-A, Dad. I like my job there, as a matter of fact. How'd you know I'm on kid duty now?" I asked. It hadn't come up when we'd spoken or texted.

"Your mother likes to talk, Dom, and she talks to your grandmother every day. Of course, Gabe told Grace that you were on kid duty, and Grace told Mom. You know, your mother doesn't like it that you've been relegated to babysitting Gabe's stepkids when you could be working for us at the shipping company," Dad got in another jab about me not working for him.

Before I could comment, he smirked and added, "I'm aware of what time kids go to school, ya know. I have three of my own." None of it really took me by surprise. Of course, Nonna told Mom what happened in New York, and yeah, they did talk every day.

I shook my head, not believing my mother and her big mouth when it came to my father—who seemed to have had a change of heart about leaving all of us in the dust, but I wanted to make certain to clarify one thing he said. "Gabe adopted Dyl and Searcy, Dad. They're not his stepkids. They're his and Dexter's *children*, and they love them very much," I defended my uncle's family.

Dad held up his hands in surrender. "That is a discussion we don't need to have, son. I accepted the fact that your mother's family is one of the privileged class who can do whatever they want and get away with it. Gabriele's children's parentage is no different. So, shall we go? I'll run you by the Victorian and then take you to lunch," Dad suggested.

Suddenly, my father's phone beeped. He retrieved it from the pocket of his suit coat and stared at the screen. "Damn. Dom, I'm afraid I'll have to take a raincheck on lunch. I forgot I have a meeting with a potential client today. I'll call you later, okay?" Dad offered as he started for the front door.

"I'll walk out with you, and yeah, we can raincheck lunch. Maybe we can make it dinner and you can meet my husband?" I suggested. If there was a chance Bruno and I were going to try to make a go of it, he'd eventually need to meet my parents and sisters, officially.

"Sure, sure. I'll be in touch. Bye, Dom," Dad said as he hurried off the front porch and down the block a bit to a black Lincoln MKX. He waved to me as he drove by while I was locking the door. I was relieved I didn't have to join him for lunch. I had bigger things on my mind.

I'd come to the realization earlier that morning that I didn't want an annulment or a divorce from Bruno Garvin. I had fallen deeply in love with the man, the reality of it smacking me in the face when I was looking out the window at the beautiful man who was double checking the fence to see that nobody had breached the yard and was snooping around the house.

What I needed to do was make sure Bruno felt the same about me. I was petrified to put myself out there in case he didn't, but—as clueless as I usually was about anything that didn't revolve around me—I had the feeling he'd been showing me that he loved me for a while. It was now my turn to do the same for him.

17

BRUNO

I still had a hard time believing that when we opened the bunker in the basement of the Victorian, Clete was sitting at the table with empty chip and cookie bags stacked in front of him. He'd consumed two bottles of water, and when the four of us had walked into the bunker, he stood and shook hands, as unaffected by me locking him inside as anything. It was shocking.

"Hey, you talk to your new bestie today?" Gabe asked me when he came into the kitchen on the second floor of the Victorian. Sabrina was answering phones, and Dex was teaching his lunchtime class, so everyone was accounted for and safe.

"I haven't and didn't plan to unless you want me to tell him something. Casper said the tracker I tagged his car with shows it's still at the Jersey Shore where I followed him to, so that's good," I answered, thinking about how that all went down. I'd have never been able to guess it.

"So, Clete, you know I meant you no harm when I rescued my husband from that club before we were married. He had no business working for Jeffrey Oswald at The Bone Yard in the first place. I didn't even know he worked there until I coincidentally walked into the place. I have no ill-will toward you," Gabe explained.

Clete, not one who was big on words, nodded.

"So, Clete, is it? What brings you to our little corner of Brooklyn?" Mateo asked the man.

"I was sent to keep an eye on Bruno. My boss knows he was at the club, and he thinks Bruno did something to the computer system there. He's pretty pissed off," Clete admitted.

Mateo grinned. "How much money do you make at your job there?"

Clete sat up a little taller. "Thousand bucks a week under the table," he announced quite proudly.

"How would you like to take a month long, paid vacation?" Gabe asked as he reached into his pocket and pulled out a large roll of bills.

"Where would I go?" Clete asked, reminding me he wasn't exactly a scholar, though I was far from one as well.

"Where's your family? Maybe your mother would like a nice visit?" Mateo suggested.

"She runs a small motel at the Jersey Shore. It's off-season now, so she's just closing up the place for the winter. She lives the off-season in a small house in Philly. That's where I grew up," Clete informed us.

"Well, it sounds like a good idea for you to go help her out, and then spend some time in Philly with her. Mother-son time is important, you know," Gabe replied, peeling off 40 one-hundred-dollar bills and counting them out on the table in front of Clete.

"Jeff will fire me," Clete stated. I knew that was probably true.

"Yeah, but there might not be a job for you to come back to. A resourceful guy like you? You'll land on your feet, no doubt," Mateo responded.

Clete nodded, collected the money, and agreed to leave the next morning. I followed him to the shore and spent the night to be sure he stayed put. The next morning before I left, I drove by to see Clete on a ladder fixing a loose gutter. A small woman was standing under the ladder, pointing at things while Clete handled the drill like he'd never seen one before. I was glad I hadn't volunteered to help him.

"I'm going to go see Jeffrey Oswald tonight," I informed Gabe. It was time to get to the bottom of things regarding Dexter, and so far, Jeffrey Oswald was my only suspect.

Gabe nodded. "I'll be waiting here. Don't talk to him, just grab him. We'll deal with him here."

"Got it," I answered before I went upstairs to find Casper. I wanted to see if he could find out who the mysterious guy was I'd seen in Venice and then at Frankie Man's house in Rome—Mr. Vanni. I also wanted to check in with Tommy to be sure Daniela and Dante were both okay.

I knocked on Casper's door, hearing him tapping away at his keyboard. "In," he announced.

I opened the door to find him sitting with Mathis Sinclair. "Am I interrupting anything?"

Mathis let out a tired sigh. "Unfortunately, no. We're at dead ends. What's up with you? Something I can help with?" Mathis asked. I closed the door. Maybe three heads were better than one?

"When I was working for Frankie Man, there was this guy who visited him a few times in Venice at Pietro's compound and then once in Rome before I left," I explained.

"Oh, the license plate to the rental car that you sent through Tommy. Yeah, I checked out all of the credit cards that had rented that particular car over those few days, and I got a list of names I haven't had a chance to sift through yet. You want me to run them down?" Casper asked.

"Yeah, if it's not too much trouble. I don't know if it'll be helpful, but it couldn't hurt, right?" I asked the computer wizard.

Casper smiled as he typed on the other keyboard connected to his large desktop computer. I wouldn't even know how to turn it on, much less use the thing. It was massive.

Casper reached into his bottom desk drawer and tossed me a box. "Got your new cell. I've added a tracker to it and transferred all of your information from your old phone to this one, so you have all your contact info back. You can dump the burner you use to contact Tommy. This one has encryption software that keeps the messages you send private and untraceable, so you're covered," he assured me.

"Thanks a lot, Casper." I took the phone and left him to his work with Mathis.

I walked down the hallway to find Willow sitting in Smokey's office alone. He had put on the silver ring I'd given him when we got married, holding his hand up and moving it around so the light hit it in a certain way.

"Have you found a lawyer yet?" I asked as I stood at the open door.

Dominic slid the ring from his finger and put it back on the chain that was coiled up on the desk. "*Why* am I looking for a lawyer?" he asked as he slid the chain over his neck and tucked the ring under his shirt collar before adjusting his tie.

I sighed. "So you can be free to start dating again. I told you that you could see other people while I was gone. I'd never hold that against you. Besides, I didn't expect you'd wait for me," I answered him.

Willow stood gracefully from his seat and walked over to me, closing the door after tugging me inside the office. He directed me to sit down in his chair and took a seat on top of the desk, his long legs resting on either side of mine as he pulled the chair closer. "You're twenty-three, correct?"

"I, uh, I turned twenty-four in March," I explained. My birthday was never a big deal to anyone in my family, so I treated it as another day in my life. Nothing special.

"I didn't know that, but we'll celebrate it very soon," Dom promised.

I started to wave him off when he took my hand, his light brown eyes staring into mine. "Do you think you know what you want out of life?" he asked, his sincerity shining through.

To me, the answer was easy—him—but I had the feeling there was more to the question. "Like career-wise or what I believe would make me happy in life?"

"Both. I mean, you're young, and you deserve to have time to make choices and decisions about what you want to do with the rest of your life. Some people can't even begin to think about what they want to do next week at your age, much less how they want to live the rest of their lives," Willow described.

I thought about his question, and I knew in my heart that I would never change my mind about my hopes and dreams for my life. If there was any way Willow would consent to be a part of it, I had to tell him the truth.

"I dropped out of high school at sixteen to work on a neighboring ranch in Wyoming. I couldn't work for my father because he hated me, but he had no problem taking the money I made to help with expenses around our place," I told him, preparing to be completely honest with him about everything.

Dom took my right hand between his and held it, so I continued. "I've told you all that sad stuff, so let me tell you something good I did for myself to help me achieve the goals I have for my future. I figured out why I have such a hard time learning—I have dyslexia. It means my brain doesn't process letters right, so I had to retrain my brain. It takes me a little longer to read things and understand them, but I practice, and I've learned how to work around the challenge. I'd like to someday get my high school diploma, not my GED, and I'd like to take some college courses so I can be a better operative," I told him.

Willow squeezed my hand and offered a sweet smile. "That's admirable. There are places in Brooklyn where you can go to night school. I can help you find one, if you'd like, and as far as college, that's doable, too. You can do online learning—" he suggested.

"No!" I interrupted. "I need to be in the class with a teacher. When I was in DC with Ben, I went to a learning center while he was at work during the day. I liked being face-to-face with the teachers. It helped me learn faster when I was able to see their faces," I admitted to him.

Willow nodded, so I continued. "I want to keep working here if that's possible, and I want to have you as my husband. I want to go through the changes and challenges I'm going to face with you there to hold my hand and tell me things will be okay, and I want to do the same thing for you. If I get stumped by something, I want to ask you to help me figure it out. You're smart, and you've gone to college," I said.

Willow looked at me—really looked at me—and I was worried

about what he was going to say. I wasn't nearly as handsome as him, but I hoped there was something about me he found attractive. "What?" I asked him. He looked like he was trying to figure out a really hard math problem, and if that was the case, I was useless to him.

"I think I've lost my mind, but I know I've lost my heart to you. I don't know when or how you did it—especially since I was such a jerk to you when we were in Kentucky—but I've fallen in love with you, Bruno," Willow said, causing me to nearly swallow my tongue.

I didn't dare move an inch or even blink for fear I'd wake up and it would all be a dream. "I've loved you almost since I saw you the first time. I never thought you'd even look at me twice," I whispered.

I stood from the desk chair and stepped closer to him. "You have to ask." I was reminding him that I wouldn't kiss him until he asked.

Dominic surprised me by placing his hands on my face and pulling me forward until our lips touched. I put my hands on his hips and pulled him into my body, feeling the sparks shooting through me as he licked the seam of my lips. My dick had a mind of its own, but I ignored it and kept kissing the beautiful man in front of me.

I opened my lips and moved my hands up to the middle of Dominic's back, crushing his slender body to mine. I slanted my head to the right so our noses stopped bumping, and I let him show me the way he wanted to be kissed.

His tongue flickered into my mouth and then swirled with mine, drawing it into his mouth where I licked all around, taking in the sweet taste of him. His hands wound in my hair, and he sank further into my arms, "*Mmmm*," he moaned.

I wanted to push him back on the desk and explore his beautiful body with my lips, but a clearing throat stopped me. *"A-hem!"*

I pecked Dom's soft lips and opened my eyes, seeing a big grin on his face. "We got caught," he whispered before he pecked my lips again and pushed me back a little.

"No hanky-panky in the office," someone announced. Gabby stood in the doorway with Smokey, Mathis, Duke, Ace, Casper, and

Dexter all standing behind him, all of them staring directly at us. My cheeks got so hot I thought I might pass out for a second.

Willow slid off the desk and stood in front of me, crossing his arms to mirror Gabby's. "You can't tell me those two,"—he pointed to Ace and Duke—"and you and Dexter haven't made out in this building. I'm sure Smokey and Parker have fucked in Smokey's chair which is why he threatens to beat anyone who tries to sit there, and I know for a fact that Maxi and Casper get down in his office all the time whether they think people are in the building or not—the noises don't lie, Casper." Dom's voice was very stern, which made me smile.

Dexter pushed his way forward with a friendly grin. "I'm so happy for you!" He lunged for me, but I side-stepped him because my dick was still hard, pushing Willow into his grabby hands.

Everyone else stepped into the office and hugged us or shook our hands. It was really nice that they were happy for us. I was still a little surprised to the point I couldn't speak, but my heart was beating a million miles an hour. Dominic Mazzola—my husband—loved me. It was the best feeling in the world.

18

DOMINIC

"I have something to finish tonight, but I'll move back home over the weekend. We can take our time getting used to living together, or I can wait," Bruno explained as Duke and I got ready to go pick up the kids from school.

Uncle Gabe had taken everyone out for lunch after the hoopla died down over the discovery of Bruno and me kissing in the office I was now sharing with Smokey since Mathis was busy with something personal.

Maxi even came to meet us, and the chatter turned toward a big party for Bruno and me. My guy sat quietly beside me, smiling like a Cheshire cat but not saying anything. I had a feeling that would be a thing I'd have to adjust to—being the spokesman for the two of us. I was pretty sure I wouldn't mind—I had that pushy Torrente gene that would come in handy for sure.

"Nope. Come stay at the apartment tonight, and we'll get your stuff over the weekend. I'm still planning to make us an Italian feast over the weekend, and you can help me do it. Maybe we can take cooking classes together?" I thought out loud.

Bruno pulled me into his arms. "We can do anything you want, okay? I'll be over as soon as this thing wraps up. Please, don't shoot me when I come in. Should I ring the bell?"

I chuckled. "No, just come inside. It's your place, too." I pecked a kiss on his soft lips before I stepped out of his grasp and grabbed my jacket to find Duke.

"Be careful," Bruno instructed as I headed down the front stairs.

"You, too," I responded before reaching the bottom of the staircase where Duke was sitting at the receptionist desk.

"Ready?" he asked me as he stood to leave. Just then, the front door opened, and my father stepped inside, which was truly a surprise.

"Dad? What are you doing here? I thought you'd gone back to San Francisco," I asked him, definitely not thrilled to see him standing in the foyer. His jacket was damp, which indicated the weatherman had fucked it up again. *Sunny and warm, my ass.*

"Not yet. My business negotiations are keeping me in town, and I thought I'd stop by to see Gabriele. Is he around?" Dad asked. That was completely inconceivable—my father hated Uncle Gabe.

"He's gone out for a client meeting. I'm Duke Chambers, Gabe's half-brother." Duke stood and introduced himself, obviously seeing the tension in my body at my father's impromptu visit.

"Oh, yes, the mysterious new Torrente son. Luci told me about you. I must say, that was quite a surprise, wasn't it? I didn't think Tomas had the balls to cheat on Grace, much less with some college whore. I had a good laugh at that one," my father commented, his sarcastic tone rubbing me the wrong way immediately.

"Dad—"

"No, Dom, it's good to meet more of the extended family. Maybe you'd like to join me and my partners for dinner before you leave town? It's always good to get to know family members in a more intimate setting, isn't it?" Duke suggested, though I could see he damn well didn't mean it. I swore I could see the hairs standing up on the back of his neck.

I heard a loud noise upstairs, but before I could figure out what it was, Duke turned to me with a tight smile. "We need to get going to pick up the kids." He then turned to my father and extended his hand. "Nice to meet you, Mr. Mazzola."

Dad took his hand, though not cordially, and they shook before Dad turned to leave. He stopped at the door and turned to look at me. "Dom, I'll be going home tomorrow. Do you have time for dinner tonight with your old man?"

"Uh, yeah... sure. I have something planned for later, but dinner's fine. I'll call you once I'm off," I offered. Dad nodded and left the Victorian, leaving me with a nervous gut.

"He's a real peach, ain't he? Let's go," Duke ordered, so we headed toward the back exit and out to the parking lot where I saw my father's rental car idling at the curb as we left to go to the school. He was talking into his phone, though he did pull down the visor as if he were trying to hide from us. My guess was he was reporting the encounter to my mother, which further pissed me off.

I had no idea what my parents' endgame might be, but something was definitely going on with them and it smelled like rotten fish.

I WAS SITTING in the living room of the apartment, waiting for my father to call me back about dinner. I'd called him a few times since Duke had dropped me off at home before he went to pick up Ace to meet Corby for drinks near the garage where Corby worked. The first time, I'd hung up without leaving a message, but the second time I left a message that I was free and ready to meet him.

I wasn't surprised Dad hadn't called me back—the way he'd acted when he met Duke was bugging the fuck out of me. It was just one millimeter short of rude, and it hadn't set well with me. Duke was a great guy, or he'd become one. Being with Corby and Ace had definitely changed the man, and he didn't deserve the way my father had spoken to him.

Of course, Gio Mazzola had always been a raging dick to everyone on the Torrente side of the family, but then again, he hadn't been too kind to his own parents. When Nonno Mazz passed away, Dad just turned his back on Nonna, leaving her to Aunt Desirée, his sister, and he never spoke to either of them again. I didn't even know if either of them were still alive.

I turned on the television about thirty-seconds before there was a knock on the apartment door. Bruno had a key, so I was sure it wasn't him, and my father hadn't called, so I got up from the couch and went to the door, looking through the peephole to see Corby.

I opened the door and greeted him with a smile. "Hey, Corby. Come on in," I invited him.

"I don't want to bother you or anything, but do you happen to have any beer or wine? Duke decided to make us a nice dinner instead of eating at the bar, and we're out of anything to drink with it. I'd rather not go out again if I can help it. It's raining pretty hard out there," Corby explained.

"Uh, yeah, sure. Come on in," I offered again.

Corby came inside and followed me to the kitchen where there was a large wine rack built into the pantry. "What's he making?" I asked Corby as I perused the selections of Torrente Vineyard's offerings.

"Chicken fajitas with homemade tortillas. Marianna has some of the most incredible recipes that she shares with us, and I didn't know we were out of beer and wine when I was on my way home," Corby explained, guilt lacing his voice.

I grinned at him. "I've got just the thing," I told him as I grabbed a basket from the cupboard. I had two limes that I placed inside, along with a special bottle of small-batch tequila I'd purchased to give to Uncle Gabe for Christmas, and I grabbed a box of salt from the pantry.

"Nothing goes better with fajitas than tequila. Oh, and beer," I told him as I went to the fridge and grabbed a six pack of Modelo that I'd had in the fridge since the previous weekend.

When I walked Corby to the front hallway to go home, he pulled out his wallet to pay me, and I laughed. "Nope. Have Bruno and me up for one of these nice meals some time. Maybe we can do a group dinner where everyone brings a different dish. I'll see if I can find a weekend that works for most of us," I suggested as we stopped at the door.

"Thanks again, Dom. I look forward to a big dinner with everyone. Keep me posted and let me know if there's anything I can do. See ya," Corby offered. I nodded and wished him a good night as I let him out and closed and locked the door.

A few minutes later, my phone chimed with a text from Bruno.

I'm not going to be by tonight. My case is taking a little longer than I thought. I'll see you at work tomorrow. Bruno

"Well, that couldn't be any chummier, could it? What the hell is going on?" I asked myself as I went to the kitchen and turned off the lights. With Bruno not coming home and me out of beer, there was no use in staying up. I decided to go ahead and go to bed. Who knew what the morning would bring, anyway.

THE NEXT MORNING, I caught a ride with Duke to the Victorian at five-thirty to work out. "How was your dinner last night?" I asked him.

He chuckled, low and gravely. "I've got a hell of a fucking hangover. Tequila? You're a sadist," Duke teased. I stared at him, seeing he looked a little green around the gills, but that big smile of his didn't falter at all.

"Corby said you were making Mexican, and as far as I know, tequila is the best accompaniment to a good Mexican meal. Nobody forced it on you, did they?" I joked.

Duke actually laughed out loud. "You'd be surprised what my guys can get up to. Anyway, I'll need to sweat it out. You feel like getting in the ring with me?" Duke asked.

"I've got a question first. You went looking for Bruno when we were in Italy, right?" I asked him.

"Yeah. He hadn't checked in, and Giuseppe was worried about him, so I went to look for him. I found him, and he was okay, but something happened to him while he'd been working for Frankie Man, and he had to get the hell out of there. Tommy got him hooked up with some other undercovers, and they kept him safe until he could slip out of Italy and get safely back to the States. Why?" Duke inquired. It was sort of what I'd already imagined had happened. I just had to find out what had gone down with Bruno over there.

"What's he working on for Uncle Gabe, Duke? I'm worried about him," I admitted. I hadn't slept worth a shit the night before, wondering what Bruno was up to. I knew he was a loyal man, which was why he hadn't told me anything about what he was doing at Gabby's direction, but now I was worried for my guy... no, my *husband*.

We got to the Victorian, and we both hopped out of the SUV. Halloween was the next Monday, and Dex and Gabby were having their annual costume party that night after trick-or-treating with the kids. I wanted Bruno to be there with me, safe and sound.

"Honestly, Dom, I don't have any idea what's going on. Gabe hasn't said a word to me, or anyone as far as I know, but I'd say you should talk to Giuseppe to see what he knows or what he can get his new tech guy to figure out for you. Casper won't come in on Gabe, but Nathaniel has no loyalty to your uncle. Call him," Duke suggested, and I knew he was right, though I didn't feel right about checking up on my people with an outsider. That didn't seem very loyal to me.

The two of us got warmed up, and then we got into the ring. Duke was kind to me—only countering my moves. He didn't try to hurt me, but he still beat the hell out of me. When I glanced around the gym, I saw everyone downstairs watching us—except Gabe and Bruno.

Ace stepped into the ring and looked me over. "Okay, kid, I'd say you're done. Let me work out my hangover with my man, please?"

I nodded and let Smokey help me between the ropes and onto the gym floor. Clearly, I was working out some aggression and worry of my own. Maybe when Bruno saw me, he'd feel bad? I hoped to fuck he felt something.

After a hot shower, I dressed in my work clothes to accompany Duke to make the school run with Dylan and Searcy. As I stood outside the SUV while Duke walked them inside, I saw a silver minivan sitting across the street and down the block.

It didn't look suspicious, but then again, people never do when they're up to no good. There was someone in the van behind the wheel, but they were wearing some sort of mask that I couldn't make out. When Duke came back out of the building, I hopped into the SUV. "Make a U-turn and go down the block to that silver van. Something's not right," I explained, relying on the feeling in my gut.

Duke did exactly as I suggested, driving the wrong way down a one-way street, and when we were less than fifty feet from the van, it made a U-turn and headed for the intersection.

We trailed them through rush-hour traffic, but we lost them when they swerved and turned against the light onto Ocean Parkway. Duke pulled into an abandoned gas station and called Casper, giving him the license plate number to see if we could find out who owned the vehicle before he turned to me. "Good call. They were definitely up to something, or they would never have taken off like that. We'll have to report this to Gabe. He might want to put another operative on the kids inside the school. Looks like someone is formulating some sort of plans."

My stomach turned at the idea that someone was planning to take the kids. We had to get to the bottom of it, sooner rather than later. I wouldn't have their kidnapping on my head, that was for fucking sure.

19

BRUNO

(THE PREVIOUS DAY...)

I knocked on the door to Casper's office after I'd talked to Willow about coming over to the apartment. I had a feeling there had to be a better way to get Jeff Oswald than Gabe beating the life out of him.

"Come in, Bruno," Casper called out.

I opened the door to see him with a friendly smile on his face, which put me at ease. "How'd you know it's me?" I asked him as I glanced around for cameras.

Casper laughed. "Nobody who works here casts a bigger shadow than you, my friend. What can I do for you?" he asked, pointing to the chair next to his desk.

I sat down, leaning forward to put my elbows on my knees—my thinking pose. "If someone was trying to hurt your husband, you'd want very much to keep it from happening, right?"

"Fuck yes! Is someone—is this about Dominic?" Casper asked.

I glanced up at him and smiled. "Thankfully, no. Jeffrey Oswald is the club owner I had you destroy the computer system of the other day. He's trying to hurt someone I care about, and short of killing him, I'm not sure what to do. I know you saw a lot of those pictures you copied. You put those files somewhere safe, right?"

Lawry opened the desk drawer and pulled out two red gadgets, placing them on the desk in front of me. "These are the files. I didn't leave them on our system. I'm sorry to say I glanced through some of them to be sure they came through okay, and I happened to run across the pictures of Dexter. I know you were trying to respect his privacy, but these have to do with the pictures Gabe already showed me, right?" he asked.

I sighed, feeling as if I'd let Gabe down. "Yes. I guess since you've already seen the other pictures, Gabe won't be mad at me. I don't want Gabe to go to jail for dealing with trash like Jeffrey Oswald. I'd do it myself, but I'm really not thrilled about going back to jail, either," I informed him.

"Well, I believe I know why Oswald sent those pictures. I believe he's planning to blackmail Gabby and Dex. I thought that might be the direction you were heading, so I did a bit of research on my own. Color me a nosey Midwesterner," Casper admitted.

"Oswald's business is bleeding money. He likes to gamble, it seems, and when he left Atlantic City and started up his business here, he continued to play the ponies to the point that he's into a bookie for about three-quarter of a million bucks," Casper explained.

"So, he wants a million as insurance, I guess," I responded.

"Wait, there was a demand for money?" Casper asked me. I'd said too much, but then again, maybe it was better if he did know. Maybe he'd be able to help me come up with a solution.

"Yes. It was written on the envelope that was left on Gabby's SUV. Why? Does that change things? Is there some way I can make this go away without Gabby getting into trouble?" I nearly begged.

"Yes, there is. I know I saw at least one underage male in those pictures. I say we threaten the asshole right back," Casper suggested.

"I'll go get him," I stated.

Casper stood from his chair and placed his fists on the desk. "No, we can't do that. If you move him from his establishment, it's kidnapping, and there's no getting around that with the cops, but I've got a better idea. Give me a few hours. I've got some work to do," he requested, so I did.

I looked up a used car rental company in Flatbush and went to pick up a 1996 Honda Prelude that had seen better days to use for surveillance, and I parked it near The Bone Yard to use that night if things went right.

I stopped at a deli I liked and got a couple of sandwiches for Willow and me to have for lunch, and as I walked back to the Victorian, I saw a black car parked in front of the building that I didn't recognize.

I took a snap of the license plate to get Casper to look into it later, and for some reason, I circled around to the back of the building and went in through the basement.

I went up the back steps that had once been used by the servants of whoever had owned the big house before Gabe bought it. They were narrow and there were spiderwebs and dust along the walls which reminded me nobody ever used them, and when I came out near the bathrooms, I made my way to the kitchen to put the food in the fridge.

I heard Duke's voice downstairs, so I walked to the top of the stairs and listened, hearing a voice I didn't recognize, but it sounded a lot like Dominic's voice, just deeper. I dropped onto my knees and crawled over to the railing where I could get a better view of who was down there.

"Oh, yes, the mysterious new Torrente son. Lucia told me about you. I must say, that was quite a surprise, wasn't it? I didn't think Tomas had the balls to cheat on Grace, much less with some college whore. I had a good laugh at that one." There stood the man I'd seen in Venice and Rome standing in front of the reception desk. He was at the Victorian...

"Dad—"

My heart nearly stopped when I heard my husband address him as "Dad." Surely that man wasn't my husband's father? He'd been working... He was the mole?

Suddenly, I felt someone laying on my back, and I turned to see Ace with a big grin. "Whatcha doin?" he whispered.

I quickly rolled him off and scrambled away. This was a horrible turn of events.

I PUT Willow's father out of my mind for the moment. I had to handle Jeffrey Oswald first, so I was sitting in the old Honda at three-thirty in the morning, having sent a text to Willow that I wouldn't make it over that night. This time, I had night vision and I was watching the drunken crowd stumbling out of the club.

I knew the routine—last call had been given at three-twenty in order to give people time to pay their tabs and leave the place. I saw a guy I didn't recognize holding open the front door for people to leave, and I had to wonder how many more were inside. I reached up to the overhead light inside the old car and popped off the cover, unscrewing the bulb and placing it in the cupholder as I slid off the night vision goggles.

After I pulled on a pair of black neoprene gloves like doctors used, I opened the car door and slid out, making my way across the street between the streetlights and around the side of the building to see if I could spot anyone who looked like a bouncer by the back door.

The back door opened and a few young guys came out—likely dancers—before the door closed again. I was sure there were still dancers inside preparing to leave, so I hid by the door and when it opened again, I held onto it.

When the stranger at the back door tried to pull it closed, I didn't let go, and when he stepped outside to see what was wrong, I grabbed him in a sleeper hold. Once he finally quit fighting me, I dragged him down the alley behind the dumpster and zip tied his hands and feet so he wouldn't be a problem. I sent Casper an all-clear text and waited for him to meet me at the back of the building.

"Psst!" I turned toward the sound to see Casper, so I rushed over to where he was hidden beside the garage across the alley.

"Okay, I got the guy at the back door secured. I still don't know how many guys are in there," I admitted.

"I'll go cause a fuss at the door and get all of them to come after me in the front, and you get inside. Take this rock with you and prop open the back door so I can get in. If I'm not back in three minutes, knock Oswald out, and then tie him to the chair. In this briefcase are folders with notes on them for the cops, so just spread them out on the desk," Casper advised.

I nodded and checked my pockets for all of the supplies we'd discussed earlier, grateful I'd written everything down.

Casper then continued. "I've got Maxi set to call the cops that there's a robbery in progress in an hour, so get out of there before they show up. I'll meet you at the Victorian unless I get arrested. In that case, call Gabe to come bail me out," Casper insisted. I nodded and took the briefcase as he ran down the alley to approach from the other side.

I waited until I heard shouting, and then I slipped inside the building, propping the rock by the door so Casper could get inside if he didn't get caught. I didn't bother to hide my face—I wanted Jeff Oswald to see who it was. I glanced into the main room to see only the bartender I'd sort of met the other day was behind the bar ringing checks as a couple of patrons waited their turn.

"*Hey! Let me the fuck inside, you assholes!*" Casper yelled, which brought the bartender with a baseball bat from behind the bar.

I hurried around the corner and let myself into Jeffrey Oswald's office. He was behind the desk with a hundred-dollar bill rolled up as a line of cocaine disappeared up his nose from the wooden top of his desk. I wasn't surprised he used drugs.

"So, that's why you want another two-hundred and fifty grand, huh? That's an expensive habit you've got there," I stated, catching him by surprise.

"What do you want, Garvin? You're not supposed to be back here," Oswald snapped at me.

I reached into the front pocket of my pants to retrieve my small Ruger, aiming it at him. "Yeah, well, you should hire better security for your club," I responded, keeping my voice low in case anyone happened to walk by the door.

"Fuck you. Go ahead and shoot me, ya stupid fuck," he demanded, and I nearly took him up on it, but I remembered my husband who was waiting for me at our apartment.

I chuckled. "Naw. There's a better place for you than hell, but I have faith you'll get there soon enough on your own, trust me."

Just then, the door opened and Casper slid inside, his lip busted and a little blood under his nose. "You okay?" I asked him as I handed him a pair of gloves from one of my pockets that he quickly slid onto his hands.

"No worries. Now, have you secured our guest?" Casper asked.

I retrieved the rest of the zip ties from my tactical pants that were left from my job with Mangello, and I walked over to Jeffrey Oswald who started to reach for something under the desk. I slapped him hard to get his attention before I reached under the desk and pulled out a Glock 19 with a full mag. "I hope you have a permit for this."

I placed the gun on the desk out of his reach and secured Oswald to the wooden desk chair before I stepped back out of the way for Casper to take over.

"Anything you want to say before I start? We have a few minutes before backup arrives," Casper let me know.

I took a deep breath and let it out slowly, gathering my nerves. "You are a bad person. Those pictures you took of Sweet Pea?" I turned to Casper who handed me the folder of the young dancer when he was sixteen. "These will get you into trouble," I told him as I put them on the desk in front of Jeff.

He looked at the pictures and laughed. "He was eighteen. I saw his identification," the slimeball determined.

I chuckled. "He was sixteen, and you raped him. Don't worry— you'll get a taste of that in prison," I stated before I stepped back and let Casper take over.

He went through the pictures quickly, pointing out the ones who were underage before he got to Dexter's photos. "Do you know who this man is?" Casper asked.

Oswald looked away without answering, so I reached over and turned his face to look at the photos, pointing to Dexter's handsome face.

"Dexter Carrington," Oswald gritted out as my thumb and index finger mashed his cheeks against his teeth.

"Wrong!" I snapped at him. "Dexter Carrington *Torrente*. You were dumb enough to piss off Gabriele Torrente. You must have a death wish," I accused the jerk.

Casper chuckled. "You should be so lucky. Gabriele isn't going to deal with you—some friends of his will be here in a minute, and then, if there's anything left of you, the police will be here shortly after that. If you'd like to avoid meeting Gabe's friends, then you can make a full confession to having photographed all of these underage men right now and it might save your ass," he urged as he put a small, digital recorder in front of Jeff and turned it on.

Casper snapped his fingers and Oswald jutted up his chin in defiance. "Fuck you, both."

Casper looked at me and smirked. "Let's go. It's out of our hands now, but we tried."

I retrieved the new roll of duct tape I'd brought from my pocket and plastered a piece across Oswald's mouth, smacking him a few times to be sure the tape wasn't going anywhere.

Casper opened the door to the office in time for Mateo and Rafe to step into the space. "Do we get to party?" Mateo asked. Casper nodded, and the two of us left out the back door.

We got into the old Honda and I drove Casper to the Victorian to get his truck. "I'll follow you to Flatbush to return the car," Casper suggested.

"No thank you. I'll take it back in the morning. I appreciate your help with this, Casper. I'll explain things to Gabby when I get home," I told him before we parted ways. Thankfully, one problem was handled. Now, I had a much bigger one to figure out—Dominic's father.

20

DOMINIC

Saturday morning, I woke to the sound of the security code being entered into the wall unit inside my apartment. I looked at the clock on my bedside table to see it was six-thirty—way too fucking early to be up on a Saturday. Bruno hadn't been to work on Friday, but neither had Uncle Gabe. When Duke and I went to get the kids for school, neither of them were at the house, and Dexter was upset. To say I was pissed, too, was a fucking understatement.

I pulled on my robe and walked down the hallway in time to see Bruno trying to wrestle a large duffel in through the doorway without making any noise. I flipped on the hallway light and aimed a steely glare his way. "Welcome home, *dear*," I snapped at him.

Bruno jumped a bit, almost falling to the floor before he dropped his bag and took off his sneakers. "I'm sorry, but I didn't want to wait any longer. I'd planned to get here earlier, but some things took a little more time than we thought they would. What happened to your face?" he gasped.

Part of me wanted to be irate at him for coming home at such an ungodly hour, but the other part of me was just so thrilled to have him home. "Duke and I got into the ring together. I'm fine," I assured him.

I walked up to him, ignoring my morning breath, and I took his handsome face between my hands and planted my lips firmly on his. He wrapped me in his arms and took the kiss further, which made my heart soar.

Our tongues swirled together as if we were dancing, and I wrapped my arms around his broad shoulders, breaking the kiss to look into his chocolate brown eyes. "I'll be mad at you later for coming home so late. Come to bed with me," I tempted.

"I really need to shower. I have dirt and mud all over me. I'll meet you there, okay?" he answered, his voice sounding confident, which was a surprise. I was the one who sounded like a nervous virgin, which was laughable because I'd been with my fair share of hookups.

I went back to the bedroom and straightened the sheets and blanket before I opened the nightstand to be sure I had condoms and lube, clearly having high hopes for what might happen between us.

Twenty minutes later, Bruno shuffled into my room in a pair of flannel pajama pants and a black t-shirt. He walked over to the side of the bed nearest the door where I was already reclined, and he stood there, staring at me. "What? Would you rather go to your room?" I proposed.

"No, Willow. I want to sleep on this side near the door. If someone breaks in and wants to hurt us, I want them to come for me first." I could see he was dead serious, so I grabbed my phone and charger from the nightstand and placed them on the matching one on the other side of the bed after scooting over to let him in with me.

Once Bruno settled into the bed, his back firmly planted against the mattress and his eyes staring at the ceiling, I wanted to laugh. He looked so worried about something, I had to know what. At least my nerves had subsided as I waited for him. I decided maybe a little chat might put him more at ease.

"Can you tell me what you were doing last night?" I asked as I turned on my side and propped my head on my hand, staring into his handsome, apprehensive face. I put my right hand on his chest and watched him as he pondered how to answer me.

I remembered back to when Bruno went to work for Nemo guarding Ben after he was elected to Congress. Nemo mentioned in passing that he had to concoct a story for Bruno to stumble into Ben organically because Bruno wouldn't lie about being there to keep an eye on Ben if he was asked outright. My handsome man wasn't keen on lying, so I wondered if he'd hedge the truth with me.

Bruno surprised me by turning to face me, a tender smile on his face as he lifted his left hand where the silver ring glinted as the rising sun shined through the window of the bedroom. He touched my face gently and let out a soft breath that fanned over my face. The minty smell of his toothpaste relaxed me, which was really a bit odd.

"I guess I can tell you now that it's over. Someone was trying to blackmail Gabby and Dexter. Back when Dexter was dancing at a club where I worked as a bouncer, a man took pictures of him without his clothes or his permission. Well, he did it to a lot of other men, and a few of them happened to be underage. I've been helping Gabby figure out who was trying to blackmail them, and it took a little more time than I thought it would. I'm so sorry I kept you waiting," Bruno admitted.

I was swept away. "I'm happy you're here now. Are you tired?" I asked, praying he said no.

The look on his face shocked me. Bruno raised himself up and moved over me, pushing me onto my back as he stared into my eyes. "No, Willow, I'm not tired at all."

When he hovered over me and gently kissed the stupid bruises on my face from my workout with Duke, I wasn't exactly sure what to say. He'd been so gentle I was shocked silent, especially coming from such a big guy.

Bruno pulled away and rubbed his nose against mine for a second before he spoke. "May I suck your cock?" Bruno asked politely, surprising the fuck out of me.

I sputtered a bit before I could organize a proper answer. "D-Do you want—do you want to?" Where the hell that came from was news to me.

Bruno chuckled. "Willow, I wouldn't ask if I didn't want to." *Well, he had a point, didn't he?*

I started to skin off my pajamas when I had another idea. "I'm not getting naked by myself." I reached for Bruno's pants and slid my hand inside them to find him gloriously naked under the flannel.

I worked them off his hips as he grabbed mine and pulled them off me until we were both naked from the waist down. "Shirts?" I asked as I tried to pry his off of him. He held onto the hem, stopping me.

"What?" I asked him.

"I, uh, I'm not as attractive as you. I have hair on my chest and uh, stretch marks from when I was fat. I don't think you want to see that," he decided without my consent.

I sat up and looked into his beautiful eyes. "Sorry, nope. We can't do that, you and me. We're married, remember? We take the good with the bad, and there is nothing we can't show each other, Bruno. We love each other. Don't ever be afraid to show me anything, please," I directed.

Bruno hesitated for a moment before he removed his t-shirt and waited for my assessment. His chest was covered in coarse, curly hair, just as I'd imagined in my dreams and there were silver streaks over his stomach as he'd mentioned, but they didn't turn me off. To me, he was quite beautiful, my bear of a man.

I leaned forward and ran my tongue over his belly, circling his navel with just the tip. He actually giggled, which sounded so cute from such a burly man, letting me know he was ticklish, and I was excited to learn something so intimate about him. I wanted to rack up things that only I knew about him as quickly as possible. We'd been married for ten months, and I was grossly behind in knowing private details about my husband, but I planned to remedy that as quickly as I could.

"*Gah!*" Bruno gasped as I moved down his body to his ample cock, sucking it into my mouth without asking permission. Short curls surrounded the member, and his scent was strong there at the base. I wanted to bathe in that scent to always have him with me.

"No, Willow, I want to have you in my... Ugh!" he whispered as I swallowed him into my throat. I bobbed on his dick, sliding my tongue over every ridge, vein, and sensitive spot. He was cut and the thick head was a bit intimidating at first, but once I relaxed, I worked him like I'd never worked a cock in my life. Hearing his groans and moans was like an epic soundtrack to the best movie I'd ever seen, and I couldn't wait until one of us fucked the other because his response to my sweet torture of his body held a lot of promise.

I nibbled on his balls and worked my tongue down to his taint, stopping when I felt a gentle hand on the back of my head. I knew he was about to come, but I wasn't done with his sexy body yet.

"*Ah!*" Bruno gasped as I offered a kiss to his hairy pucker before I pulled away.

"Was I doing it—" I started, but when Bruno flipped me onto my back and pressed his body to mine, slotting our hard rods together, I was a little stunned. I'd never figured him for being aggressive in bed.

"You're doing everything right, but I want to show you how much... I want to take a turn first if you don't mind," he requested. I'd never met a person more polite in my life.

"Bruno, you don't have to..."

Before I knew what was happening, the man pulled my legs over his shoulders and dove face-first into my crotch, gobbling my cock into his mouth like I'd never had happen to me in my life.

Bruno picked up my hips and shoved my dick down his throat, not stopping the glorious sucking I hadn't expected. "*Mmmm*," he groaned as he continued to work me in and out of his mouth, moving my whole body instead of his head.

When he pulled off and pushed my hips up so he had access to my ass, I wanted to die. It was absolutely the best sensation in the world. When his tongue circled my hole, I had a hard time not screaming in ecstasy, but I didn't want to scare the man and have him stop what he was doing. The feeling had me ready to explode.

Bruno's tongue slid inside my hole, sending my mind over the moon at the unrelenting stimulation. The burn was enough to remind me I was alive, but when he continued to lap at my pucker and pressed his tongue further inside me, I felt my body tense and then completely relax because I'd never had so much stimulation overtake me at one time as it had when Bruno went at me.

"God, can you fuck me? *Please!*" I begged him, loudly.

Bruno stopped abruptly, gently lowering my hips to the mattress. "I don't like *fuck*."

The sexy man sat up and stared at me for a moment. My eyebrows shot up into my hairline and I was certain he could tell I was a bit worried at his comment.

Bruno chuckled as he stared at me. "I don't mean I won't have sex with you, but I don't like the term, *fuck*. With you, I want to make love. Does that bother you?"

I'd like to say I was surprised by his comment, but I wasn't. It was fitting that Bruno would be more romantic than me, but I damn well didn't want him to stop all of the shit he was doing to drive me wild.

I chuckled. "Make love? Isn't that something old married people do? Oh, wait... We're married, and we're not getting any younger, are we?" I teased.

Bruno smirked and changed the subject quite handily. "Do we have condoms?"

I pointed to the nightstand, and when he opened the drawer and pulled out the strip of foil packets and the half-empty bottle of lube, he looked up and smiled. "This should get us through today." My eyes had to be as big as dollar coins.

Finally, I got my wits about me to ask the important questions. "Do you only top?" I asked him. It was probably a question I'd have asked earlier if the man hadn't put those sexy moves on me and shocked me stupid. Then again, we were just embarking on our sexual relationship, weren't we?

Bruno hovered over me, his dimpled cheeks flushing a little as he stared into my eyes. I was so surprised to see his adorable smile, I was dumbstruck for a moment. "It's okay for me to say I love you while we make love, right? I want to be inside you, and I want to feel you inside me, too. I think that's the best way for us to show each other—I want to feel you inside me," he explained quietly.

It was something I hadn't actually anticipated, though I'd hoped it might be possible. I was versatile, and if Bruno was, as well, I saw a wonderful future ahead.

"Oh, love, I want to be inside you, but I'd love to have you make love to me first, if that's okay?" I suggested as I pulled him down to kiss me, smelling my scent on his face from where he'd kissed me so intimately. If I was only having another dream about Bruno and I fucking, I'd die when I woke up.

We worked to slide on the condom and slick up Bruno in record time, both of us breathing hard. He started to push lube into my hole, but I stopped him. "I'm more than ready to feel you inside me, love."

Without further hesitation, Bruno looked into my eyes and melted my heart as he slowly pressed the head of his glorious cock inside my first ring of muscle. The burn was perfectly biting before he leaned down to kiss me, closing his eyes as he pressed forward. His lips were soft, and his tongue was aggressive. Once he bottomed out, he stopped and opened his eyes. "It feels like home."

The tears rolled down my temples and I couldn't stop them. It was truly the single most beautiful moment in my life. Bruno did make love to me. It was like we were gently being rocked together as he moved the whole bed while he was showing me how much he wanted me. I could feel the love he'd spoken of earlier, and with every stroke of his inside me, it was as if he were erasing every one-night stand I'd ever had, searing himself into my heart and mind for the rest of my life.

November

21

BRUNO

"*Holy Fuck,*" Dominic shouted as he pounded my hole until he released into the condom inside me. We had only stopped pleasuring each other long enough to go to Gabe and Dexter's Halloween party on Monday night, and now we were going after each other again.

I'd already climaxed, and when I collapsed onto the bed, the cold, sticky goo was the last thing I wanted to feel against my overheated skin. "Gross," I groaned as I rolled over to face him, seeing his big grin as he peeled off the last condom in the box and tossed it into the trash can by his side of the bed—which was overflowing after the weekend we'd had.

The party at Gabe and Dexter's with the trick-or-treating had been a lot of fun. I was certain that no two children were safer that night than Dylan and Searcy Torrente.

All of our co-workers—including Willow—were armed in case someone tried to cause trouble. With Jeffrey Oswald out of the picture, there was one less thing to worry about.

"*Noble, help us put him in the van, will you? We'll take care of it from there, and you don't need to worry about anything,*" Mateo told me as Rafe continued to flip that jackknife he had in his hand, making me nervous for him. If it landed wrong, it would slice through the chef's hand like warm butter.

"I thought sending him to jail was what we were planning to do," I reminded the two of them. They both looked a little too eager for my liking, and Casper and I had set it up so that Jeffrey would go to prison for a very long time, based on the minors he'd photographed naked. It seemed like the best place for him, unless it was underground, but I wasn't pressing that option.

"Do you really want to put those kids through the trauma of a trial? Having their pictures passed around a courtroom for this stronzo viscido to argue they did it consensually? I wouldn't want Teo to have to go through that," Rafe explained as he used his brother as an example.

I hadn't thought about what a trial would be like for Sweet Pea and the others. Of course, they were right.

I picked up the desk chair Oswald had been tied to and slid it into the back of the Bianco Catering van before I turned to look at the Torrente brothers. "What are you going to do with him after..." I didn't finish the sentence, trying hard not to think about what after would be.

Rafe chuckled. "That's my area of expertise, amico mio! No worries."

With that, Rafael hopped into the driver's seat and started the van. Unfortunately, he'd parked it in a puddle, and when he started to pull forward dirty water and mud flew all over me.

Mateo started laughing as I reached for my handkerchief to wipe my face. "Thanks a lot," I reacted.

Mateo walked over and hugged me. "Send your dry-cleaning bill to the stronzo in the van. Thank you, Bruno, for getting to the bottom of this ridiculous issue. Oswald will never be a problem again."

"Hey, lazy bones. We need to get ready for work," Willow reminded me that Tuesday morning.

His phone buzzed on the nightstand, and he picked it up. "It's my Dad. He's still in New York and wants to have dinner with me. You want to come?"

That was the bigger problem I had on my mind—Willow's father. Giovanni Mazzola, the traitor of the Torrente family. I hadn't told anyone what I knew about the man because I wasn't sure what to do with the information. I was sure when Mazzola saw me, he'd remember me from my time working for Frankie Man in Italy. What would that mean for Dominic? Hell, what would that mean for me?

"Did you tell him my name? If your father runs a background check on me, that won't look favorably on your taste in men," I questioned as politely as I could. I got up from the bed, taking the sheets with me to toss into the washer before my shower.

Dom was already in the master bathroom turning on the water. With all of the exercise we'd gotten over the weekend, we had decided to skip the workout that morning, especially after I saw what Duke had done to Willow in the ring the previous Friday. We were going to have to talk about that, Duke and me.

"My father doesn't care about anyone but himself. I don't know if I ever told him your name, but as far as him running a background check on you, don't let that bother you. He doesn't really have those kind of resources," Dominic assumed.

I knew for a fact that he *did*, so I decided to contact Dante to ask if he or Daniela had heard anything about Mr. Vanni wanting to know my identity. I prayed the man was too busy being self-involved to give a care about me, but I really couldn't take that chance.

Once we were both dressed, we went downstairs to the Honda I hadn't yet returned. I'd called the rental office on Sunday morning and left a message that I was keeping the car over the weekend. It reminded me that we really could use a car.

"Where'd this come from?" Willow asked as I unlocked the driver's door and walked around to open his door for him.

"Some cut-rate rental place. It's actually not a bad car. The power steering is a little loose and it needs new brake pads, but I can do that myself," I explained to him.

I got into the car and saw the surprise on his handsome, bruised face. "What? I can fix cars and other things with motors. I had to learn how to do it on the farm," I told him before I started the car and directed it to the Victorian.

It was early enough that most of the operatives would still be working out, so Dom wouldn't be late for kid duty. I needed time to figure out my dilemma, too, but I needed some privacy to make a few calls to Italy. I needed to talk to Tommy, for sure.

"I get the impression you'd rather not meet my dad. Am I wrong?" Dominic asked me. His voice sounded sort of sad, and I didn't like that at all.

"How about not this time. Find out when he'll be back in New York, and let's take him to one of Rafael's restaurants in Manhattan. Maybe he can bring your mother, and I can officially meet them together. I think that's a better idea. It'll give me a chance to get a nice suit to wear. What do you think?" I questioned. It would definitely buy me some time to figure out what to do about the traitorous man who was trying to take down the Torrente family.

AFTER DOM and Duke left to get the kids, I went to Duke's new office and closed the door. I didn't want to use my new cellphone to call Tommy, so I used Duke's office phone, thinking no one would find it odd that he'd called Tommy since they were friends.

The phone rang several times and I was about to hang up when it was answered. "Torrente Vineyards, Tomas speaking."

"Hey, Tommy, it's me—Bruno. Can you talk?" I asked.

"Our hours are ten in the morning until six in the evening, Sunday through Thursday, and ten until eight on Friday and Saturday. If you'll hold, I can take your reservation," Tommy told me, confusing the heck out of me.

"O-Okay." Music began playing over the line, so I stayed connected. I sat in Duke's chair for six minutes, wondering if I should hang up and try again later because Duke would be returning any moment now.

"Hey, Bruno?" Tommy finally came back onto the line.

"I'm here. What was that about?" I asked.

"Papa and I were in the tasting room, and I knew whatever the call was about, I didn't want him to hear. He's not feeling well," Tommy explained.

I suddenly felt bad for calling. "I'm sorry to bother you. I'll, uh, I'll figure it out myself."

"No, no. Tell me what's going on?"

"Is it safe to talk?" I asked him.

"Safe from who?" Tommy asked.

"I know who the mole is, Tommy, but I'm afraid to say it over the phone. Can you ask Daniela if anyone has contacted Frankie about my identity?" I asked.

"If anyone has, Daniela would have told me. Can you give me a hint who it is?" Tommy asked.

I thought about it for a moment and finally settled on an answer. "It's someone in the family."

Tommy was quiet, too. I was sure he was thinking about everyone with the name Torrente, or anyone married to a Torrente, remembering behaviors that might have been some sort of a sign that they weren't loyal—that would have been what I would be doing, anyway.

Finally, he spoke. "I'm going to go talk to Giuseppe. We need to get Daniela and Dante out before this all blows up. I'll be there on Friday. Be safe and try to stay out of sight, Bruno. I won't have you putting yourself in danger for something we should have seen coming. Stay in touch." With that, he hung up.

I put Duke's phone on the cradle and decided I'd keep an eye on Giovanni Mazzola. I had to wonder how I could find out how long he'd been working for Frankie Man and if his involvement with the Mangello organization went further than just selling information, if that was what he was doing.

For me, it all boiled down to Dominic. How would it affect him if he found out his father was the one who had been keeping Frankie advised of family movements? Was Giovanni really interested in repairing his relationship with Dominic, and if he was, could I keep such a secret from Dom to keep from hurting him? *God, my head was spinning.*

22

DOMINIC

I stood outside The Palms restaurant in Tribeca waiting for my father that Tuesday night. We'd agreed to meet for an early dinner, but he was now running thirty-minutes late. I had sent him two texts to ask his whereabouts, but he hadn't answered. I'd called his number, and it had gone directly to voicemail, which pissed me off.

It was cold enough that I could see my breath, so I decided to go into the lobby and wait for my dad inside the building. I checked my topcoat with a nice lady in the front before I went into the bar, taking a seat at the end. I pulled out my phone to send a message to Bruno.

Whatcha up 2? I'm w8ing for Dad at The Palms in Tribeca. He's 30 min L8. What's the appropriate amount of time 2 wait b4 u tell someone 2 fuck off?

I saw the three little dancing bubbles on the screen, and my heart sped a bit. This love stuff could wreak havoc on a guy's cool factor if he was willing to let it.

I'm at the apartment watching a romantic movie to pick up some tips for when my husband gets home from his dinner date. I'd say 30 minutes is more than enough time. Come home and we can cuddle in bed. xoxo

I smiled at the text, knowing he used speech to text because of his dyslexia. I sent him back a heart emoji before I ordered a whiskey neat, deciding to give my father another fifteen minutes before I threw in the towel.

Bruno's offer was damn tempting to be sure. After another five minutes, I decided to shoot back my drink and get a cab home when I felt a hand on my shoulder.

I turned to see my father with a big smile, so I grinned in return. "I'd just about given up on you," I told him.

"I've been waiting for you up front and just decided to check at the bar. You ready? We can get another drink at the table," Dad suggested.

I followed him to the hostess stand, and we were seated in a booth near the front windows. Once we were settled and ordered drinks, the waiter winked at me and left us alone.

"So, how're the girls—and Mom?" I ask him, deciding to dive in.

"Your mom is the same, Dom. I know the two of you don't see eye-to-eye on much, but believe it or not, I had the same relationship with Valentina," Dad admitted.

My grandmother, Tina, always seemed to hate my father. Dad took Mazz's side when he and Tina divorced because Nonno had a girlfriend. Tina and Dad never reconciled, even after Mazz died. Nonno left the shipping company to Dad alone, cutting out Tia Desirée completely. It seemed to be an unforgivable sin to Nonna, and she refused to ever speak with my father and us kids by extension.

"You and your mother didn't get along because you didn't give Tia Des part of the shipping business, and it pissed off Nonna," I reminded him. It was funny how my father liked to rewrite history.

"What does a woman know about the shipping business? Hell, your mother is listed on the paperwork because of taxes, but she has no say in the business. No, my father built that business for me, and I've kept it going for you. I want you to come on board at Mazzola Shipping, Dominic. I'll teach you everything you need to know about the freight hauling business. I have a client who uses Mazzola Shipping exclusively, and he pays us a lot of money," Dad tossed out, likely attempting to get me to follow in his footsteps.

"Who is it?" I asked him, curious who this mystery client might be. As I mentioned, I've never really given a shit about my father's business, but the hard sell had me a little suspicious as to his actual motives.

"That's confidential until you sign an employment contract and a non-disclosure agreement," he answered.

"Is there something wrong with you that you're not telling us? Are you ill?" I questioned. If he was sick, it would make sense that he wanted to get all of us back into the fold and wanted me to go to work for him at the shipping business. Dad always seemed to be envious of how close Mom's family was and how they all worked in family businesses even though he honestly hated the Torrentes.

Dad looked up as the waiter approached, and we ordered our food—shrimp cocktail for an appetizer; Caesar's salads; and steaks with Au Gratin potatoes to share. Dad ordered a bottle of Pinot Noir —a non-Torrente vintage—and we sat back, me still waiting for him to answer.

Dad sucked down his drink and held up his glass for another. He looked at me, but I waved him off. I still had half of my drink left, and I wasn't trying to get shit-faced and let my father talk me into something I didn't want to do.

We sat at the table for a few minutes before our server brought our appetizer. I thanked him, seeing Dad had ostensibly dismissed the guy the second he put the dish down on the table. It brought back so many memories of his elitist behavior when we went out for dinners—and none of them were pleasant at all.

When we finished our salads, Dad stared at me for a moment before he chuckled. "So, you're not going to tell me anything about your husband? Not even his name? How the fuck did you end up married, Dominic? Can't you annul it? Your mother isn't happy about it at all," Dad stated, feeling those drinks—and however many more he'd had before he'd arrived.

I placed my fork on my empty plate and wiped my mouth with

my napkin. "Yeah, that's not a surprise, Dad. What do you think about it? I told you I was gay, and you said you didn't care," I reminded him.

Dad smirked. "I remember how it is to be your age. Hell, I nailed anything that stood still long enough—girls, guys, in-betweens. There was a guy in college who I let suck my dick, but I didn't marry him, for hell's sake. Look, I don't really give a flying fuck who you sleep with, Dominic, but I'd appreciate it if you'd be discreet with this shit. I have a business to protect, and if you go prancing onto the dock in platform heels like Elton John, then…"

I tossed my napkin on the table and stood, throwing a hundred-dollar bill next to my father's glass of non-Torrente wine. "I've heard enough, thanks. I definitely don't plan to move back to San Francisco to take over the family business, so don't make any plans along those lines. I might have given it some thought before your last comment, but now? No thanks," I told him as I buttoned my jacket and headed to the coat check to get my topcoat.

There was a wonderful man waiting for me at home, and suddenly, I couldn't wait to get to him. I wanted to kick my own ass for thinking my relationship with my father could have been anything other than a disaster. It was right there in our history as father and son.

My phone started ringing before I could hail a taxi. I checked to see it was my father, so I answered it. "What?"

My dad's deep chuckle echoed in my ear. "I should have expected you to run off in a snit. That's my fault. Come back and eat your meal, Dominic. We need to talk about things, okay? Come back, please."

Part of me wanted to tell him to fuck off, but a feeling in my gut told me to go back and finish hearing him out. My love for my sisters and desire to have them in my life told me I needed to hear more of what my father had to say. Their future depended on the shipping company, and I wanted to ensure they were safe and that Ava would be able to attend college. If the company was losing money, I'd have to do something, wouldn't I?

One thing I'd learned from Uncle Gabe and the other operatives at GEA was to gather as many facts as possible to create the best plan of action. That was the mission now. Find out what the fuck my father was actually up to.

"I HAVE to go pick up Tommy at the airport this morning. I borrowed Smokey's truck, so I'm going to take a cab over to pick it up. You'll be okay getting to work this morning, right?" Bruno whispered into my ear as we lay in bed, early on Friday morning.

We'd traded blowjobs the previous night on the couch while we'd watched a football game that it turned out neither of us gave a damn about, and after, we'd cuddled under a blanket and turned on *The Office*. Bruno had never watched it, and he immediately became a huge fan of Dwight Schrute and his brother, Mose. We laughed through three episodes before we decided to turn in. Having my hunk of a man snuggled up to my back was everything I'd been missing before Bruno came along.

Suddenly, lightening cracked through the sky and rain pounded the bedroom window. "God, I hate this kind of weather," I complained as I turned onto my other side and snuggled into Bruno's hairy chest. Scrape of the coarse, curly hair against my flesh was like little sparks of electricity skittering over my skin. I definitely second guessed why we had to get up so early and hell, why we had to have jobs in the first place.

Just then, Bruno's stomach grumbled, which made both of us laugh and reminded me that we needed money to eat. That was why we worked. I looked up at him through my lashes, seeing he was studying me very intensely. "What's wrong?" I asked as I moved up a little to kiss his soft lips.

"I never, ever, want to do anything to hurt you, Willow. I'd rather hurt myself than see you in pain," he whispered before he kissed my forehead. He pulled me closer and buried his face in my neck. I felt wetness on my shoulder, but when I tried to pull away, he gripped me tighter.

"Is there something you need to tell me?" I whispered, not sure what the hell was bothering him. He shook his head but didn't move, so I let it go. I'd learned he was the type of guy who wouldn't keep a secret from me—he'd stew on it for a while and tell me when he was ready, and I would patiently wait.

We were still figuring out how to be together, but I knew more than anything that being with Bruno was exactly what I needed, regardless of what my father had said earlier in the week when we'd met for dinner about me being discrete. That was bullshit, and all of his attempts to kiss my ass after I returned to the table fell on deaf ears.

I wanted everyone to know I was the lucky guy who had the love of the large man currently crying on my shoulder. He looked like a brute, but I was certain beyond a shadow of a doubt the man was a sweet, teddy bear. That was all I needed to know.

23

BRUNO

My heart was as heavy as a hundred-pound bale of hay. If I was right, and I'd tried to convince myself I wasn't, then I was going to have to hurt Willow by confessing that his father was the rat. That was something I never wanted to do, but I feared it was no longer in my control to keep the information to myself.

I'd parked down the block from the restaurant Willow and his dad had met at in Tribeca for dinner. I'd seen my husband rush out of the place and try to hail a cab, but then his phone had rang and he'd gone back inside, which made my stomach sink.

Dom had finally come out of the restaurant with his father and the two men had hugged as a black sedan pulled up to the curb. They'd argued for a moment, Mr. Mazzola had pointed to the car, seeming to offer it to Dom who'd protested. In the end, Mazzola had ridden away in it, and Dominic had hailed a cab.

I'd sped over the Williamsburg Bridge and had gotten to our neighborhood ahead of Dom's cab, having parked the car down the street and running up the stairs to the apartment so it had appeared as if I'd been there the whole evening.

When Dom had come inside, he'd seemed to be a little troubled, but he hadn't mentioned why, and I hadn't known what to say, so I'd left things alone.

We'd watched a couple of episodes of a television show Dom enjoyed that I'd found to be funny, as well, and then we'd gone to bed. Sleeping next to him had brought a comfort I'd never known. I'd prayed I'd get to do it every night for the rest of my life.

My phone buzzed on the console in Smokey's vehicle as I headed to JFK to pick up Tommy. It was still raining, but it was mostly drizzle, not the thunder and lightning storm we'd had earlier that morning. Lying in bed with Dom as the rain pounded the window was my new favorite thing to do.

We're at baggage claim. We'll meet you at the rideshare pickup. Tommy

I didn't know who the *we* was, but Smokey's truck was large, so things should be fine. There was even a new cover on the truck bed so Tommy's luggage wouldn't get wet. I was grateful Smokey trusted me to borrow it.

I wound my way around the airport, finally finding the rideshare waiting area. There with Tommy were two people I couldn't make out. They were wearing hats and heavy coats, so I had to hope they were friendly.

I honked the horn twice before I pulled into an empty spot and hopped out, pulling my hood up to shield me from the rain. I fired off a text to direct Tommy to the truck, and when I saw him look at his phone and point in my direction, I opened the hard shell on the truck bed and waited for them to come to me.

I was surprised to see Dante and Daniela were the two with Tommy. "Bruno!" Dante greeted, pulling me in for a tight hug. I happily returned it, clapping him on the back while Tommy loaded luggage into the bed of the truck.

Daniela pulled her brother off of me and gave me a hug of her own, pulling back to look at me, her black hat shielding her face from the rain. "Bruno, it's so good to see you again. I've missed your smile," she offered kindly. I gently hugged her and opened the rear passenger side door of the truck, extending my hand to help her inside.

Dante climbed in next to me, and Tommy got into the back with Daniela. I'd have to wipe down the seats of Smokey's truck because we were all wet, but I was glad they were safe.

"Where are you staying?" I asked, looking in the rearview at Tommy's reflection.

"Daniela and I are staying in the apartment over Blue Plate, and I was hoping Dante could stay with you. I want her hidden somewhere Frankie's men can't find her, and worst-case scenario, Dante can help you with the rat. Now, I'm here. Who is it?" Tommy demanded.

I glanced around at the three of them and then remembered I was in Smokey's truck. With finding out that Gio Mazzola was working for Frankie, I had no idea who I could trust. "We'll talk at Rafe's apartment," I decided.

I drove us to Blue Plate and helped Tommy carry their luggage upstairs. I'd thought it was all storage up there, but it was a really nice apartment. "I didn't know this was here," I commented as I took off my shoes so as not to tramp water onto the hardwood floors.

"I think Rafe uses it to hide out in when he's dodging a former lover. He lives in a place on the Upper West Side, but he makes the mistake of bringing his conquests to his place, and some of them have stalker tendencies, he says," Tommy explained as he took Daniela's hat and coat to the bathroom.

I took mine off and grabbed Dante's, hanging them over the railing on the covered back porch before we went into the dining area to sit at the table. I wasn't sure that I was doing the right thing, but I honestly had no idea how to handle the situation myself.

"Giovanni Mazzola is the mole," I announced quietly. I wasn't proud of the fact that I'd found out Dom's father was the person causing so many problems and feeding Frankie information. It made me heartsick.

"Giovanni Mazz—you mean Lucia's ex-husband?" Tommy responded, his face showing shock. I could see his fingers clenching into fists, and I completely understood if his anger was getting the best of him.

"Yes. I'm guessing she's been unknowingly feeding him information about the Torrente family for years, and he's used it against them. He's also my husband's father, so I'm sure you can see the position I'm in. What are we going to do?" I asked Tommy.

"First, we cut off the flow of information. I need to talk to Gabriele and Mateo about this," Tommy advised.

"Not without concrete proof," Dante offered wisely. I was relieved he saw the issue we were facing even if Tommy didn't. We couldn't accuse the man of being a traitor without having evidence of it.

"I don't need concrete proof," Tommy snapped.

Daniela walked up to Tommy and put both of her delicate hands on his chest, her long brown hair swaying with her movements. "Tomas, *amore mio*, we need foolproof evidence." Daniela then turned to me. "Show me a picture of this Gio Mazzola. I saw Mr. Vanni several times when he came to visit Francesco, so I can identify him," she suggested.

"Do you know why he was visiting Mr. Mangello? I think we need to keep you out of it if possible," I told Daniela.

Dante chuckled. "I've seen him at the gate a few times. I can vouch if it's him."

"If you come forward and identify him, Frankie will know where you are, and he'll come after you and Daniela," Tommy mentioned.

"Sure, he will, but we'll be ready for him," Dante replied.

Daniela turned to Dante and smirked. "Yes, brother, we'll be ready."

Things had definitely taken a dark turn. I walked over to Dante and Daniela and pulled up the picture I'd snapped at the Victorian the day Mazzola stopped by to see Dominic. "Is this him?"

They studied the photo, Daniela making it a bit larger before looking at Dante. The two of them nodded together and turned to Tommy and me. "That's him. He's involved in a shipping contract with Frankie," Daniela advised.

"What's he shipping?" Tommy asked the two of them. They were near in age, but in my opinion, they didn't look a lot alike. The two of them were around the same height, but Dante was definitely more muscular than Daniela, who was slender but curvy. She came up to Tommy's shoulder, and they looked good together, much like Dom and me.

Dante put his hand on my shoulder. "Anything and everything, I'm afraid. Drugs, human trafficking, you name it. Frankie Man is old-school mafioso, and not one of his businesses is legitimate. The Italian authorities know it, of course, but they're being paid off well enough they won't do anything about it. He's basically *intoccabile* —untouchable."

That wasn't good news at all. "How can we stop him?" I asked.

"*Uccidilo!*" I knew that word—*kill him.*

DANTE and I returned Smokey's truck to the Victorian. I took him in through the back door by way of the palm reader, and when the lights flashed as we walked inside, there were footsteps behind us. I turned to see Duke and Ace standing in the hallway, Duke reaching behind his back where he had started keeping his weapon.

I held up my hands. "Just me. This is Dante, a friend of mine. He's visiting us for a while," I explained, leaving out a few details, but it was enough of the truth that I didn't hesitate to tell Duke.

Duke extended his hand to shake Dante's, followed by Ace who offered a big grin. "Nice to meet a friend of Noble's."

My face heated at the nickname Mateo had given to me when we were in Kentucky nearly a year ago. I definitely didn't feel it was called for—I was just a normal guy. There was nothing special about me—other than my husband.

Dante chuckled as he looked at me. "Yeah, I see it. Anyway, nice to meet you guys. Nice gym you have here," he offered as he talked to Duke and Ace. I took the chance to slip away and look for Dominic. I needed to tell him we were going to have a houseguest for a few days.

I hurried upstairs and down the hallway to the office he shared with Smokey, knocking on the door before I opened it. "Hi, Smokey. I wanted to return your keys and thank you for letting me use your truck." I put the keys on his desk and turned to find the other desk empty. "Where's Wil—Dominic?" I asked him.

"He's having lunch with his daddy. The man is an asshole, you know," Smokey stated, surprising me. He rarely ever spoke poorly of anyone.

I noticed papers on the desk with lots of numbers on them that I could never hope to understand. "What's all this?" I asked him.

"Close the door, please. No use gettin' everybody up in arms quite yet," he requested.

I did as he asked and sat in the chair Smokey had pulled closer to his side of the desk. "These are the chemical compounds found in the botched bomb—wait, you weren't around for that. Okay, so someone planted a bomb here in this office that Mateo was sharin' with Sherlock at the time. Here in the US, we use C4, which is detonated with a blastin' cap. It's pliable and can be damn effective at blowin' shit up," Smokey explained.

He then went on to explain to me that a more popular explosive in Europe is PE-4, which is a very similar compound. "So, the bomb that was put in here was made from PE-4. It wasn't rigged properly at the time, so it didn't go off. It would have killed us all if it had," Smokey told me.

"Okay. I hope there's no test on this," I joked, trying to keep up but failing miserably.

Smokey chuckled. "This paper is the analysis of the explosive device that blew up Blue Plate a few years ago and nearly killed my husband. It's the same shit. Same batch number, even. It was traced back to a manufacturer in Italy..."

"*Fuck!*" I gasped, slapping my hand over my mouth at the curse word I let slip. Ben's voice echoed through my head—"If you can't get your point across without swearing, you'll never be taken seriously."

"Yeah, *fuck!*" Smokey repeated. "These two explosions are closely related, though the fire marshal probably wouldn't agree because we never showed him the first IED we found in the office. How the fuck are we ever gonna figure out who did this? It was speculated that Carlotta Renaldo did it because she was jealous or some shit, but now she's disappeared and Sherlock is gone, and even Sierra, who was seeing Sherlock, is nowhere to be found. I know there's somethin' here, but I don't know how to connect them or who to blame," the man stated, frustration heavy in his voice.

"What was the occasion when Blue Plate had the explosion?" I asked. I hadn't been invited to any parties held by the people at GEA-A back then because I didn't really know anyone very well, so I wasn't offended.

"It was an engagement party for Maxi and Casper. The whole family was there, too, which was a surprise, really. Parker was working under Rafe back then, and... Hell, that was the night Sally Man was killed. I've gotta talk to Gabby," Smokey stated as he stood and headed for the door.

"Wait. Give me the weekend before you tell anyone about this, please. I need to do something, but I have to be careful about it. Can you do that?" I asked the man.

"Let me help you with it," Smokey pushed.

I shook my head. "If anyone gets in trouble for this, I want it to be only me. This is my problem to fix. Please give me your word," I urged him as I stuck out my hand. Smokey shook on it, and I hurried down the back hallway to the secret passage and down the rickety old stairs.

I found Dante still chatting with Duke and Ace, so I interrupted. "Dante, we need to get your things to the apartment and then get to work on that case," I outright lied. My chest clenched at saying it, but I wanted to keep everyone who I cared about clear of any wrongdoing. If anyone was going to be blamed for what I was about to do, it would be me.

24

DOMINIC

"So, are you and Mom going to get back together—married again?" I asked my father as I sipped a cappuccino at an Italian restaurant in the Village where we'd just finished lunch. He was leaving town for the rest of November, and I had a feeling he was trying to guilt me into returning to San Francisco for Thanksgiving.

Dad chuckled. "No. I can't forgive that your mother cheated on me while we were apart, but I still love her. I just want us to be a family, Dominic," he responded, sipping his espresso.

"Hang on—you cheated on *her* over and over while you two were *married*. Now, you're going to hold it against Mom because she dated a guy *after* the two of you got divorced," I challenged him.

"It's a matter of loyalty, son. You took a vow to love your husband until you die—I still find that strange that men want to marry each other and limit themselves to one man, but it's your life—and if he slept with someone else, could you ever forgive him?" my father asked me.

"One, you don't know much about gay guys, and two, if we were divorced, it's within his right to—" I started to explain.

"No! I sent Salvatore to date your mother as a test of her loyalty, and she failed miserably. The whole Torrente family is filled with liars and cheats, son. Be glad you only have half of their blood in your veins," he ranted, drawing the attention of those within earshot.

"That's the most ridiculous thing I've ever heard in my life," I replied to him, keeping my voice down.

"That's not a topic up for debate. Tell me, how are Gabriele's children? Do they feel cheated at having two fathers and no mother in their lives?" Dad asked. The venom in his voice wasn't anything new, though it made my stomach sour immediately.

"Why? Why do you care about Dylan and Searcy?" I asked him as I motioned to our server for the check. I fished out my wallet and found my credit card. The food was like a lead ball in my gut, and I could already feel the burn of acid in my chest. As much as I didn't want to talk to my mother about her relationship with my father, I had to know if she condoned this bullshit Dad was spouting so freely.

I RAN a few errands while I was in Manhattan and took a cab back to the Victorian in time to accompany Duke to pick up the kids from school. Smokey was sitting at the reception desk when I walked in the front door, appearing to be very bored. "Hey, how'd you get suckered into phone duty?" I asked him.

"Sabrina is teaching Dexter's class. He and Gabby were called to the school, and they took Duke and Bruno with them," Smokey told me.

I chuckled. "What did Dyl do now?"

Smokey stood abruptly, sending the chair into the half wall behind the large desk. "A woman who claimed she was *your* mother tried to sign the kids out from school today, saying they had a dentist appointment. Thankfully, the list of who can and can't sign out the kids is up to date, or she'd have taken them without anyone's notice."

My throat closed, cutting off my laughter. "This morning? My mom's not in New York," I stated, though I wasn't sure if I was trying to convince myself or Smokey.

I quickly retrieved my phone and called my mom's landline, surprised when it was answered on the first ring. "Hello?" It was my youngest sister, Ava.

"Hey, Aves. Is Mom there?" I quickly snapped.

"What's she done now? She's been spying on Daddy, hasn't she? I know he's in New York for business. Mom was going out to the port today to try to go through the accounts. She says Dad's behind on child support, and he told her he was barely able to keep the ships in the water. Mom says that's bullshit and she's going to find out what he's up to," Ava explained.

"Wait, did she get back with Dad to get more money out of him?" I asked her.

"God, seriously? I mean, he spends the night here on occasion, and let me tell you, they get loud. It's disgusting, but surely she's not sleeping with him for money, right?" Ava suggested exactly what I was thinking.

"You're sure she's in California, right?" I asked, exasperation engulfing my soul.

"Yeah, yeah. In fact, she should be home in a few minutes to take me to school. I only have a half-day today. You want me to have her call you?" Ava offered.

"No, it's fine. Have you talked to Gina lately?" I asked, covering my bases. I was pretty sure my middle sister wouldn't have anything to do with some half-baked scheme to kidnap Searcy and Dylan.

"She's busy with finals. Are you coming home for Thanksgiving? I'd love to meet Bruno," Ava gushed a little, which made me smile.

"Probably not for Thanksgiving, Aves. We have a full caseload right now, but you'll be coming to New York for Christmas, right?" We always got together as a family for the holidays, and I hoped to hell we were finished with the shit with Dad and Mom by then. It was nerve wracking to say the least.

"I guess," my sister answered, sounding a little disappointed.

"Okay, brat. I'll talk to you soon. You could call me, ya know.

Phone calls go both ways," I guilted her, having learned from the best, Lucia Torrente Mazzola.

"You really wanna hear about me trying to figure out if I wanna go with a guy or a girl to the winter formal?" Ava taunted.

I laughed. "Oh, lord! That's gonna set Lucia off. Call me when you tell her so I can listen over the phone." Ava giggled, which was nice to hear. It felt like so long since we'd had any reason to laugh and cut up as brother and sister. I hoped to fuck things went back to normal soon.

I disconnected the call and turned to Smokey. "My mom's in Frisco, apparently running an audit of my father's books at Mazzola Shipping. Seems dear-old-dad is behind on child support," I recounted.

Smokey rolled his eyes, and I chuckled. "I know—my family is a clusterfuck. Where's everyone else today?"

"Ace and Mathis went over to Gabby and Dex's to take a look around and be sure the alarm system is up and workin'. Sinclair's workin' a book signin' today at a bookstore in Times Square, and Nemo's down in North Carolina to deal with his daddy. His aunt Hazel called to say the old man's actin' up again. Thank God we've got Momma to keep Daddy in line," he answered as he went back to the papers in front of him. As I started to walk away, Smokey called me back, extending two pieces of paper.

"Tommy called for Bruno, so tell him when you see him, and someone named Dante Barba called to speak with you. Here are the numbers," Smokey told me as I took the two pink message papers.

"Thanks a lot," I replied before I hurried out of the Victorian, only to figure out I didn't have a ride, and no taxis ever came by the building without being called for in advance. Bruno and I needed a car, that was for damn sure.

I called a rideshare and paced on the sidewalk until it arrived. Once I was in the car, I dialed the number for Dante Barba, unsure of who the hell was calling me or why.

"Yep." That wasn't really impressive, but at least the person answered.

"Dante Barba? This is Dominic Mazzola returning your call," I responded.

"Thank you for calling back. I'm a friend of your husband's, and I need to speak with you as soon as possible. Bruno is going to be pissed about this, but he's going to need your help," the man told me.

"Go on," I prompted.

"I'm at your place. Come here so we can talk. It's very important. I'll see you in a bit," the man instructed before the line went dead.

My rideshare driver was headed to the school, but that wasn't where I needed to go. "I need to change my—"

"Change it in the app," the guy announced without waiting, so I tediously redirected my destination from Mosby Academy to our apartment. When the update went through, we changed direction.

For the life of me, I couldn't figure out who Dante Barba was or what he had to tell me that was going to piss off Bruno. I hoped to fuck my man wasn't hiding things from me. That would be a fight of epic proportions for certain.

When I arrived at my apartment building, there was a police barricade just down the block. I saw cops everywhere, crime scene tape blocking access to my building, and a guy looking out the curtain of my apartment. When he saw me looking up, he stepped back out of view.

"What's going on?" I asked a nearby uniformed officer.

"Ongoing investigation," he answered, so I figured I'd never find anything out from them. I made my way around the side of the building to the parking garage and entered that way.

When the elevator stopped on my floor, I got off and went to the door. I reached under my jacket to find my Sig wasn't in the holster, which pissed me off because I'd left it at the office. I hoped to fuck I got better at being an investigator, or I was going to get my ass shot off.

I rang the bell to alert whoever was inside that I was coming in, and I shoved my key into the lock, opening the door. "I'm unarmed," I called out, holding my hands in the air as I went inside.

I walked into the living room with my hands still high and in plain sight, and I stopped when I saw a short guy standing by the windows with a gun pointed at me. "Dante Barba?" I asked. He offered a curt nod. His eyes looked red, as if he was crying.

"I'm Dominic Mazzola. This is my apartment. What are you doing here?" I asked him.

"My sister was shot down there on the sidewalk. She was coming here to help me talk to you. She was with Tommy," the guy told me.

"Tommy? My cousin Tommy?" I asked. The guy nodded again.

"I'm going to take off my topcoat. Don't shoot me," I informed the man as I quickly slid the black wool garment down my arms, draping it over the arm of the couch.

"Lower the gun, okay? I'm not armed like I said," I reasoned with the guy, pulling open my suitcoat to show him the empty holster.

"I've called Bruno several times, but I can't get him on the phone. There's new information I need to tell him," Barba stated.

"I'm gonna take out my phone and call him now. I'll put it on speaker, okay?" I asked him. The guy didn't look too stable if anyone wanted my opinion on the matter, but if he had information that Bruno needed to hear, I wanted to hear it, too.

25

BRUNO

I paced in Dex and Gabby's kitchen while they were upstairs with Searcy and Dylan, trying to calm Searcy down. She wouldn't let Dylan out of her sight, even though the kid wanted to stay downstairs with me for some reason.

I got myself a glass of water and began checking the doors and windows for lack of anything better to do. I knew Ace and Mathis were on a perimeter watch outside after Smokey sent them over when they were finished with their previous assignment, but I hated being in a holding pattern, so when the house phone rang, I answered it. "Torrente home."

"Thank god you're okay. Your phone must be off." I recognized the voice right away. My Willow.

"Where are you? Are you okay?" I asked as I retrieved my cell from my pocket, seeing I'd forgotten to turn it back on. I'd turned it off on the way to the school after the school secretary called Duke to tell him a woman named Lucia Mazzola was at the school to pick up Dylan and Searcy for a dentist appointment.

Duke grabbed me and the two of us ran upstairs from where we'd been rearranging the gym for lack of anything to do until it was time to pick up the kids from school.

I ran upstairs to get Gabby while Duke grabbed Dexter, and the four of us raced to the school. The kids were in the office, Searcy in tears and Dylan looking very worried. He had tried to get me off to the side, but in the scramble Gabby picked him up, and we left the school.

"I'm fine. Someone got shot outside the apartment building, and there's a man here who looks really jumpy. He says his name is Dante Barba," I informed my husband.

"Bruno, man, someone shot Daniela. Tommy's with her now. I don't think she's hurt badly, but the cops are gonna ask questions," the man informed.

"Babe, what are you mixed up in?" Dominic questioned me.

"I'll be home in ten minutes," I responded.

I ran upstairs and down the hallway to where Duke and Gabby were standing, looking in Searcy's doorway. "I've gotta go. A friend of mine has been shot outside the apartment building," I whispered.

Dylan saw me and ran through the bathroom and out his bedroom door. "Tio Gio was with the woman. I saw him driving the car," Dylan gasped out, running into my arms.

I knelt down. "Are you sure?" I asked him, my worst nightmare coming true.

"I was looking out the window in my classroom and saw the car double parked in front of school. The lady got out and headed for the steps, and then Tio Gio got out and opened the door on the back passenger side of the black car and waited. That's when the office called for me to leave for the dentist, but I knew we didn't have a dentist appointment, so I told Miss Carr something wasn't right, and she got the hall monitor to watch the class and took me downstairs. When Mrs. Jarrett told me Tia Lucia was there to get us, I told her that wasn't my aunt," Dylan explained to us.

Gabby looked at me and cocked an eyebrow. "What's going on, Noble?"

I turned to Duke. "Call Smokey to come over and stay here with you all," I instructed as I pointed to Dex and Searcy on the bed where she was still crying.

I then looked at Gabby. "You better come with me."

Without hesitation, he went to his bedroom and came back with two guns, shoving the Glocks into the holsters under his shoulders. The two of us ran downstairs, Gabby grabbing his coat on the way. We went to the garage and got into Dexter's smaller SUV, and we sailed through traffic on the way to the apartment building.

"Cops probably have the front roped off because Daniela Barba got shot in front of the building, so take the alley behind and park in the garage," I suggested.

"Tell me what the fuck is going on," Gabby ordered in a very no-nonsense way.

"It involves Dom's father, which is why I was trying to look into it myself. If I was wrong, then Dominic would never forgive me," I stated.

"Yeah, yeah, tell me."

"Giovanni Mazzola is the mole. He's working for Frankie Man. I saw him in Italy a few times, but I didn't know who he was back then, though now I see Dom looks a lot like him. Daniela and Dante Barba work for Giuseppe. They were undercover like me, though none of us knew it for a while. Tommy's engaged to Daniela, too. It's a really long story, but Mazzola was using your sister to get information for Frankie, and I think he's trying to do the same to Dom," I explained, trying hard not to freak out.

Gabby slammed both of his hands on the steering wheel, making me question whether I should have let him drive in his current state. He then let out a string of curse words in Italian, "Mother fucking... *Figlio di puttana! Ucciderò il bastardo!*" Yeah, that wasn't good.

Gabby slowed down when we drove past our street so we could see if the cops were still there before he pulled into the alley and into the entrance for the garage. The gate lifted because Dexter had a transponder on his Chevy Equinox, and Gabby parked it in a handicapped spot.

We both rushed out of the vehicle and up the adjoining stairs, not wasting time with the elevator. Once we reached our floor, I stopped Gabby. "Let me go first." I bent down and retrieved my Ruger from my ankle. I opened the door to the hallway and rolled into it, checking for anyone who might be unfriendly. Thankfully, it was empty.

We both hurried down the hallway, and I opened the door with my key. "It's me," I shouted before we rushed in, guns still drawn.

Tommy was sitting on the couch looking all kinds of worried. Dante wasn't there, which had me worried. My Willow was sitting in the chair next to the couch, staring into space. I was guessing Tommy had filled in some of the blanks for him.

I hurried over and knelt next to Dom's chair, holstering my weapon before I pulled him into my arms. "I'm so sorry, Willow," I whispered as he put his left arm around my shoulders and buried his face in my neck. I knew it had to be a shock to him, his father betraying his family like that, but I also knew that if Mazzola had shot Daniela, he'd be looking for a way out of the country as quickly as possible. That was when something struck me as odd.

I pulled back from Dom and kissed the tears on his cheeks. "Dom, what time did you leave your father after lunch?"

Dom glanced up at the clock over the entertainment center. "It was just after one. I ran a few errands while I was in Manhattan, but I had to get back to the Victorian to pick up the kids with Duke. Are the kids okay?"

"Yeah, they're at home with Duke, Smokey, and Dexter. So, if your father was at the school after one, he couldn't be here shooting Daniela. We have another problem. Mazzola's not alone," I stated for the benefit of Tommy and Gabby.

"Fucking hell," Gabby snapped, grabbing his phone from his pocket before he walked into the kitchen.

"Where is Dante?" I asked Tommy.

"Daniela went to lay down in the back bedroom, and he's with her. She refused treatment. The shot grazed her arm, thankfully. The car's tires squealed when it rounded the corner, and we both turned to see a shooter out the window. I think it was Tony, Bruno," Tommy answered, referring to Tony Ricci.

I slowly stood and headed toward our bedroom to change. I would find Gio Mazzola and finish it. What he'd done to my husband

and had tried to do to Dylan and Searcy deserved the devil's wrath and a trip to hell.

After I was changed, I walked into the living room to see Tommy and Gabby were gone. "Where'd they go?" I asked as I checked my pockets to see I had everything I might need.

"They went looking for Gio and Tony Ricci, but you and I are going to find my father first. I know just how to get him to come to me," Dom offered.

"You're not going without us." I turned to see Dante and Daniela standing in the hallway together. Daniela had changed out of her dress and into a pair of black jeans that looked way too big on her. She'd pulled her hair into a low ponytail, and she was wearing a long-sleeved, black t-shirt that was also big on her. Dante was dressed the same.

"You need to stay here," I told them, thinking of her close call and what it might have done to her nerves.

Daniela stepped forward, a small Beretta Bobcat in her hand as she slid a loaded magazine inside. "I can take care of myself. Let's get going."

I looked at Dominic, seeing the anger in his eyes as I expected. "Look, how about you stay here but set a trap for him and we'll handle it. I won't kill him yet, but I *will* make him pay for the hurt he's caused you and your family."

"No. You know, you truly are a noble man, but this is my father, and he's hurt the family long enough. He will pay for that hurt, you can count on it," Dom vowed as he retrieved his phone from the pocket of his pants and made a call.

"Son? Are you okay?" the voice of Gio Mazzola echoed in the quiet of our apartment.

"Mom called Uncle Gabe and he fired me, the asshole. I can't afford to stay in New York without that job," Dominic lied.

He reached into my pocket and grabbed my smartphone, pecking out a text before handing it to me.

Mom—it's me, Dom. Don't answer Dad's calls until you hear from me. He tried to kidnap Dyl and Searcy from school. I'll be in

touch when I can.

I read it and hit the send button for him, nodding in understanding of his strategy. He was going to turn the tables on Gio Mazzola, and I was going to be right there with him every step of the way.

26

DOMINIC

My father's deep laugh over the phone caused chills to skitter down my spine. He was truly evil, and how I hadn't seen it before had me completely flummoxed.

"I told you they were liars and trash, but I'm glad you've seen it for yourself. Meet me at Teterboro tomorrow. I've already chartered a plane to take me back to San Francisco, and you can come, too. Will your husband be joining us?" Dad asked.

I looked at my handsome brute who was nodding like a bobblehead. I touched his soft beard and leaned in, quickly kissing his mouth. "No. He's loyal to Gabe. I just want away from them all," I stated, seeing Bruno's face crumble before me.

My father laughed. "Well, well. It seems the prodigal has seen the light," Dad remarked sarcastically. He then added, "You know, Dylan and Searcy are Frankie Man's grandchildren, and he wants them back. If you're serious, bring them along so we can return them to their rightful family, son. Frankie will pay handsomely for his grandchildren." My father confirmed what everyone else already seemed to know.

"It will take me a little time, Dad. Someone tried to take them from school today. They're all freaking out right now, and Dexter and Gabe won't let those kids out of their sight," I admitted. Of course, my father would know that I knew about what had happened at the school earlier, so I couldn't skirt the issue.

"Ah, yes, I put too much trust in young Poppy, but she failed me. She won't get the chance to do that again. I'll give you until tomorrow evening at nine to get Dylan and Searcy and meet me at Teterboro. I'll text you the hangar number when you text me that you have the kids and send a picture, Dominic," my father instructed, not sounding like the man I grew up knowing at all. " I don't want to be as disappointed in you as I am in your mother. She won't get a second chance, either."

"Are you planning to make Mom pay for not being loyal to you? Is she really worth it?" I asked, trying to sound disinterested in my mother's safety and as if I were on his side and didn't care about Mom at all.

"I'll be in touch, Dom. Love you," Dad responded to me, not offering any additional information.

"Okay, Dad. Love you, too," I threw in for good measure before we disconnected the call. I so wanted to wash out my mouth with bleach at having uttered those words.

I looked at my three companions. "No doubt he's got someone watching the house, so you guys need to get out of here and find Tony Ricci," I suggested to Dante and Daniela. "I need to get someone to look out for my mom and sisters."

"I'll go with them. If someone is watching the place, I need to be seen leaving as if we've broken up," Bruno suggested. He started to walk away, but I followed him down the hall.

"You know, I'm not letting you go. We're not getting an annulment, and we're not going to let my family come between us. I love you, and I want us to have a long and happy life… together," I assured him.

Bruno gently pulled me into his arms, looking deeply into my eyes. "I'm glad to hear you say so, Willow. I'll take the Barba's to the Victorian and get them something a little more powerful than that little Beretta that Daniela is carrying. I'll sneak back tonight, okay? We can work on a plan to end this and clean up the mess. Please don't go anywhere without me."

With that, he gently kissed my lips, our tongues sliding in a familiar pattern. His strong arms held me carefully, as if I were breakable, but that wasn't what I needed from him. I needed to feel every inch of him inside every inch of me.

I broke the kiss. "I'll be here waiting for you. Try not to get your ass blown off while you're gone," I joked.

Bruno chuckled. "I *knew* you liked my ass," he teased, which made me laugh. He would never cease to surprise me, I was sure.

"I love you," Bruno told me before he went to our closet and threw a few things into his duffel to make it look like he was moving out. He took my hand and led me out into the hallway, stopping before we reached the living room and the windows which weren't covered by curtains.

Bruno turned to me and gently touched my cheek before he kissed my forehead, sending warm feelings through my body. "We'll need to make it look real, Willow. Will you move your arms around and make it look like you're yelling at me, then slap me across the face. I'll storm out after," he detailed as he leaned into my body and kissed my neck, taking away my breath yet again.

"What about Dante and Daniela?" I whispered to him. Bruno glanced across the living room to see them quietly talking in the hallway that led to his old bedroom, neither of them paying attention to us.

Bruno snapped his fingers to get their attention before he made some sort of hand gestures. Dante nodded, and he and Daniela both dropped to their knees before crawling to the door to wait for the Bruno and Dom show, I was guessing.

"Be very, very careful. We haven't talked about having kids or where we want to live. Hell, we need to get a car, and I wouldn't mind a honeymoon, you know. I know exactly where to go," I listed off.

Bruno pulled me closer to him and aggressively kissed my mouth again, our tongues wrestling together for too short a time. "Come on, man. You can fuck later," Dante complained, making me laugh.

"I can't wait to do all of those things with you. Ready?" Bruno prompted. I nodded, and we both took a deep breath.

"Three, two, one," I counted and then Bruno stormed down the hallway with me hot on his trail, flailing my arms in the air for any slimy bastard who was watching.

I grabbed Bruno by the arm, and slapped him across the face, seeing the shock settle in before he reached up and touched his cheek. "*You really hit me!*" he gasped.

"I was just trying to make it look real," I told him before I stormed over and opened the door, dramatically pointing toward the hallway like a silent film star while Dante and Daniela crawled out, hidden by the table in the dining room.

Bruno briskly walked toward the door. "I love you. I'll be back," he said as his back was toward the windows.

"Me, too," I told him before I slammed the door and went into the kitchen, taking a seat at the island in clear eye shot of the large windows. If anyone was watching, they'd see me making phone calls as if I were preparing to leave town as well.

I finally grabbed a bottle of the Torrente Reserva Chianti from the wine rack and poured myself a glass as I dialed Uncle Gabe's number. "Anything?" he answered.

"No," I lied. As my Nonna Grace always said, too many cooks would definitely spoil the gravy.

I STAYED at the island until the sun disappeared and the apartment was pitch dark. I sent Bruno a text to flip the switch to turn off the hallway lights on our floor before he came into the apartment, and I slipped back to our bedroom, closing the drapes in case anyone was still watching.

I decided to take a shower and do a little prep for when Bruno returned. I wanted him to make love to me in the most morbid kind of way because I was worried about the outcome of our situation. If we died, I wanted to be sure we'd solidified our connection. The man... how did I ever get by without him?

My biggest issue was figuring out how I could ever convince my father that I had Dylan and Searcy with me. There was no fucking way Gabby and Dex would let me use their kids as bait because if I had kids, I'd never do it. I'd have to figure out another way to make it appear as if I had them.

The best way to catch my father was by using the element of surprise. I couldn't chance him getting to Teterboro and getting away from Bruno and me before we could find him. I'd have to hide my husband because I was guessing my father would recognize him easily, which had me worried. I truly needed more devious minds than my own, and based on one night in that bunker at the Victorian, I knew exactly who to call.

Once I was finished with my preparation, I pulled on a pair of flannel pajama pants in case Bruno brought Dante and Daniela back with him. I made my way back to the living room and lowered the blinds over the large picture windows before I turned on the kitchen light and sat down at the island again, grabbing my phone to call Mateo.

"*Ciao, cugino,*" Mateo answered.

"Hi, Mateo. Have you spoken to Gabby or Duke?" I asked him before I began detailing the issue.

"*Si!* I just returned from a scouting expedition with them. Gabriele went home to be with his babies, and we have Casper trying to track your father's cell phone, but we're having no luck," he caught me up.

I might have been making the biggest mistake of my life, but I needed help with something neither Bruno nor I had expertise in. "Remember the night you thought I was working with Nick and Sierra and you locked Nick and me in the bunker?"

Mateo chuckled. "Again, I apologize for my overabundance of caution."

"That's not what I'm calling about. I need to get my hands on something to make someone tell the truth. Well, first, I need to immobilize them, then I need to make them tell the truth. I remember you had Corby knocked out that night, so what did you use and where did you get it?" I asked him.

"That was a most unfortunate night. It taught me a lesson in jumping to conclusions without all of the facts. So, tell me what's going on," Mateo insisted. I knew him to usually have a clear head, though I knew he was deadly—as Cyril Symington would attest to from the great beyond. I hadn't told one soul what happened that night, and I never would. The skeletons in the Torrente closet were damn full.

For the next ten minutes, I gave Mateo the rundown as I believed it to be, answering his questions as best I could. I didn't have all of the details, but I was sure my husband had those that I didn't, and once we put our heads together, we'd have the whole story. There were some pieces of information I was determined to hear from my father himself.

"Dom, forget that shit you see on television about sodium pentothal. It's unreliable at best. The only real way to get the truth is by fear—you have to scare it out of your captive. That's where a professional comes in, and that's why you need someone from our Italian office. It just so happens I'm in town," Mateo stated, chuckling before he continued, "I'll bring something along to make Giovanni easier to manage. Tell me when and where."

Had I been discussing someone other than my father, I'd have climbed on board immediately to drug a mother fucker. Unfortunately, it was a little harder because it was a member of my family.

I was coming to realize the family I had through GEA-A was more loyal and supportive than my own parents. I had to wonder about Bruno's parents, but for the moment, I was on board with Mateo's suggestions.

"Okay. I'll text you tomorrow. Thanks, Mateo," I responded before we hung up.

My phone chimed as there was a knock on the door of our apartment before it opened and the code was entered. I stepped into the hallway to see Bruno slipping off his shoes, the common hallway dark behind him.

"You okay?" I asked him as I walked to the door and took his wet sweatshirt from him, carrying it to the laundry room. I felt his strong arms around me as I filled the detergent dispenser and turned to him. "Pants, please."

Bruno's handsome face turned a bit red as he began unloading his muddy tactical pants. He emptied pockets and stacked his wallet, a small handgun, a Swiss Army knife, and a set of keys on top of the dryer before he skinned off his pants and his boxer briefs.

I looked at the stack of stuff on the dryer, and I laughed. "When you were a kid, did you carry random shit in your pockets?" I asked. He gave me a shy nod before he smirked.

I tossed his tac pants and underwear into the washer and turned to look at his semi-hard cock swaying from side to side. It was a beautiful sight to see. "So, can I help you with that?" I offered as I pointed to his prick, seeing Bruno's sexy lips curve into a happy grin.

"How do you think you could help me, Willow?" Bruno teased me, lighting up my insides.

"Well..." I dropped to my knees and sucked his thick dick into my mouth. His manly scent drove my lust level to the top, and I enthusiastically kissed and licked him like it was lifesaving.

"*Oh, Willow,*" Bruno moaned, which only made me want to hear more from him. He was such a sweet soul, and nothing about him gave off a filthy vibe, but when I got my man going, he turned me on like nothing I'd ever experienced before.

Bruno put his large hands on my head and pushed his hard cock into my throat, thrusting in and out with speed as he fucked my mouth with joy. "God, yeah, Willow," he groaned as he continued ramming his rock-hard rod between my lips.

I swirled my tongue over the bulging mushroom head, feeling it heat in my mouth as I reached up and gently tugged on his heavy balls. I wanted to drain them, and as I continued to bob on his dick, I could feel Bruno surrendering to me. It wasn't like he hadn't before in the times we'd been together, but with what we were facing, I wanted to be sure the two of us were one.

I pulled off. "Please, give it to me," I urged him as I sucked him back into my mouth.

Bruno pulled me off of him gently. He sank to his knees and stared into my eyes. "We're not going to break apart over this, are we? I'll stop pursuing your father and tell everyone I was wrong, Willow. I don't want to lose you."

I sucked in a hard breath before I looked at him, sinking closer to his beautiful body. "I'll admit that when I first met you, I didn't see how the two of us could be compatible, but I'm sorry for my short-sightedness now. I know there were times when I was a complete jerk to you, and I can't tell you how sorry I am for that. Right now, I can't see how we weren't perfect for each other from the beginning," I acknowledged.

The man I didn't expect to come into my life grinned at me. "So, we have a future?"

I exhaled. "I believe we have a very good future if you're willing to give me a chance."

Bruno pulled me up from my knees and hauled me into his strong body, bracing me against the laundry room wall. "Give you a chance? Willow, I love you more than anyone I've ever met in my life. I still don't know why you're willing to be with me, and if you want me to leave you alone after this situation with your father is settled, I'll do it."

I stared at him for a moment, thinking about what I really wanted in life. I suddenly realized that I couldn't begin to imagine my life without the man. "Naw. You'll stick with me."

Bruno kissed up my neck until he settled his lips on mine, picking me up and wrapping my legs around his strong body as he carried me back to our bedroom and into the master bath.

He gently placed me on the vanity as he turned on the water and left me there—his hard cock wagging like a puppy's tail—and placing his toiletries in the shower on the bench next to mine. He also reached into the medicine chest next to where I sat and pulled out the waterproof lube.

I hopped down and went to the bedroom, opening the drawer to see there were no condoms left. I was suddenly very disappointed, but not defeated. I walked into the bathroom to see Bruno taking off his socks. "Bad news. No condoms."

"We don't need 'em. We've both been tested, and I'm negative. You are, too, right?" he answered, surprising me for a moment. The thought of us being negative hadn't even entered my mind!

"Yeah, I am. Damn—I wish we'd have thought of that sooner," I joked. His gorgeous smile rekindled the fire that was burning inside me.

Bruno took my hand and pulled me closer as he reached to push down my pajama pants, stopping to kiss my stiff cock on the way, and gently lifting my right then my left foot out of my garment before he kissed his way back up my body, starting at my feet... then knees... then thighs, where he licked the crease where my legs were attached... then sucking each ball into his mouth before he stuck out his tongue to gather the precome beginning to run like a river.

He then swirled his tongue in my navel and continued his kissing trek up my body, biting each nipple gently before he placed his hands on my face and looked into my eyes. "You are so beautiful. I want to worship your body, but first, I've got to clean up. I smell sweaty, but I got Dante and Daniela set up somewhere safe, and we found Nardo in that building across the street where they're doing renovations. He was watching our place, but he won't be doing that anymore. Come with me," he coaxed as he gently pulled me with him into the shower.

I nibbled at his neck, the salty taste of him fueling the fire inside me and honing an addiction to the man right there in the humid shower. I reached for his body wash and filled my palm before I washed him from head to toe, loving the giggles when I found his ticklish spots. I did my best to block his comment about Nardo and my question of what happened to the man from my mind. There would be time to discuss it but standing naked in the shower with him wasn't that moment.

"Turn," I ordered before I took the shampoo he used and began washing his hair. The moans and groans as I massaged his scalp filled the room with sound and made me wonder if Mr. Prugh, our neighbor, could hear us. I seriously didn't care, but I knew he'd call Uncle Gabe and then I'd hear about it. Hell, if we were going to get yelled at, we might as well have a very good reason.

I grabbed the beard shampoo from the bench and looked at my man. "How long does the conditioner need to stay in?" I asked him as I squirted a dime-sized dollop into my hands before I pecked a kiss on his sexy lips and went about washing his beard.

"Let me get it," he insisted as he washed his handsome face before he held his head under the spray and rinsed himself from head to toe.

"Now, the conditioner stays in about two minutes," he informed me as he stroked my hard cock with a sudsy hand.

That sounded perfect.

I reached for the conditioner and coated his beard before I grabbed the lube. "I'm damn glad we don't have to worry about condoms anymore," I reminded him as I squeezed lube on both of our jutting cocks and gathered them in my fist.

"Gah," Bruno gasped when I began to stroke us together.

I pulled out all of my best moves—the slow-and-soft stroke, the piano player, the squeeze and pinch, the tunnel-of-love, the reverse sausage wrap, and the bottle cap, which really did him in. He mimicked my moves, and when we exploded all over each other, it was as if we'd base jumped from a mountain together. The freefalling feeling when my balls emptied was something I'd never experienced with another man, and it was magnified by the look of love in Bruno's eyes.

We rinsed off again, and I reached for towels on the rack outside the shower door while Bruno turned off the water. "Please tell me you're staying here tonight," I nearly begged as I stepped out and wrapped the towel around my waist.

Bruno chuckled. "Dynamite couldn't blast me out of here, Willow."

Bruno finished his night-time routine, officially moving his things into the master bathroom, where the comforting mint and vanilla scent now wafted through. When he wrapped his arms around me and pulled me into his body, I fell into a blissful oblivion...

27

BRUNO

Once Willow was sound asleep—and after I'd held him long enough that night and early morning so that I would still feel him in my arms as I went about my day, I slipped out of bed and got dressed in running gear. I definitely had a bounce in my step as I jogged to the Victorian where I'd stashed Nardo the previous night after Dante knocked him out. I wanted to get there before anyone else arrived at the building that morning and needed to get into the weapons vault.

When I opened the back door and the lights flashed, I stepped inside, not surprised to see Mateo sitting on the stairs. "A little early for a workout, isn't it?" he asked me with his big Torrente grin in place.

"I, uh, I couldn't sleep," I lied—well, only half. My adrenalin hadn't stopped pumping, even with the good pumping Dom and I had given each other in the shower, but there was no way I'd have been able to sleep.

"There's the twitch. You're right eye twitches when you lie," Mateo informed me.

I knew my eyes got as big as silver dollars. "Really?" I questioned.

He chuckled. "Naw. I'm just fucking with you. So, who's the guest of honor?"

"Leonardo, or Nardo, as Frankie and Tony called him. I found him in the building across the street from our apartment spying on us through the picture windows. Dante knocked him out," I informed Mateo as I placed my hand over the reader after pressing the panel.

The door sprang to life, and when it opened, I saw Nardo was still out, which seemed unlikely. I hurried inside and felt for a pulse, barely getting one. The air was stale in the bunker, and when Mateo joined me, he dragged Nardo out into the hallway. "Fucking Gio Mazzola trying to kill another one," he remarked as he administered a few chest compressions to make Nardo take in some air.

The man began sputtering and fighting the zip-ties around his wrists and ankles. "Stop. You'll hurt yourself," Mateo insisted before he looked at me. "Is he a good guy or a bad guy?" Mateo reached for a Tanfoglio behind his back and slid a suppressor out of the pocket of his jeans, twisting it on the barrel of the gun.

"I never had a problem with him, but I don't know if he's good or bad," I answered honestly.

Mateo smirked before he turned to the man, gently tapping the gun on Nardo's cheek. "Are you a good guy or a bad guy?" he asked again, removing the duct tape in one quick, painful-looking pull.

"Argh!" Nardo complained, shaking his head as if to stop the sting I'm sure was strong.

Mateo tapped the suppressor against Nardo's skull, watching the man very carefully. "So, Leonardo, tell me. Are you a good guy who would love to wander the US to save his own life? Because if you go back to Italy, Frankie will probably skin you alive. Or are you stupid enough to think you can talk yourself back into his good graces?"

"I don't think he speaks much English," I volunteered quietly.

Mateo chuckled. "They all *parlare inglese*, don't you?" Mateo tapped the gun on Nard's crotch, and I actually saw his face turn ghostly white.

"Yes, yes. I speak English," Nardo admitted. I wanted to kick him in the nads because he always acted like he didn't understand me when I said something.

"Ask me questions. I'll answer," the man quickly agreed.

Mateo let out an eerie laugh. "Frankie must be scraping the barrel for you."

"I'm Rosa's brother," the man informed us.

I looked at Mateo, who was shaking his head. "It's always the family, isn't it? So, Leonardo, you came here to assist who in kidnapping Dylan and Searcy?"

"Mr. Vanni," the man answered.

"That's what Mazzola called himself when he visited Frankie," I explained. I didn't like Nardo, but he wasn't lying.

"And you knew you were to kidnap two children? What else were you supposed to do?" Mateo quizzed.

"Kill Mr. Vanni's ex-wife. He tried to do it when he blew up a restaurant here in New York a few years ago, but he didn't use enough explosives. His partner back then took half of it and tried to blow up another place, and she didn't leave him with enough to do the job properly. That's what he told me." The man moved his head between Mateo and me so quickly I was sure he was going to get whiplash.

I looked at Mateo, who was scowling. "It was Carlotta Renaldo. She's been dealt with."

"Smokey has the chemical compound of the two devices and said they are identical," I volunteered in support of the man's statement.

"So, you *can* tell the truth," Mateo said to Nardo. The restrained man nodded quickly.

"Mr. Vanni, whose real name is Giovanni Mazzola, tried to kill you while you were inside the bunker, did you know that? Not very much of a team player, is he? He disconnected the air compressor the same way he did when he killed a young woman who was most likely misguided into believing his lies. Do you know where Mr. Vanni is staying? How did he check in with you?" Mateo asked him.

"He didn't. I'm supposed to meet him and the Torrente children at a place called Teterboro. Do you know where that is? I'm supposed to be there at twenty-one hundred," Nardo stated.

Military time. Nine o'clock tomorrow night. I had until nine o'clock to catch Giovanni Mazzola to keep him from harming the people I cared about—one I loved with my whole heart.

A dark haze seemed to overtake my mind and body, one I'd felt a few times in my life—when I'd shot the man who was trying to harm Parker Howzer; when I'd tried to choke the life out of two men on the metro in DC who had decided they were going to do harm to Benjamin Hoffman, and now, when I thought about Giovanni Mazzola and his intentions to do harm to people I loved.

I looked at Mateo. "If we let him go now, he'll warn Mazzola. Can we leave him here until we have Mazzola," I questioned.

Mateo shook his head. "Too many loose ends," he stated before he aimed the gun and pulled the trigger, sending one shot into Nardo's forehead. The action caught me off guard, but I was glad I didn't have to be the one to pull the trigger this time.

The man didn't make a sound, just staring into the distance with unseeing eyes. At the end of the day, he had agreed to assist Mazzola in kidnapping two children who had the unlucky fate of being born into the Mangello family. They shouldn't pay for it for the rest of their lives.

Mateo had called Casper, who was hacking into Nardo's phone to see if he could locate Mazzola to find the man before he could do harm to Dominic or the kids.

I hauled Nardo's body out of the Victorian after Mateo and I rolled him in the rug from Duke's office, and I drove him down to the river, dumping his body into the Hudson after I tied weights from the gym to his arms and legs to sink him into the bottom sludge. I was sure Duke would be unhappy to find the large weight disks missing, but there was nothing to be done about it.

I put the rug back into Mateo's SUV and hauled it back to Duke's office, seeing only one spot of blood had seeped out of the plastic bag Mateo had tied around Nardo's neck to contain the mess. I wasn't even sure if the blood was Nardo's, but I went to the supply closet to find spot remover and went about cleaning the rug just the same.

"What position would you like to have with GEA-A?"

I turned to see Mateo standing in Duke's doorway where I was on the floor, having put the rug back in place to clean it.

"I like what I'm doing now," I answered him as I continued to scrub the plastic bristled brush over the spot.

"I appreciate that, but there are certain types of situations where a cool head and a willingness to do the unthinkable are necessary. You've proven yourself to all of us, Bruno. Would you be willing to take on some rather unpleasant tasks?" Mateo stated.

I sighed. "When I was working on the blackmail case, Gabby mentioned cleaning up my record so I could get an investigator's license and a gun permit. Would I still need to do that?" I responded to the man.

"Yes, but that's not as difficult as it might sound. Would you be willing to spend time in Italy?" Mateo asked.

I inspected the spot again to see I'd done as much with removing the drop of blood as possible, so I moved the desk over it and returned Duke's chair to its usual spot. I gathered my cleaning supplies and walked to the hallway, turning off the light and closing the door.

"Only if Dominic will agree to come with me," I answered honestly.

Mateo nodded. "That shouldn't be a problem after all of this. You would both be very useful to Papa's organization. As you know, the Italian authorities turn a blind eye to certain activities. Once this matter is in hand, we'll discuss things in more detail."

I held up my hand. "I have to talk to Dom about it, and I'd like the two of us to take a few weeks off to have a honeymoon."

Lawry came running out of his office with two phones in his hand. "I don't know whose phone this is and where they are now, and I don't want to know, but I've found Mr. Vanni. He's staying at a

Hampton Inn in Paramus. Should we call the New Jersey State Police?"

"*No Police!*" Mateo and I shouted at the same time.

Casper smirked. "My bad. So, what's the plan? Do I need to sound the alarm and rally the others?"

Mateo looked at me, and I could read his face. "No. We've got this," I announced as Mateo grinned in agreement.

I WAS WALKING home when a black SUV pulled up next to me. The passenger window rolled down, and someone whistled at me the way construction workers whistle at pretty girls in the movies. I glanced to the left to see Willow in the driver's seat. "Hey, baby! How about a ride?" Dom called out, making me laugh.

"Were you out driving around to find hot guys, or were you looking for me?" I teased as Dom stopped at the curb, motioning traffic around him as I walked up to the SUV. It looked like Duke's—there was a safety seat in the back for Searcy, so I was sure I was right.

"You're the only hot guy I'm looking for. Come take a ride with me. I've got candy..." He waggled his eyebrows, which made me laugh more than I'd laughed in a week. I hopped into the vehicle and pulled on my seatbelt, taking his hand that was resting on the console between the seats.

"Where are we going? Did you eat anything today?" I asked him. My stomach growled right then, making Dom laugh.

"We can get something after our appointment. What have you been up to?" Dom asked me. I didn't want to say, "Disposed of a body." That seemed a bit harsh to me.

"I was helping Mateo with an issue at the Victorian. Right now, it might not be the best time to bring it up, but he mentioned that maybe we'd want to move to Italy. I could take his old job as a wine salesman, and you could work for Mr. Torrente in some capacity," I explained to him.

"Like, permanently move there, the two of us? What about Frankie's people?" Dom reminded me.

"Yes, that's a good point. Maybe we should give it some more thought?" I responded to him as I really considered what I was asking of him. The people I'd met in Italy who worked for Giuseppe were all very nice, but that didn't mean they'd like the two of us, and there was the Mangello threat until Frankie was dealt with for good.

I put it out of my mind and turned to see Dom merging onto I-87 South. "Where are we going?" I asked him again.

"We're going mannequin shopping in East Brunswick. I talked to the owner, and she thinks she has what we need," Dominic informed me.

"What do we need?" I questioned, not sure why we needed mannequins. I found them to be creepy when I saw them in the stores. I couldn't imagine why we needed some.

"The only way I can convince my father that I have Dylan and Searcy is if I have mannequins that look like them in the back seat. I'll borrow some of their clothes, and we'll have them strapped in. Dad just needs a glance at them and then we grab him," Dominic told me as if it were simple as A-B-C.

"Is he that stupid?" I mumbled.

Dom chuckled. "Maybe? Mateo will be there to jab him with a sedative, and we'll throw him in the back after you tie him up. Then we'll take him to the Victorian and get him to admit what he's been doing and for how long, and who else is involved in his scheme to take down the family," Dominic detailed.

"Then what? What will we do with him after he admits to being a bad guy?" I asked him, very curious about his answer. It was his father we were talking about, after all.

Dom glanced in my direction. "You know what we'll probably do with him, but it will be Gabby's call because my father is a threat to his children. So, what do you want to eat?" Dom quickly changed the subject, but I knew his father was weighing heavy on his mind.

"How about a good hamburger? You still owe me your grandmother's braciole, you know," I teased him a bit, sorry to have taken the smile from his handsome face. I wanted to see him smile as much as possible.

I wasn't sure if Willow's weird idea of mannequin children would work, but I was in it with him—always.

28

DOMINIC

I turned Duke's SUV into the parking lot of an average, gray-block building I'd seen in about a million slasher films over my lifetime. There was a chain link fence around it with holes cut here and there, and the gate was broken from the hinges. Thankfully, it was propped open so Bruno and I could enter.

There were two cars on the lot aside from ours—one of which was an old hearse and an old Volvo with oxidized black paint and a bumper sticker for Dukakis/Bentsen. A shiver of fear slid down my spine at the sight of the hearse. I glanced around the property to see it looked completely deserted, and I wondered if it was wise to pursue the mannequin idea at all.

I pulled up the message on my phone to double check the address, and yep, it was correct. The building gave every indication that we would die there, but "God hates a coward," as Nonno Tomas always said, so we were going in.

I reached under my jacketed arm to double check I had my Sig. Bruno went into a pocket in his running shorts and pulled out a small Ruger which surprised me, checking it before he slid it into the waistband of his shorts and turned to me. "This place is kind of creepy, ain't it." It wasn't a question; he'd already read my mind.

I laughed. "Yeah, I only take you to the best places. I promise I'll feed you after this." *If we're still alive...*

The two of us got out of the large, black SUV and met in front of the somewhat dilapidated building. The gutters were sort of sagging on the north side of the building, which only added to the spooky-as-fuck effect, especially with the sun beginning to set behind it, giving it an ethereal orange glow—like we were entering a portal to hell.

I glanced at Bruno, who swallowed. "You ready?" I asked him, offering my hand.

"Yeah—let's go," he said as we walked toward the only visible entrance in the front. I pressed the buzzer by the door twice, and we waited.

Bruno checked his pistol before leaning to his left to kiss my cheek as the heavy sound of footsteps indicated someone was approaching. Of course, the mother fucking door creaked when it opened.

Standing there was a massive man with a bushy white beard. He was dressed in an old-timey tuxedo, complete with tails and a top hat that had a pair of goggles around the brim.

His face was made up with a white base and dark circles around his eyes. His lips were painted black and it looked like he had ashen shading on his cheeks to make him look really old. My mind immediately went to that Svengoolie dude on late-night television. He was, however, wearing extremely cool, high-heeled black leather boots that laced up to his knees. "May I help you?" the man asked, his voice a deep bass that reminded me of Lurch from a show I used to watch as a kid.

"Uh, yeah, sure. We're here to see Roxy," I informed him, which not so coincidentally was the name of the place—Roxy's Mannies. I'd thought it was kitschy when I found it on the internet and spoke to the woman, but now I was kind of freaked out.

"Ah, Mr. Mazzola, I presume," the man stated slowly. I nodded.

"Please, come inside. Roxanne is setting things up in the back. Follow me," the man, who was as tall as Nemo but much thinner, invited, so Bruno and I stepped inside.

Never in my life did I expect to see hundreds of mannequins of all shapes and sizes facing our direction—some with faces and some not; some with arms and legs, and some without. The absolute worst were the lifelike ones with realistic expressions and no genitals. It had to be one of the creepiest things I'd ever seen—or so I thought for about two minutes...

Bruno swallowed loudly next to me, so I squeezed his hand. "Let's get this over with," I whispered, bracing myself for what we'd find *in the back.*

We followed Lurch through the mostly dark warehouse toward an illuminated area, stopping when I saw a tiny woman with white hair in cascading ringlets down her back. She was dressed in a brown leather dress with black fringe, an equestrian top hat with a black lace train perched on top of her head at a kicky angle. She looked like something out of a Madonna video.

"Mr. Mazzola, welcome to my studio," the older woman greeted us, her hands extending with a flourish like a spokesmodel. Her blood red lips were hypnotizing.

I stood there with my mouth gaping like an idiot, so Bruno cleared his throat. "Thank you for seeing us, Miss Roxy. Willow mentioned you might have what we needed," Bruno remarked as he squeezed my hand.

I snapped out of my stupor, breaking my gaze from her sparkly red lips. "Yes, uh, sorry. I guess I didn't expect to see you—so many mannequins in one place. It's a little overwhelming," I corrected. The woman smiled, her perfect teeth glowing in the scant light. Her canines were filed to a point that would definitely pierce skin, which had me wanting to protect my throat.

"Forgive us, but we're going to a birthday party for a friend, and we wouldn't have time to change after your visit. Follow me, please," Roxy insisted as we hurried back toward the light where two sets of mannequins were posed together. The boy mannequins were tall like Dylan. One was wearing glasses and the other wasn't. They had short hair, but their flesh was a shade or two apart.

The girl dolls were the same way, so lifelike that they creeped me out. They definitely looked like Searcy—with a little adjustment to the hair, but then again, my father wouldn't give a flying fuck about her hair, would he? He wanted the real thing for the fortune they would likely bring him when he turned them over to Frankie Man.

"From the picture you sent, this was the best I could do on short notice," Roxy admitted.

"No, no. This will definitely work. How much?" I asked as I pulled cash from my pocket, remembering that was the only way she'd see us so late in the evening.

"Not so fast. What are you planning to do with them?" Roxy asked us as her gaze scanned over the two of us.

"They're for a display," Bruno responded quickly.

Roxy put her hands on her bustier covered waist and stared at the two of us. "What does that mean, exactly?"

"It's a display at our kids' school," I tried to cover.

The woman continued to assess us, finally sighing loudly. "Tell me you're not going to drill their mouths open and use them for some twisted photo shoot. You look like decent guys, but I won't let you have them if you're perverts."

I glanced at Bruno, who stood a little taller. "Miss Roxy, we're using them as bait. A very bad man is trying to kidnap the two children we're guarding, and we want to catch him and see that he's brought to justice. If we can make him believe these are our primaries, we have a chance," Bruno honestly admitted, which surprised me.

The woman offered a slow grin. "That's brilliant! Do you need outfits?" It was then I noticed a bit of an Aussie accent I hadn't picked up before. She was definitely an enigma.

"No but thank you. We'll get the clothes from the children's wardrobe. We want them to be as authentic as possible," Bruno answered, surprising me yet again with how incredibly astute he was under the circumstances. He had the woman eating out of his palm, while I looked like an idiot—a role I was too used to playing.

"That'll be two fifty... Gents, let's just call it two bills even, shall we?" she answered. I peeled the money off the wad I'd taken from petty cash at the Victorian and nodded to her as she shoved the money between her tits.

Bruno held up his hand and she extended hers in return. He leaned forward and kissed her knuckles, the elegant bastard. "Thank you, ma'am. Can I ask how you make the mannequins?"

Roxy giggled at us and waggled her thin eyebrows. "We make plaster casts of attractive cadavers. Ervin used to be an undertaker," she answered. I felt my blood run cold at her words, but when Lurch—uh, Ervin—laughed his deep spine-chilling laugh, I had no idea what to believe.

Bruno and I each grabbed a mannequin and headed back through the factory to the parking lot. We put the kids in the back seat and Bruno took my keys to drive us back to Brooklyn. I was too fucking freaked out to argue.

WE GOT HOME ABOUT EIGHT, and I ordered us a pizza from a great pizzeria in the neighborhood. Bruno went to shower, and I poured us each a glass of wine, walking back to the bathroom to talk to him.

"Can I bug you?" I asked as I went into the room without knocking.

"Always. What's up?" he asked as I opened the glass door and handed him a glass of wine. He took a sip and nodded before handing it back. "That's good. Now, tell me what's got you bothered. Is it still that mannequin place?"

I grinned at him and shook my head. "You know how to work on cars and other engines, right?" I asked, thinking about Mateo's offer for us to move to Italy and for Bruno to maybe take over the salesman position at the vineyard.

It wasn't that I didn't think he could learn the job, but Bruno wasn't an arrogant man like Mateo. He was a genuine person who liked simple things. He wasn't sophisticated, but that was what I loved most about him. I also knew Mateo's primary job wasn't to sell

Torrente wines—it was far more nefarious, and I had to wonder if Bruno knew it, as well.

"Yeah. I've been working on motors all my life. Why?" he asked as he shampooed his hair and beard. The scent of vanilla filled the room, and once again, I was under Bruno's spell.

"Corby Barr and I have sort of become friends. He's Duke and Ace's partner. Well, he's a mechanic and left GEA-A to pursue it as a business, and I thought maybe the two of you would have some things in common. Maybe you'd like to leave GEA-A, too, and go to work with Corby… Or maybe the two of you could open a garage together? I have some money saved," I explained to him.

I remembered seeing Ace's Camaro that Corby was refurbishing, and that damn thing was amazing. Duke and Corby were giving it to him for Christmas, and I was sure the man would lose his mind over it. I could definitely see my Bruno enjoying something like that much more than killing a stranger because Uncle Giuseppe deemed them a bad person. I couldn't fathom Bruno doing that, ever.

The water turned off and the door swung open, Bruno standing in front of me in all of his sexy, naked glory. There was a scowl on his handsome face that put me on edge.

"Do you think I can't do the job? Do you think I wouldn't be a good salesman?" Bruno asked, his face verging on hurt, which I hated to see.

"No, no, honey. I just know you're not a fan of wine, and could you sell wine if you don't really like it?" I suggested, trying to save the conversation as I placed the wine glasses on the vanity top behind me.

Bruno wrapped a towel around his waist and stepped between my legs, shaking his wet hair at me. I batted at him and rifled my fingers through his short brunet strands to squeeze out some of the water. "Stop it!" I chuckled at him.

"If you don't want to go to Italy, I'm fine with staying here, and I might talk to Corby about doing some side work for him. I really want to stay on at GEA-A, Willow. Those guys are like family to me, and I didn't really have one," he answered, his honesty shining in his eyes.

I reached up and gently combed his beard with my fingers, reaching for the beard oil he used. I sprayed some on my hands and carded my fingers through the coarse hair, stroking his gorgeous face at the same time.

"Maybe one of these days, we can have a family of our own?" I whispered to him as I reached for his black comb that was sitting on the white marble vanity top, combing back his hair before I attempted to tame his beard.

Bruno stopped my hands, holding them to his lips after he took the comb and put it on the counter again. "Why would you want to make a family with me? I'm not smart like you. I didn't go to college, Willow. I can do manual labor, but I'm not as classy as you."

I felt the tears pool in my eyes as I realized that for me, Bruno was the total package. He was everything I didn't know I wanted in a man. His gentleness with those he loved; his calmness in the face of the unknown that I'd witnessed at that fucking mannequin factory earlier; and the fearlessness I saw in him. He would truly lay down his life for the benefit of another, and I was in awe of it. My Bruno did nothing halfway.

I tugged his large hands, which were rougher than mine, to my lips. "What makes you think I want a guy like me? I want you. I want a man who isn't afraid of hard work. A man who appreciates simple things. A man who is willing to work toward goals with me. I believe you're that man, Bruno," I told him before I kissed his knuckles as he'd kissed Roxy's earlier that afternoon.

"I want to be that man for you, Willow, but I'm worried I won't be enough," he told me as he placed his hands on the countertop on either side of my thighs.

I scooted closer to him. "I love you. We'll figure out our life together. Don't worry about being enough because I know for sure you're everything I'll ever need," I told him as I wrapped my arms around his strong neck and leaned in to brush a kiss to his soft mouth.

Bruno wrapped me up tight and lifted me from the counter, taking me back to the bedroom and plopping me on the bed. "How long before the pizza?" he asked as he unbuttoned my navy slacks and pulled them off, leaving my black briefs riding low on my hips.

When he leaned over and captured the waistband in his teeth, pulling them down my legs and off my feet, I gasped. "*Bruno!*"

"Pizza?" His deep laugh lit a fire inside me, bringing my prick to attention before he bent forward and sucked it into his hot mouth.

"Twenty minutes." My hands wound in his silky hair without my permission, and I pulled his mouth closer to the base of my cock. He swirled his tongue around the ridge, zinging to life the nerve endings to drive me wild.

Bruno continued to show me what his mouth could do, and I appreciated every lick, nibble, and slurp. "Please, don't stop," I moaned as he continued to pleasure me with abandon.

"God, I want you in my mouth," I groaned as my balls pulled closer to my body, ready to fire off.

I slid across the mattress away from him, pulling my throbbing cock from his mouth. "Get up here," I demanded as I grasped the towel and pulled it off of him before I yanked my shirt open, buttons scattering over the bed and floor of our room.

I moved to the foot of the bed and rested my head over the end, my tongue sliding between my lips to lick the end of Bruno's leaking cock. He quickly rammed forward, shoving his hard member into my mouth. I swallowed it down, and we went after each other relentlessly. I was glad we'd decided to forego rubbers. I needed that full feeling again—both ways.

29

BRUNO

I woke with Dom on my chest, both of us having slept like rocks to the point we hadn't moved after we'd eaten the cold pizza the delivery guy had left by the front door. I was relieved Dom had tipped him on the app, or I wouldn't have chanced eating it because I didn't know what he'd do to it when we didn't answer the door. People were vengeful these days.

Willow's smartphone buzzed loudly, skittering across the nightstand, which must have been what had woken me in the first place.

I kissed Willow's forehead, hearing a cute snort from him as he turned away from me. I wrapped my arms around him and grabbed his phone, holding it in front of him. "Willow, your phone is buzzing," I whispered as I covered his neck with kisses.

"It's too early, love," he whispered back, which had me smiling.

"It's six," I whispered to him in return, my sweet husband.

The phone buzzed again. "Damn," he sighed as he slowly opened his eyes and blinked a few times before he glanced up at me.

He let me hold the phone and put in his passcode, which made me laugh. "That's not very secure," I teased him.

"One, three, five, seven—all prime numbers—is as secure as

anything else I could come up with. You ready to start the day?" he asked as he brought up the text message from Gabby.

I've got the clothes you asked for. I sent Dex and the kids out to Long Island with Duke and Ace. Come over when you're up and park in the garage. Let's get this done.

I looked at the message and slowly sat up with Willow still in my arms. "I wish you'd let me do this without you," I nearly begged him. His soul was pure, and mine wasn't. Besides, I knew what was in store for Giovanni Mazzola, though I wasn't sure if I wanted it to be at my hands. I feared that was a thing Dominic could never forgive me for.

AN HOUR LATER, Dom and I took Duke's SUV over to Gabe's house, parking in the garage as he'd instructed. We got out of the vehicle and went in through the laundry room, surprised to see no dog or cat to greet us. Gabby was sitting at the island, looking very worried.

"Good morning," I greeted him.

He glanced up from his coffee. "Bruno. Dom," he responded.

He stood and walked to the coffee machine that wasn't like the one at the Victorian. He made two cups of coffee for Dom and me before he placed them on the large white marble island and pulled out two stools for us.

Anyone could see that Gabby was upset about the situation, and I couldn't blame him. Someone was trying to take his children, and I was sure if I had any of my own, I'd feel the same way.

I turned to my husband and offered him a smile. "Maybe you go get the mannequins so we can dress them? Gabby, where are the clothes Dom asked for?"

Dom grinned and gave me a quick wink. "Yeah, I'll get the mannequins. I'll warn you, Uncle Gabe, they're creepy as fuck," Dom responded before he left through the laundry room.

I looked at Gabby. "I don't want him involved. This is his father, and we both know what needs to happen, but Dominic can't be there. I'll handle it. I'd rather you not be involved, either. Then you can tell your sister that you have no idea what was going on or what happened to him, and it won't be a lie," I tried to convince the man.

Gabby looked at me and offered a tired smile. I wondered if he'd even slept the previous night. "This is a hell of a mess, isn't it? I have two of the most incredible children ever to grace a family, and we went through all of the channels to make sure they were ours. We endured that fucking adoption process, and those two are my babies as much as if I fucked... Well, they're mine and Dexter's, and god willing, we'll find out within the next few weeks if we're going to give them a brother or a sister."

He took a sip of his coffee and scowled, pushing the mug away before he looked into my eyes. "I absolutely refuse to allow that fucking prick Gio Mazzola to take anything more from me. He's already poisoned Lucia's mind about our family, and I won't let him do anymore harm to the people I care about," Gabe stated with conviction. I definitely believed the man. He was more than sincere in his vow.

"I understand but let Mateo and me handle it. It's for the best, Gabby," I replied, hoping he saw it as the best option.

"My hands aren't clean by any means, Bruno, so don't worry about me. It will be my pleasure to end that son of a bitch," he stated.

He glanced out the large kitchen window that faced the front yard where a fountain was covered, likely having been winterized for the season. "You know, don't you, that you definitely are a noble man... Oh, that reminds me, we've gotta get you a new identity so you can get your private investigator's license and a gun permit. Casper's ready to make the changes, but he needs you to pick a new name," Gabby explained.

Just then, Dominic returned to the kitchen with those two weird dolls, one under each arm. "Okay, Gabby, we need clothes," Dom stated, a big smile on his face.

He placed the dolls on the floor facing the counter, and Gabby stood, walking over to them before he knelt down to look at them.

Dom came to stand by me and wrapped his long arm around my shoulders. "Creepy, yeah?"

Gabby chuckled. "Yeah, a little. So, what's the plan?"

"We get outfits from Dyl and Searcy's wardrobes and dress them like the kids. I put them in the back seat of Duke's SUV, and I call Dad to meet me at Teterboro, telling him I have the kids, and sending a picture to him like he insisted, the untrusting jackass. Bruno can hide in the back of the SUV, and when Dad gets inside after he sees the dolls, we'll tie him up," Dom explained.

I glanced at Gabby to see he didn't have a lot of faith in our plan. "What?" I asked him.

"I have a better idea," he stated before he lifted his phone and made a call.

"*Si!*" It was Mateo who answered.

"*Serve un piano migliore,*" Gabby stated.

"What's wrong with the plan? Dad has a jet chartered at Teterboro to take us to Italy where we turn over the kids to Frankie Man. I'm supposed to call him today to confirm I have the kids, and he'll tell me which hangar to meet him. It can't be any simpler than that," Dominic defended his idea.

"We know Tony Ricci is still around somewhere," I threw in.

"You two can't do this alone," Gabby determined. I started to disagree, but maybe he had a point? Nardo was dead, but we didn't really know how many people Mazzola had brought with him.

Thirty minutes later, we had a *new* plan, though Dom wasn't thrilled with it. "He's my responsibility," he'd protested a few times, but I stood by my decision... Dom wouldn't be a part of it.

"You gotta swear this won't hurt him," I questioned Mateo for the third time as we geared up in the bunker of the Victorian. He had come to Gabby's home and picked me up, the two of us deciding to get a little more firepower in the event a war broke out. I'd changed into more appropriate gear from the stash I had in my locker in the gym, and I was ready for whatever was coming our way.

"*Sulla mia vita,*" he swore. *On my life...* I put the syringe in one of the pockets of my tac pants, and Mateo and I returned to Gabby's house, both silent as we prepared ourselves for what we had to do that evening.

Mateo had stopped at a deli to grab sandwiches for all of us, but my stomach was too nervous to eat as I considered all of the ways in which things could go wrong.

My biggest fear was that Dominic would somehow be hurt—physically if there were some sort of shootout, and emotionally if his father were killed in front of him. That was why I had a secret Plan B in my pocket. I'd never forgive myself if anything happened to my Willow.

We arrived at the house, Mateo parking his SUV in the driveway. I did a quick check of the neighborhood to see if we had picked up a tail anywhere, relieved to see everything looked normal.

I went to the back of the house and into the garage where Mateo had gone to situate the mannequins in Duke's SUV just as he was turning on the tablet as if Searcy were watching a movie.

"Dom's inside trying to find a game for the Dylan doll. Its head adjusts so it's not just staring at the back of the seat, which is really fucking weird. Where'd you get these things?" Mateo asked as Dom came out of the house with one of Dylan's handheld games. I reached into a pocket and pulled out a length of two-sided tape to secure the device to the male doll's hands to look as though he was playing a game.

"Dom can take you to the place if you're really interested in seeing it. All of your mannequin needs can be fulfilled there, I'm sure," I joked, looking up to see Mateo and Dom both chuckling.

"He jokes now? When did Noble become a comedian?" Mateo asked Dom, who offered me a big grin and a wink. That would be all I needed for the rest of my life.

I glanced at the male doll that was wearing a black t-shirt with a video game hero on the front and a hooded sweatshirt I remembered seeing Dylan wear a lot, just in case Mazzola had kept eyes on the kids before we were aware of their plan. I couldn't help but worry that we might be walking into a trap of some kind, but I had more confidence since Mateo, Gabby, and Rafe were going to be with us for backup.

We put up the third row of seats so I could be hidden in case Mazzola insisted on opening the back, and I had a black blanket to pull over me when we arrived at the airport.

"Okay, they're as safe as can be. Rafe and I chartered a jet to Las Vegas out of Teterboro that will fly empty, and Gabe's already gone to Long Island. He'll meet us at the airport from there, and then we all have our alibis established," Mateo stated.

I stood back and looked inside through the windows to see if everything was believable. Dominic adjusted Searcy doll's hair a little, bringing it more toward her face to hide its lack of life, and everything was as set as it could be.

Mateo looked between us and then at the phone in Dom's hand, all three of us nodding in unison that we were ready. I was holding a new burner in my hand with Mateo's number in it to send him the details once we had them. Dominic touched his father's number on his smartphone.

It rang once before it was answered. "Son. Do you have news for me? Are you ready?" Mazzola answered.

"I'm actually babysitting right now. Uncle Gabe took Dexter out to a bed and breakfast on Long Island for the night, and I volunteered to babysit the kids. How's your end of the plan?" Dom asked.

"Let me say hi to my niece and nephew. I thought you were going to send me a picture of them," his father demanded. The look of panic on Dom's face told me the secret plan Id made was doing the right thing.

"Tell him they're at the neighbors on a playdate," Mateo whispered.

Dom quickly scanned through his phone for the picture of the Dylan and Searcy dolls and sent it to his father. "Dad, they won't talk to you. You scare the crap out of little kids, remember? You're not exactly Mr. Rogers, you know. Besides, they're next door playing. I took that picture earlier when I got here but forgot to send it. What time?" Dominic lied.

After a moment, his father cleared his throat. "You'd do well not to double cross me, son. I know exactly who your husband is, and I have someone with a rifle aimed at his head as we speak. Did you think I wouldn't find out the man was working for fucking Giuseppe, the coward? He worked for Frankie for months, and everyone knew he was a spy. It was only because of me that they didn't kill him," Mazzola bluffed. If they'd known who I was, I'd have been dead after a day.

Dom exhaled. "I don't care. When and where?"

Mazzola offered an evil laugh. "Dominic, I promise you that if you double cross me on this, I'll deliver your husband to Mangello just short of death. Frankie doesn't like betrayal, either, and he'll send your husband back to you in small pieces, just like the Torrentes did his son, Giancarlo," his father threatened again.

Mateo grinned and shook his head in disbelief after hearing Mazzola's empty threats, putting a comforting hand on my shoulder. "He couldn't find the handle on the shithouse door. I heard Smokey say that before." We both quietly laughed at the comment, which sounded exactly like the cowboy.

Dom chatted with him a few more minutes, and Mazzola promised to call him back with details in an hour. "Okay. Bye, Dad. Love you," Dom signed off. He then looked at Mateo and me. "The miserable piece of shit," he stated, a flash of sadness crossed his handsome face, but then he offered a pointed look in my direction. "You're not going."

I chuckled as I reached down to touch the syringe in my pocket. It was sweet he was trying to protect me, but I was ready. "I'll be fine, and the plan only works if we're both there. Stick to it, and we'll keep each other safe."

Dominic took the left exit from the interstate to NJ-17 South. I glanced out the window from my spot on the floorboard of the SUV between the second-row bucket seats where the mannequins were posed.

"Can you tell me where we're going on our honeymoon?" I asked Dom to get his mind off of what we were actually going to do. I'd sent Gabby the details as Mazzola had given them to Dom, and he'd sent me back a thumb's up emoji. It didn't make my heart slow down at all.

"Okay, but I haven't made reservations yet, so things are subject to change. Have you heard of the singing group, The Tex-Sons? The lead singer is Kelso Ray Anderson, and GEA-A has done some work for him. Anyway, I met him when I was in Italy and he came to see Gabby about a case. He owns a place down in Texas with his husband and his brother, and he was telling me about some great places to stay—oh, it's in South Padre Island, Texas. I've looked it up, and there are some really great rentals and small hotels, so I thought we could go down there for the week after Christmas," Dom explained.

"That's around our anniversary," I reminded him.

Dom glanced into the rearview mirror and grinned. "I know, and I don't want to spend it with our co-workers. I want it to be you and me. We may not be able to swim in the Gulf, but evening walks on the beach holding hands or a bonfire with hot dogs and s'mores sounds pretty romantic. Beats the hell out of capture the flag, doesn't it?" Dom suggested, referring to some of the games we played in Kentucky during the New Year's weekend when we got married.

As we drove along, Dom humming along with the radio, I thought about the last year—most of which I spent away from Willow. I was determined not to repeat that pattern. Back then, knowing he was out there somewhere kept me going, but now that we were living together and beginning to make plans together, I couldn't imagine how I'd made it—and that was why I was going to do something I was certain would piss him off...

30

DOMINIC

I double checked my father's message to be certain I was taking the right route to Signature FSO East, the only hangar on that side of the small airport. It was just after seven, and thankfully, darkness had fallen. Bruno had unscrewed the dome light in Duke's SUV, and we were ready for whatever lay in store.

"You in place?" I whispered for Bruno's ears. He'd been wiggling around back there, but I couldn't see what he was doing—which would be an asset to our mission, if not for my sanity.

"Yes," he gave a muffled answer, leading me to believe he was under the blanket.

I pulled the SUV near the door to the hangar but not under the light, and I put the vehicle in park and turned off the motor. The vehicle suddenly jostled, alarming me.

"I love you with all my heart. Please forgive me for this, but it's for the best." Before I could look in the rearview mirror, I felt a pin stick in my neck...

31

BRUNO

After I gave Dominic the sedative, I wiggled under the blanket and waited. There was a knock on the front driver's window. "*Dominic! Yo, Dom!*"

Suddenly, the knocking stopped and a minute later, the back tailgate of the vehicle opened. There stood Gabby and Mateo, each holding an end of Gio Mazzola. They dropped him into the small luggage space behind the third-row seats and closed the gate while I pulled Dominic into the second row. I tossed the Dylan doll on top of Gio Mazzola and lifted Dom into its place on the seat, strapping him in for a nice little nap before I went to the back and zip-tied Gio's hands and feet. I then closed the tailgate and straightened my clothes in triumph.

I got into the driver's seat and unlocked the doors, Rafael joining me in the front. "Where are we going?" I asked him.

"We're going to a warehouse owned by Francesco Mangello. It's the place where Dino took Dexter when they kidnapped him. It has a certain sense of irony, doesn't it? The man who was out to kidnap the kids about four years ago gets what's coming to him in the warehouse where he tried to kill Dexter. I love shit like this," Rafael stated, bouncing in his seat a little.

I glanced in the rearview to see my Willow with a sweet smile on his sleeping face. If we did it right, he'd sleep straight through all of the ugliness.

"Make the left up here but turn off the lights," Rafael ordered.

I did as he'd said, seeing Mateo and Gabe standing next to Gabe's SUV. "How'd they beat us here?" I asked.

"Oh, uh, I took us the long way to make sure we didn't have a tail, but we're here now," Rafael admitted shyly, making me laugh. We hopped out of the vehicle and I punched the button on the key fob to open the tailgate.

"Let me guess—you got lost again," Mateo predicted.

Rafael began making hand gestures I didn't understand. "*Vaffanculo, Teo!*" Gabby and I both chuckled at their antics as he walked over to the door carrying a crowbar. He swung it up and broke the overhead light, shielding his face from the flying glass before he pried open the door and stepped inside.

I went to the back of the SUV and helped Mateo grab Mazzola while Rafe pulled down the gate and quietly closed it. He hit the flashlight app on his phone to guide us through the door and deeper into the warehouse to a single chair in the middle of the room. Gabby rushed past us and returned a minute later, carrying a few camping lanterns with him that he put in a semi-circle around the chair.

Mateo and I put Mazzola into the chair and Rafe taped his arms and legs to it, his head flopping to the point his chin rested on his chest. "How much longer will he be out?" Gabby asked Mateo, who had been the one to inject the sedative into Mazzola as I'd done to Dom.

"I didn't give this *stronzo* the same amount as you gave Dom, who'll be out for about another eight hours and won't remember anything about the day. This *cazzo traditore* should be waking up *now!*" Mateo informed as he backhanded Mazzola across the face. I truly envied him, wishing I'd have had the chance to do it first.

Mazzola's head snapped back and his eyes popped open, taking a few seconds to focus before he looked around and scowled. "What the fuck is this, Gabriele?" He seemed to single out Gabby who was standing to the side, which was a surprise to me. Rafael was standing next to me in front of Mazzola, flipping a Balisong butterfly knife in the air with skills I'd never witnessed in my life.

When the knife was coming back down, I reached out and snatched it before Rafe could get it, bringing it down, knife point first, into Mazzola's thigh. His shriek of pain echoed through the whole building.

"I was told that the only way anyone gives up information willingly is through fear, so I'm going to scare the fuck outta you, and you're going to tell me why you've suddenly taken an interest in Dominic when you've ignored him most of his adult life. If you don't tell me the truth"—I pulled the knife out of his thigh and held it over his forearm—"I'll see how many times I can drive this blade into your body before I sink it into your skull," I threatened as I moved my hand up to his temple and scraped the blade there, making a small cut with the sharp tip.

"Did he just curse?" Gabe whispered from behind me.

"He did. Hell, now *I'm* scared," Mateo answered. It barely registered in my brain.

The adrenaline and anger had taken over my mind and body, turning me into a man I didn't recognize. I'd never dared imagine having a man like Willow in my life, much less that he'd love me. The idea of his own father planning to harm him had me out of my head with rage. I was going to make sure Gio Mazzola knew I would end him without regret.

"Fuck you. Sierra Conti told me all about my son's fucking around with her brother, Nick, who one of these assholes killed. I owed you for taking care of that problem for me—Frankie was getting suspicious about the shortages in the heroin shipments thanks to Nick's skimming off the top. He almost pulled his shipping business from me over that idiot, so thank you for tying up that loose end for me." Mazzola didn't look scared at all.

Mateo actually laughed, which pissed Mazzola off. I could see he was getting angrier by the minute. "In return, I took care of a problem for you, *Gabby*—Sierra Conti—Nick's sister," Mazzola remarked, sarcasm thick in his voice.

Of course, he kept talking as any man facing death would do. "She had a big mouth, that one. She's not talking anymore, is she? It was genius of you to put the ventilation system outside the bunker, Gabriele. The way I see it, we're even. Let me go, and no hard feelings," he attempted to reason with us.

I turned to see that my friends weren't buying into his line of thinking, so I came down with the knife on his forearm, sinking the sharp, steel blade through the tissue of his right arm and into the wood of the armrest. That certainly got his interest back on the things that mattered.

"You planned to blow up Blue Plate to kill your wife—you're whole family, didn't you? You didn't have enough PE-4 to do the job right, though, so you failed, didn't you? How many men did you bring from Italy to help you because you weren't man enough to do the job yourself?" I snapped at him.

Gabby stepped next to me and offered a scary smile. "Toss the mannequins in the parking lot, will ya? I'll take care of them after I take care of this. I don't want you doing more, Bruno. Take Dominic home. We'll talk about this on Monday at the office. Go, now..."

I started to protest, but Mateo and Rafe grabbed me by the arms and pulled me backward. "Leave the rest to us. We owe the bastard a little play time. Thank you for all of your help, Noble," Mateo offered quietly.

The brothers pushed me out of the door and pulled it closed, locking it from the inside. I stood outside the door to listen for a moment. "So, after all these years, you've turned your back on our family. What did you think you'd accomplish? Huh?" It was Gabriele talking, and a second later, there was a blood-curdling scream that was definitely Mazzola's.

I turned around to see Duke's SUV, so I got those freaky dolls out and put them next to Gabby's vehicle as he'd asked before I got into the other SUV and turned around to see my sweet husband was still asleep with a small grin on his face.

I drove us home and carried Willow inside, sliding off his shoes and socks before I pulled off his jeans and relieved him of his jacket, shoulder holster, and Sig Sauer. I stripped down to my boxers and pulled back the blankets on our bed.

I moved the sheet and thick quilt over Willow and joined him, pulling him close to my body to hold tightly and thanking the universe that he was safe and didn't have to witness what I was sure Mateo, Rafael, and Gabby were doing to his father. Dominic didn't need that guilt. His father was the only one who should pay for his actions, and that shouldn't be on my husband's conscience.

I woke to kisses smothering my face and the smell of bacon nearby. I opened my eyes to see Dom in a t-shirt and pajama pants. His beautiful brown hair was damp, and he was sitting on my groin with a plate of pancakes and bacon balancing on my chest.

"Are you mad at me?" was my first thought that I put voice to that morning. We'd arrived home about midnight, and Dom hadn't woken. I got up a few times throughout the morning to check his pulse and breathing, thankful that he was fine. I was guessing the shot I'd given him had knocked him out but good.

"God, no. Are you mad at me that I passed out on you? How much did I have to drink?" he asked as he held up a piece of crispy bacon to my mouth. I took a bite, watching his actions.

"Why do you think you passed out from drinking?" I asked as I chewed his offering.

"Uncle Gabe sent me a text that I shouldn't be crabby with you, no matter how bad my hangover is. You tried to stop me from doing tequila shots with Mateo, and I wouldn't listen, so I'm really sorry, love. I didn't make this—I ordered it—but we're going to take cooking lessons like we talked about, right? I want to be able to make my man a proper breakfast in the future," Dominic explained before he moved the plate to the nightstand and leaned forward to kiss me gently.

I wrapped my arms around him and flipped him onto his back, ready to love him as much as he'd let me. I wasn't sure when, or if, he'd remember what happened the previous night, but until he brought it up, I wasn't saying a word.

After we ate, Dom made love to me, and I kept pinching myself to be sure I was awake. It was more than my simple imagination could come up with.

We took a shower together, and my mouth wouldn't leave his skin. Once we were finally drying off, I saw a text from Gabe.

Don't ask him any questions until you meet with me in the morning for a workout at five. No more worries, though we won't let our guard down again. I'm going to have Duke put you and Dom on kid duty going forward. Thank you for saving my children, Noble. Gabby

The rest of the day found Dom and I watching The Office, laughing at the crazy show, and then that night, I took my husband to Solé for dinner at Rafe's invitation. After dessert, we took a carriage ride through Central Park before we rode the subway back to Brooklyn, holding hands as we walked home. It was a perfect night, and I forced myself to enjoy it, but in the back of my mind, I couldn't help but worry about what might be coming next.

Frankie Man was still out there, and Tony Ricci, his head of security, was around somewhere and would need to be dealt with. Our work was far from over.

I FINALLY GOT out of bed at four on Monday morning, not having slept well because my mind was racing. I wrote Dom a note that I'd see him at the office and ran all the way to the Victorian as fast as I could. I let myself in through the backdoor and quickly opened the bunker, surprised *not* to see the dead corpse of Giovanni Mazzola inside.

When I was able to open the door with my code, it should have been a sure sign nothing was in there, but at that point, my heart was pounding in my ears and all I could think about was getting Dom's father out of there before my husband showed up for work.

As I closed up the room, the lights flashed that someone was coming inside, so I sat down on the stairs and waited. Casper stepped inside first with Gabby behind him. "I knew he'd be here before us," Gabby commented as he flipped on the lights and grinned at me.

"Come on, Noble. It's the first day of the rest of your life," Gabby told me as he pulled me up from the stairs and put his hand on my back, guiding me to Casper's office on the second floor.

"I'll get us some coffees. Casper, go ahead and get him started, will you?" my boss requested before the man looked at me. "I told Mateo to fuck off with coaxing you and Dom into going to Italy. You're part of *my* family, and I want you here. If you wanna freelance for Uncle G from time to time, well, we'll make it work," Gabby said before he left.

Casper led me to his office, turned on the lights and his computer station, and pulled out a yellow tablet. "So, I found out that Tony Ricci caught a flight out of Newark on Saturday night headed to Frankfurt, Germany. That puts the ball in Giuseppe's court, according to our fearless leader. Anyway…"

Casper tossed the tablet on the desk and grabbed a pen from the top drawer of his desk, looking up at me with a big smile. "There have been several times in my life when I wished I'd done this very thing, but those are stories for another day. So, Bruno Garvin, what's your new name going to be?"

Gabby had mentioned a name change to me once before, but I was a little caught off guard when Casper asked me the question. "Uh, I don't know."

Casper nodded. "I'll give you a minute. You'll get a different social security number and a different birthplace, but you can keep your birthday. First, give me your old information," he requested.

I had only one question for him. "What does that do to my marriage to Dominic? It won't annul it, will it?" The panic settled in my chest, and I felt as if I was going to be sick as I stood there before I started to pace the small office.

Casper stopped writing. "Hey, Bruno, man, calm down. If you and Dom wanna stay married, I can make it happen. If you don't, then I can fix that, too."

I retrieved my phone and started to call Dominic, but then I stopped. I'd been fortunate to get him to marry me once. Did I want to chance it a second time? "Can you just change my name on it, or do we need to get married again?"

Casper smirked. "I can just change your name. I don't blame you —I wouldn't guarantee Max would marry me again, either. So, name?"

For a minute, my mind went blank. How did parents ever choose a name for their kids? I didn't hate my name—Bruno—but that poor idiot had a truckload of baggage, and if I wanted to work with the operatives at GEA-A, I needed to unload the wagon. I needed to make a choice.

I glanced at the clock to see it was still too early to call Dominic to ask his opinion, so I thought about the people I'd met throughout my twenty-four years of life. Bruno had been my father Arnold's grandpa. I never knew the man, so I really had no tender feelings over the name, but I did like the way it sounded on Dom's lips, so maybe that was something to remember?

There were a few people I'd met over my life who had been good to me—Dexter and Gabby, Ben and Nemo, and Tommy, Daniela, and Dante, but as I considered it, I thought about the first person who I actually remembered being nice to me—Louisa Austin. Mrs. Austin was my fifth-grade teacher back in Wyoming. She read the tests to me and always complimented my memorization skills, and back then, it meant a lot to me.

And then, of course, there was the Torrente family who had treated me like one of their own. That was when it came to me. "Austin B. Torrente. Not Bruno, but B because I still want to remember the guy Dom married," I announced, feeling a sense of pride course through me as I stopped pacing and let the name settle.

I looked at Casper to see a big grin on his face. "I think that's a very good name, Noble. Now, let me get to work. Mateo and Rafe went to Vegas, according to an email I got from them, but Mateo has a guy for documents if memory serves me. Let me try to track him down. Enjoy your day. I'll get back to you very soon, my friend."

Casper stood and wrapped me in a hug, and before I teared up, I left his office and went downstairs to shower. I sent Dom a text before I got undressed.

I forgot to bring clothes. Can you please bring me something? Love you—sorry to bother you!

I went to my locker to find some clean workout clothes, and I grabbed a towel from the large rack by the wall and headed to the shower stall but before I undressed, something popped in my mind.

One thing was bothering me, so I turned off the water and stepped out of the stall, heading upstairs in search of Gabby. He was in the office he'd moved into since he'd surrendered his old office to Duke. The man was flipping a butter knife in the air, mostly catching it by the blade. Thankfully, he wasn't being cut.

I knocked on the doorframe twice, and when the knife landed on the floor instead of in his hand, Gabby cursed, "Fucking hell."

He glanced up at me and waved me inside. I closed the door because the discussion I wanted to have wasn't really meant for everyone—especially my husband.

He pointed to the chair at the end of his desk and sat back, hands resting on his abs. "What can I do for you besides thank you for your help on Saturday?"

"Tell me what happened. Why doesn't Dom remember anything about it?" I asked him, aching for the answer.

"Mateo, the mad scientist, laced the sedative with Rohypnol, which is used to help erase short term memories. Teo didn't just pull it out of his ass, Bruno. He contacted a shrink friend of his to ask about it before he did it, so don't worry—there will be no lasting effects on Dom except he won't remember anything about Saturday," Gabby assured, though I was still worried.

"He thinks he got drunk on tequila," I replied.

The large man smirked. "I liked that touch. He was a blank, okay? He remembered nothing, so I gave him an alternative reality that took his father out of the mix completely. Oh—he won't be a problem ever again. You don't need details, but I was fucking impressed when you caught that knife and jammed it into that prick's thigh. How the hell did you do that?"

I chuckled for a moment, though the answer wasn't really funny. "My father used to like to toss knives at me when he was drunk. It stuck a couple of times until I learned how to catch them," I answered him before I really thought about it. "Please don't say anything to Dominic. I want to explain those things to him over time—not all at once."

Gabby nodded. "Does that mean the two of you are going to stay together?" He sat up, folding his hands on the desk and staring at me. His intense gaze made me nervous.

"Yes. Is that a problem with you?" I asked as his phone chimed. He picked it up and looked at the screen, glancing at me for a moment before he chuckled.

"If you're taking my family name, I get to kick your ass. How about we go a couple of rounds in the ring, nephew?" Gabe suggested.

"Casper told you?"

Gabe typed something into his phone and tossed it on the desk. "He asked for permission to insert you into my family tree, and I said I'd be honored to have you as a relative. Welcome to the family, Noble Austin B. Torrente." Gabe had a bit of a grin as he stood and extended his hand. I took it and he pulled me up from my seat and into a bear hug, surprising me.

"I can't hurt you in the ring, Gabby," I protested, thankful he was offering permission for me to take his family name.

Gabby, too, was still dressed in his workout clothes. "Oh, that's what I'm counting on," he responded with a laugh.

He clapped me on the back, laughing as we left the office and went downstairs. I'd probably be bruised when I stepped out of the ring with him because I wouldn't raise a hand in defense, but it was a small price to pay to have Gabe accept me into his family in a very official way. How could I say no?

December

32

DOMINIC

"Rise and shine, Honeybee," I whispered as I licked my husband's balls, trying to wake him on a cold December morning. It was the day of Dylan and Searcy's school holiday concert before the Christmas break—and our honeymoon in Texas—and I was anxious to get on with it.

Bruno—or Bee as I now called him because of his name change—and I had been assigned as the official guardians of Dylan and Searcy Torrente. It wasn't just to keep them safe, but to legally care for them in the event anything were to happen to Gabriele and Dexter.

It had blown both of us away when they'd asked us at Thanksgiving and later brought a lawyer into the office that Friday to have us sign the documents, and we were both grateful they had faith in us to care for their children... though we prayed nothing ever happened to either of them that would cause us to act in that capacity.

Gabe and Dex had become both of our surrogate parents since the ones we were born to were worthless, and we'd come to depend on them as sounding boards for almost anything that came up. Bruno and I put a lot of stock in their advice, and I knew Uncle Gabe was proud of us for our diligence with looking out for the kids.

Austin, as Bruno had asked everyone to call him after he officially changed his name, brought joy to our daily task of accompanying the kids to and from school. We had Gabby and Dex's permission to stop for ice cream as we wanted or to bring them straight home and discipline them if they'd been in trouble at school. That usually meant we'd make them listen to Bee and me read excerpts from my husband's favorite books. It wasn't really punishment because they didn't hate it. It was as if we had kids of our own, and it had both of us thinking about *our* future.

"Oh, damn, Willow," Bruno—now Austin—gasped as he buried his cock in my throat before he pulled me off him. The man loved a morning blowjob.

He scooped me up and turned me onto my back, amazing me with his brute strength, yet again. "How much time?" he asked.

"Time for mutual blow jobs and showers. Coffee to go, and we work out after we drop the kids at school," I explained to him.

The smile I loved more than life split his handsome face in two, and I was flipped in a one-eighty over his body like a rag doll. I did love the fact that the man could toss me into the air with no effort at all.

"Now, we start the clock," Bee stated as he sucked my hard cock into his mouth. I returned the favor without fail, and we embarked on a fantastic morning. It was the way I never imagined my life would be, and it was beautiful.

Austin had taken the place of Duke in the carpool parade, driving the four of us to Mosby Academy in the morning and escorting Dylan and Searcy Torrente into the building while I waited patiently outside the vehicle for his return, gun at the ready under my left arm.

We then ventured to a brand-new bakery on the next block over and had breakfast together, and we were happier than I ever thought I'd deserved to be.

That particular morning, we were discussing plans for our honeymoon. "So, we go to the family party on Christmas Eve at Solé, and then we're expected at Nonna's for Christmas Day. I have reservations for us on the nine o'clock flight on the evening of the twenty-sixth to

Brownsville. We'll have to spend the night there because we can't pick up the car until the next morning. That okay? You ready for it?" I asked my honeybee as we left the school that morning.

Austin only nodded as he drove us to the coffee shop, spotting an empty space on the street, which was a rarity. He precisely maneuvered the new SUV like a stunt man and shifted into park. With Uncle Gabe assigning us a GMC Denali to use for transporting the kids to school, our need for a car of our own was put on the back burner for a while.

I reached for the handle to hope out, but Bee took my hand, squeezing tight to stop me. "You know, don't you, that if you don't want to stay married to me after I tell you this, I'll give you a divorce." He kissed my palm before he released my hand and we got out of the vehicle and headed inside.

We took a seat at a small table, and I stared at him, still stunned by his comment. He was set to start night school after the new year to get his diploma—his high school diploma—and we were planning to take Saturday morning cooking classes the second week of January. To me, everything was going forward in wonderful ways, but what if he was having second thoughts about our marriage?

"Are you really starting with this shit again before I even have a fucking donut?" I snapped at him, not wanting to hear him list off the reasons why he didn't deserve me. It was like a broken record at that point.

I definitely didn't mean to complain, but I was always afraid Austin would find a reason to cut me loose. With all of the wonderful things I was learning about him, it was hard for me to believe he'd chosen someone as self-centered and spoiled as I used to be—according to Gabby when he and I sat down to have a heart to heart at Thanksgiving before he and Dexter asked us to be the legal guardians of Dylan and Searcy in the event of an unforeseen disaster.

"I'm not going to belabor this, but I'm impressed with all of the changes I've seen in you, Dom. When you first moved in with me before I met Dex, you used to have study groups at my house and ruined my favorite chair with cheese curl dust, remember?" Uncle Gabe reminded me.

I chuckled at the memory. "Yeah, and I remember you making me stay up to clean that chair. Where is it, by the way?" I asked as I looked around his office.

"You know damn well that Dex hated it and made me sell it. Anyway, I wanted to congratulate you on what a fine man you've become, Dominic. I was worried about you, but not any longer. I trust you with my life, but more importantly, I trust you with that of my children. Dex and I want you and Austin to take over kid duty."

I happily accepted the responsibility. I was busting my buttons at his confidence in me.

A scraping chair brought me back to reality. I glanced up to see if Bee had noticed I was daydreaming, and there he was, looking at me as if I were something special and he was afraid I'd disappear.

Bee lifted his finger in the direction of the counter, and a really cute girl wearing elf ears and a Santa hat rushed over to us. "Hi guys. What can I get you? Oh—we have red velvet donuts with red and green sprinkles," she offered, a lilt in her voice that made it sound as if she was only letting us in on the secret.

My husband of nearly a year offered her a kind grin. "We'll take a dozen of those to go, but we'll share one of the giant glazed donuts and two hot cocoas, please."

The young woman nodded and skipped away, leaving us alone. "So, what's got you ready to throw in the towel this time?" I asked him, remembering our earlier topic.

"It's about your father, Willow," he confessed before the young lady returned to drop off our massive donut that had been cut in half and served on two separate Santa plates with a cute, iced holiday cookie included on each plate. There was a sprig of mistletoe decorating the top, and it made me smile.

"Thank you, CC," I offered, glancing at her nametag. She smiled and her cheeks turned pink, much like Bee's did on a regular basis. It was absolutely adorable.

After she left, I turned to my husband. "What about my dad? I'm not sorry he hasn't called me or even bothered to check in with Mom and the girls. It fits his MO perfectly. Really, it's fine. You're my family now, so don't worry about him, okay?"

Bee sat there staring at me for a moment before he leaned closer and took my hand. "What if something happened to him? Something permanent?"

I couldn't lie and say I wasn't sure my father was dead, because there was no way Gabriele would behave as lighthearted as he had over the last few weeks if he didn't know my father wasn't a threat any longer. I didn't need direct proof of his demise; I was just happy the threat was temporarily gone.

I lifted Bee's large hand and placed a quick peck on his knuckles. "I would never blame the person who made sure my father was no longer an issue for handling a situation I'd have handled myself had I not decided to drink my weight in tequila that night. I don't need any more details than a confirmation he's not going to blow up my sisters' or mother's lives," I stated.

I knew there was something fishy about the night I had no memory of, but for reasons I didn't examine too closely, I didn't really want any answers. No looking back was my new motto.

I took a sip of my cocoa and continued. "I realize it was fortuitous that my father left my mother as co-owner of the shipping company after the divorce and made her a corporate officer on the official paperwork so the shipping company can continue to function. I want no part of it, and when I have the ability to discuss this with Lucia without biting off my tongue to keep from screaming at her stupidity, I'm going to tell her to turn over her client list to the FBI. I'm sure they'd be interested in it," I explained, heading him off of any confession he was considering.

Austin stared at me for a moment before my favorite smile lit up his face. "Okay. I won't bring it up again. So, will you marry me?" he asked as he pulled out a little blue box from the pocket of his wool peacoat and placed it in front of me.

We both wore our silver rings now with pride. I'd come to love the symbol—if not the actual ring—and I wanted everyone around to know Bruno Garvin/Austin B. Torrente/Honeybee was mine.

I flipped the lid to see two gold rings—one with diamonds inlaid into the gold, and the other, larger one, was just plain. "These are beautiful," I told him as I glanced up to see his happy smile.

"I picked them out myself. I'm sort of a plain guy, so I got this one for me," he told me as he touched the shiny gold band before removing the diamond band from its nest in the bird's egg blue lining.

Austin held it up to me and whispered, "I got this one for you, Willow. You are graceful and beautiful, and you sway with the winds, regardless of how harsh they may be. I will do my best to block them, but I know they won't break you. I'm very lucky to be sheltered under your strong branches. I'll love you forever."

I was stunned silent for a moment as he slid off the silver band and replaced it with the golden one. Finally, I found my voice. "Is that a quote from someone? It's beautiful."

"I've been working on it since we got married. I sent it to Ben, and he helped make it sound prettier, but he only changed a couple of words. The idea is all mine," he told me, pride puffing up his chest. I was in awe of the man.

I picked up the gold band that was so much like my Bee—simple but shining brightly among all of the dullness of those around. "This band is just like you. Not fancy or ornate, but unable to hide a golden light. I love you and... we're already married, Bee," I teased a little.

I slid the silver band off his large finger and replaced it with the golden band before I squeezed his hand. I bit into my donut to keep from crying right there in the middle of a coffee shop. When the sun popped out of the gray clouds, it was as if its light was shining just on the two of us as a sign that together, we could accomplish anything.

On Christmas Eve, Bee and I settled into the large round table at Rafe's restaurant, Solé, with our family—Gabe, Dex, and the kids; Duke, Ace, and Corby; and Shep, because Parker was helping with the meal. Mateo and Shay were at a table behind us, and the rest of the family was scattered around the room. I could feel their closeness, and it warmed my heart.

Maxim was flitting around lighting centerpiece candles on the ornately decorated tables, and the atmosphere was quite festive. Of course, my mind wasn't on the party that night or the dinner at my Nonna's the next day. I was focused on the trip we were taking the day after Christmas—South Padre Island.

I'd found a great house on the beach for the first week of our honeymoon and had rented us a convertible for tooling around town. Bee and I weren't exchanging gifts—we were spending our money on the honeymoon. What he didn't know was that we weren't coming back to New York right away—we were going to Cancun for a week after our time in South Padre.

He was going to kill me, but I'd bought him a skimpy bikini swimsuit that could only be classified as a banana hammock, and I had concocted all kinds of ways to tempt him into wearing it. I'd have to be covert about it, but I was getting a picture of him in it if it—or he—killed me.

A soft kiss on my neck brought me back to reality. "Where'd you go?" Bee whispered to me, his arm around the back of my chair.

I looked at him and offered a peck to his lips. "I was on a beach with a handsome man," I teased.

"Gross! We're all here, ya know. If I can't nibble on my man instead of the appetizers, then none of y'all can either," Smokey protested, making all of us laugh.

"Speak of the devil," Uncle Gabe said as Parker and Rafe walked out of the kitchen together, each carrying a glass of Torrente prosecco, which was also being passed by the staff.

Everyone tapped their butter knives against their water glasses until Rafael held up his empty hand. *"Benvenuto alla mia festa!* Welcome to my party!" Everyone applauded, including me and Bee.

Bzzz! Bzzz! Uncle Gabe reached into the breast pocket of his suit and retrieved his phone. He leaned to his right and whispered to

Dexter, who nodded, and then Gabby got up from the table and hurried away.

"Where's he going?" Dyl asked. He was sitting between Dexter and me, and I was interested in the answer as well.

"To take a call. Shh!" Dex scolded, turning to look over his shoulder to see Gabby outside.

Dyl looked at me and Bee, and we both shrugged. Suddenly, Casper hopped up from a table to the right, along with Duke and Mateo, all of them heading outside into the cold Christmas Eve air. I didn't know what was going on, but I was determined nothing was going to ruin our honeymoon.

A few minutes later, everyone returned inside and sat down in their respective seats. Rafe looked at Mateo who nodded. "Thank you all for coming to celebrate with our family. Here's to a *Buon Natale e un Felice Anno Nuovo! Saluti!*"

I turned to Bee, my beautiful husband, and whispered, "Merry Christmas, *amore mio*," before I kissed his lips, and we drank to the future. With Austin B. Torrente by my side, I was excited to see what our happily ever after looked like. I knew it would be better than I could ever imagine.

EPILOGUE
BRUNO / AUSTIN

"*Hey—you can't just storm in here!*" Sabrina yelled from the reception desk, the sound echoing up to the kitchen where I was doing homework for my night school class until it was time to go pick up the kids from school.

Dom had taken the day off to do errands and get the house ready for company—Nemo and Ben were coming to Brooklyn for the weekend, and they'd agreed to stay with us when I'd asked. I was excited to see them again—it had been almost three months.

I stood from my seat and walked to the railing by the stairs to look down, seeing a guy dressed all in leather standing on the bottom step with a motorcycle helmet under his left arm as he pinched off leather gloves. His appearance was angry and combative, so I lifted my left ankle and double checked that I still had my Ruger in the holster that was now like a part of my body before I began walking down the stairs.

Things had been in an uproar since Christmas Eve. One of our own had been killed that night as he was crossing the street to come to Solé to enjoy the Feast of the Seven Fishes with the family. We all felt like chaos had consumed our very souls, and the sooner we knew what had actually happened that night, the easier we'd all breathe.

"Hi there. I'm Austin. What can I do for you?" I addressed the guy. At the sound of my voice, he looked up, appearing to be surprised. He studied me as I walked down the stairs until I was on the step above him, waiting for an answer.

"I want to talk to Gabe Torrente," the man snapped at me.

Just then, Smokey came out of his office and ran down the stairs. "Hey, Kelly. How are ya, man? I didn't know you'd been released," Smokey addressed the man before extending his hand.

The stranger shook it, seeming to lose some of the anger I'd seen on his face earlier. "Hey, Shep. Good to see you. I, uh, I got discharged last week. There was paperwork, of course, but I just got to Queens last night and I tried to call—"

"Yeah, uh, let's go up to my office, Kelly. Oh, Bru-Austin, this is Kelly Brown, Mia Brown's brother. I'll fill ya in on details later, but he's a client of ours," Shep explained.

The three of us walked up the stairs and down the hall to the conference room. Shep opened the door for us, and we walked inside and took a seat at the table, each of us flanking Kelly Brown in case he became angry again.

"Tell me what happened," Kelly insisted.

The funeral had been awful. Willow and I had put off our honeymoon in South Padre Island for two days to be there to mourn with our family. The church community he belonged to and depended on had joined us in our grief, and I didn't think I'd ever seen so many grown men weeping without shame.

After our wonderful South Padre stay—where we made some new friends—we jetted off to Cancun for a week, which was a total surprise to me. My husband, who I found out was a nasty boy at heart, bought me a swimsuit that barely covered my junk, and when it was just the two of us together in our private villa with a plunge pool, I wore it for him. I even let him take a picture of me, but I made sure he put it in a password protected album. I was no cover model, but for my Dominic, I found myself doing a lot of things I'd never imagined.

Unfortunately, when we arrived home, our bubble of bliss was popped by the reality that someone dear to all of us had been run down on a busy street on Christmas Eve. Finding the driver of a black 1978 Plymouth Fury that had been described as a former police car had become our number one mission at Golden Elite Associates-America.

Dante Barba gently rapped on the glass of the conference room and motioned for me to step out. "Will you excuse me for a moment? Smokey, you'll be okay, yes?"

He glanced over his shoulder and offered Dante, our newest hire at GEA-A, a small wave before glancing at me. "I'll be fine. Kelly and I go back a few years. Go see if St. Michael is around, will ya?" I nodded and stepped out of the room.

"What's up? You okay?" I asked Dante as I pulled out my phone and sent a text to London St. Michael.

You around? Conf room—Smokey needs you.

I then shifted my attention to Dante, who was nervously pacing the gray carpeted hallway. Finally, they stopped and looked up at me. "I gotta go back to Italy. I can't live in the dark, B. Daniela and Tommy are in hiding right now, but they can't stay away forever. Tommy has parents who miss him, and the two of them want to get married soon, so I'm going back and doing something about this bullshit," Dante insisted as St. Michael hustled down the hall.

He pointed to the conference room, and I nodded before I took Dante's arm and led them over to the kitchen, thankful it was empty. "You know they'll find you. It's a suicide mission, Dante," I stated. I could tell they knew and believed what I was saying, but their body language told me that my words were falling on deaf ears.

Dante sighed, playing with the pearl necklace they were wearing that had been their mother's. They had on a white lace blouse and a blue suit with fancy sleeves. They always looked really nice, and Gabby had made sure Dante knew they were more than welcome to be themselves—which included wearing makeup—in the office and in front of our clients. We were who we were, and we wouldn't hide ourselves for anyone.

"Maybe, but if I'm careful, maybe not. I can't live like this," they said as they held their hands out at their sides. I knew Dante loved the dangerous side of things, and the cases we had at GEA-A likely bored them to tears.

I hugged my friend tightly, trying to gather my emotions before I embarrassed myself in the office. "We're a phone call and a jet ride away if you need us. If you don't want me to come over there looking for you, you better stay in touch," I threatened as I hugged them again.

Dante offered a big grin. "I'll hold you to it. Ciao, my friend," he whispered before he bounded down the stairs and out into the early spring morning.

I reached for my phone and called Dom. He answered on the first ring. "Honeybee? Miss me?" he joked.

"Every minute of every day that we're apart," was my answer, and I'd never said anything more honest in my life. To my bones I felt his absence, but thankfully, I knew it was short lived. My husband—soulmate—was my other half. A man couldn't live without his other half.

"Dante is going back to Italy. He doesn't like living in limbo here in the States, and I think he really misses Daniela," I explained to Dom.

"You're not going with him, are you?" he asked me, worry immediately changing his voice.

"Not yet, but I told him if he needs us, you and me, we'll be there as quick as we can," I replied.

Dom sighed. "You're my hero, Noble. And I think everyone else knows it, too."

It was nice to hear, but the only person I wanted to be a hero to was my Willow. That was all I needed to know...

WAIT!

There's more to Dom and Bruno... read on for a secret bonus scene!

If you enjoyed Bruno and Dom's story," look for "Avenging Kelly," the next book in The Lonely Heroes series,
coming soon.

After the painful loss of one of GEA-A's own, Kelly Brown is released from the United States Disciplinary Barracks in Kansas, determined to make someone pay for the wrongs done to his friend and family. Who can keep him from avenging the loss and losing himself?

PREORDER NOW

SECRET BONUS CROSSOVER SCENE
FOR "ABSINTHE MINDED"

"Absinthe Minded, On the Rocks, Book 3", is the final book in the On the Rocks series which has guest appearances by our Lonely Heroes. It is the story of Bailey Marsden, the alias for Marsden Dempsey, and Cordon March, the Master Distiller at Ima-GIN-ation Distillery. All of the gang from the previous two On the Rocks books are back for a final adventure, and a few new people come into the mix to turn things upside down. Don't miss it!

READ ON...

May...
Dominic Mazzola
"Beaver!"

I was so tired of Gabby stomping around the damn office because he was bored. It was the middle of May, and things were a little slow at the Victorian. We'd suffered a huge loss, all of us, and we'd run out of leads to find out who was responsible. It had been hard on everyone, but the crew was slowly getting back to normal—whatever that was.

After Austin and I had returned from our fantastic honeymoon in Texas and Mexico, we'd gone back to work, but it just felt wrong. I was surprised when Duke had pulled me into his office one day in February and closed the door.

"Beav—Dominic, I spoke to Giuseppe, Gabby, and Mateo while you were out enjoying your honeymoon with Noble, and we all agreed it was time to turn over the reins to the next generation. As of this very minute, you are in charge of scheduling and human resources at Golden Elite Associates-America. Here are the keys to the office and the desk. Casper can hook you up with anything else you need, and I'm going back to the gym. If you need anything... talk to someone who is *not* me—oh, and put me on the schedule to take cases part of the time. Good luck, and don't let the incessant bitching about the schedule get you down," Duke had instructed before he'd run out of the office like his ass was on fire.

That had been a few months ago, but just like that, I'd been elevated to the administrative position at the Victorian because Duke had tired of it pretty damn quickly. For the time being, I was in charge of things at GEA-A, and while I didn't always know what the fuck I was doing, I was learning—and I had Uncle Giuseppe's cell phone number on speed dial, which he didn't give out to everyone. He had been all kinds of help to me.

I stood from my chair and made my way down the hallway to find Nemo in Gabby's new office instead of my uncle. "Goddamn, you sound just like Gabby!"

Just then, my uncle stepped from behind the door and scared the shit out of me. "It was me, dipshit. What are you working on?" Gabby asked.

"What do you think? Scheduling. Vetting cases. Keeping up with operatives. Trying to figure out a way to deal with Frankie Man. You know... shit nobody else seems to want to do," I reminded him, unable to keep the sarcasm from my voice.

"Yeah, that's on hold for now. We have a situation we need to think about," Gabby explained as he extended his hand for me to enter the office before he closed the door. I stood in the middle of the room and crossed my arms over my chest, looking at Nemo and nodding for him to proceed because he seemed to have something to say. He'd returned to Brooklyn after all hell had broken loose in the aftermath of the unthinkable, and he'd been hanging around more with Ben flying up every other weekend. Nemo had been a rock for all of us, and I knew for sure my husband appreciated having the man around. He stayed with us when he was in town, and I was glad he was there.

"Okay. Do you remember when we did a job for Kelso Ray, the country singer? We helped get a friend of his husband's…" Nemo started to explain.

"Yeah, yeah, of course. Bee and I got to hang out with them when we were down there at the beginning of our honeymoon. Cool bunch of guys. We had fun with them."

I then turned to Gabby. "Tanner's friend became a witness for the prosecutor in Smith County about the shit that went down in the prison there with the black-market ring. We helped with the relocation of the kid from Smith County Prison to a minimum-security facility out of state. He went into WITSEC under an alias. Nemo went down and moved the kid to South Padre when he got out of Johnson, yeah?" I recalled from the case file. That one, Nemo took on pro bono. He liked the kid and wanted to make sure he was staying somewhere safe until he could get his footing outside of prison.

Nemo stood and walked around the desk, leaning his ass against the edge as he looked at me with a smirk. "Good job, Beaver. So, we have a problem now. I got a call from the lawyer we used to get Marsden Dempsey moved and cut the deal for his early release," he began, and my gut sank. It definitely couldn't be good, and things had been going along so well since I'd been put in charge…

"He got a message from the Smith County prosecutor that Beryl Rollings, the perp, is in the wind, and it's assumed he'd going to go looking for Marsden Dempsey. The kid got out a few months ago and is in hiding with a new identity," Nemo explained.

"How the fuck did Rollings get out?" Gabby asked. I could definitely see him working himself into a tizzy over what he perceived as incompetence. Even though Marsden Dempsey wasn't technically ours to protect, I could see both Nemo and Gabby weren't going to leave the kid unprotected.

"Rollings was stabbed by a fellow inmate in prison—a friendly they presume so there wasn't much damage. The prison took him to the hospital in Tyler, Texas. Somehow—and nobody will admit that someone fucked this up—the bastard managed to escape from custody there, even with thirty-five stitches in his gut. Word is that a nurse helped him escape, but that's unconfirmed. I'm going to guess he's looking for Dempsey to make the kid pay for turning on him since the kid's testimony put him away for life," Nemo informed.

Nemo stood and handed me a paper from his printer. "On this one, Dominic, I'd say Tanner Bledsoe is our primary because the people at Smith heard Rollings swearing he was going to kill the queer who took away his goddamn slave. We have two secondaries this time—Leo Anderson and Kelso Ray," Nemo announced.

"Wait… One person can't watch three assets. We'll need backup, right?" I determined.

Nemo nodded. "You're right—we need help with this one. We need to find Rollings before he finds Dempsey. I happen to know his contact at the Marshal's Service, and he's a standup guy. He mentioned in passing that he's been temporarily relocated to Corpus Christi to keep an eye out for Marsden so I'll reach out and check in with him. He mentioned maybe leaving the Marshals Service soon, and he might be a good fit with us," Nemo informed.

I was a little overwhelmed with all of the information, but Nemo was right. We'd eventually need more operatives—especially since we'd lost one—so if we had a line on someone, why not reach out? If the guy vetted well, then that was one less worry on my plate.

"Okay, so what's his name?" I asked as I looked between Gabby and Nemo.

"Fitzgerald Morgan. He's been with the Marshals Service for twenty years and looking to retire soon, and I think we can get him to come on board," Nemo asked..

Much to my surprise, they were looking at me. It was now my call, and I was more than worried, but… "Yeah. Let's see if we can give him a hand."

God help me if I made the wrong decision. It sounded like the kid's life might be hanging in the balance…

Ready for more? Check out "Absinthe Minded," coming August 2022.

PREORDER NOW

MABRY'S MINOR MISTAKE

And an excerpt from "Mabry's Minor Mistake," coming this holiday season, 2022.

If you missed previous parts of Mabry's story, read them in -

IMA-GIN-ATION
ORPHAN DUKE

[...]

"As I was going to say, I own AdvanTech," Jimmy announced.

That caught me by surprise. "The gaming company?" I asked. It was then I remembered receiving about fifty letters from AdvanTech during my time in the NBA, more frequently since I'd retired. My agent, Luke Schoenfeld—who also used to manage major league baseball MVP, Cash Mitchell—had told me about the letters when they started rolling in after we won the NBA championship, but I'd ignored them. After I'd decided to take my career in a direction away from the court, I'd had to let Luke go. There was no use spending my money on him when I had no plans to be in the public eye for more than three new commercials a year for the dealership.

"You wanted to use my likeness or something?" I responded, vaguely remembering the conversations with Luke about it. The letters didn't really say more than that, so I blew them off and Luke quit mentioning them.

"Yes. We contacted you through your agent several times, but when we heard nothing, we decided to table the idea and moved on to Cash Mitchell, who is the star of "MVP Challenge—Baseball." Maybe you've heard of it?" Jimmy tested me.

I'd never been a video gamer, but I also didn't live under a rock. Of course, I'd heard of the series of video games. They'd won awards and had been the hot ticket for Christmas gifts for several years. Kids made their parents stand in line in the Chicago cold to get the damn game according to the news I'd been listening to that morning when I accidentally hit the car in front of me who had crossed three lanes of traffic to make a left turn. The accident was his fault, but I didn't want to fuck around with him, so we agreed to handle the accident individually, not calling the police or exchanging insurance information.

"Nope, sorry. Never heard of it," I lied. I wasn't about to give the arrogant jerk the satisfaction I knew anything about his business—which I didn't know was his. It wasn't really a surprise because the kid had proven he was a tech genius when he wiped away my life. I suppose I was impressed he'd gone on to use his powers for good.

Of course, the smart little asshole saw through me, rubbing his index fingers against each other in a shaming manner. "Liars go to hell. Anyway, we have Christmas this year on lock, so now's the time to start working on Christmas next year. We'd like to do a limited version of "MVP Challenge—Basketball" to be available on-line by the beginning of this season's playoffs to build a fanbase for the release of the full version in time for the holiday buying season, which now begins at Halloween," Jimmy explained to me.

"So? You just wanted to tell someone, or what?" I remarked, hoping I could rile him up.

"You were MVP of the league for three years in a row and—" Alby began to further explain.

Jimmy waved him off. "You want me to say it? Fine. I want you to be the face of MVP Challenge—Basketball, Mabry. You were the brightest star on the court until you got hurt, and I still say it was a foul that took you down. The ref was blind, but we can't rewrite history. The future is—" he pitched. I was having none of it.

"No thanks. Remember all of the damage you did to me my senior year of college? My life was hell that whole year," I reminded the runt.

Jimmy chuckled. "I apologize. What is it they say about a young man scorned? Anyway, I thought you'd outgrown that nonsense by now."

My blood pressure went up about fifty percent as I stared at him. His brown hair was perfect. He still wore those damn cute glasses, and the khaki pants and button-up shirt had been traded for an expensive suit with all the trimmings. The beat-up Vans he used to wear were now expensive loafers—the total package was stunning.

Unfortunately, the young, bashful guy with the adorable smile was missing. That was the guy I was attracted to the day I met him—before I found out he was seventeen. Even with the possibility of a prison term over my head, I'd have given him the time of day. We might have even been friends while I waited for him to tick over to eighteen and then maybe we'd see where things went, but then... Jimmy Lewis nearly tanked my life. That was unforgivable.

"No thanks," I answered again.

Jimmy snapped his fingers at Alby, who scrambled to retrieve another folder from the messenger bag, handing it to Jimmy. He flipped it open, and his eyes moved up and down as he looked at something.

"Ah, yes. You're sitting on top of a seven-hundred, fifty-thousand-dollar mortgage here. You pay... Wow! Who's Kiernan O'Day? You pay him a hundred-and-fifty grand a year to do what?" Jimmy glanced up at me, that smirk I was coming to hate in plain sight.

"What, are you stalking my finances now?" I griped, standing from my chair and sending it into the wall of shelves behind my desk, the awards I'd won from the Chamber of Commerce and other civic and charitable organizations, along with the plaques from Ford Motor for record sales, rattling with the force.

Jimmy glanced at Alby, handing him the folder before he offered a fake smile. "Alby, will you please go hunt up Mr. Caldor and me some coffee?" The guy scrambled from his chair and was out the door like a shot.

Jimmy then turned his attention to me. "I wasn't stalking you, *per se*, but I never go into a business venture without all the facts," he pointed out. I wasn't surprised with his logic. I couldn't imagine what he was worth. I'd seen things in the business pages and on television about the wunderkind, JJ Lewis, but I never put it together that he was the runt who nearly sunk *me*.

"You found a way to channel your hacker energy, then?" I asked him. I studied Jimmy, seeing he was starting to get nervous, and I smiled, a small bit of satisfaction settled into the pit of my gut.

"Mabry, I'm very sorry about all of that. I was young and stupid back then. I had a massive crush on you. You'd been nice to me and taken me around to parties—"

"Where you proceeded to get hammered behind my back," I reminded him. His cheeks flushed an adorable pink, and for a damn minute, I was looking at the cute young guy I'd met ten years ago.

"Look, that's all—"

"No, no. You have every right to be pissed about what happened back then. I was an impetuous brat. My parents were overbearing, and I looked at every authority figure as substitutes for them. I was stupid for doing what I did, and I'm awfully sorry," Jimmy offered as an apology.

My heart nearly melted, but then I remembered having to vacate my dorm room for a month and sleep on a couch in the apartment Grayson March shared with Quincy Thompson, biting my tongue every time they laughed when they walked by me and all my worldly belongings.

The devil on my shoulder wanted to tell Jimmy Lewis to fuck off, but that one better angel—who sounded a hell of a lot like my mother—told me to give the adult Jimmy the benefit of the doubt. I came out of that ordeal a much stronger person, didn't I?

I sighed, tapping my fingers on the desktop. "Fine, Jimmy—JJ—I accept your apology. Now, thanks for dropping by," I offered and stood to escort him out.

"Wait. I seriously want to work with you on this game. You're an incredible athlete, and you've done a lot of charity work in the southside of Chicago—paying to rehabilitate an abandoned warehouse to make a community center that you solely support; donating vans and vehicles to charities around town to help those in need; all of the stuff you've done at children's hospitals..." Jimmy recited my charitable accomplishments. It was my turn to blush.

"Most of it was done under anonymity. How'd you find this information?" I growled at him and remembered exactly why I disliked him in the first place.

"Your accountant had to provide substantiating evidence for the dealership to take the tax deductions. It's not hard to find, Mabry. I didn't mean to violate your privacy—"

I cleared my throat. "Again."

Jimmy began wringing his hands, "Again, but I want to help you—yes, and myself in the process. Look, please have dinner with me and let me make my case. I have a very lucrative offer for you that can wipe away all of your debt, and I'll use my influence to get your father into a top-notch rehabilitation facility that my family's foundation sponsors. I don't know what happened to him, but based on what I found about Kiernan O'Day, he's a rehabilitation nurse who you pay a hefty sum to take care of your father. We—you and I—can help each other in many ways, Mabry."

He reached into the breast pocket of his suit jacket and retrieved a folio, flipping it open and pulling out a business card. "My cell number is on the back. Think about it, and please, call me. I owe you for what I did to you back then. Please let me make it up to you. I'm dying…"

"May, there's an emergency call from your mom. She's been trying to call your cell." It was Gloria over the intercom on my desk, so I quickly picked it up.

"Mom, what's wrong?" I asked.

"Dad's had a seizure. They're taking him to University Hospital," Mom rattled off quickly, the commotion in the background making it hard to hear her.

I plugged my other ear, not that there was any noise in my office… except the closing of the door as Jimmy left.

Look out for "Mabry's Minor Mistake"
this holiday season!

ABOUT THE AUTHOR

I grew up in the rural Midwest before moving to the East Coast with a dashing young man who swept me off my feet, and we've now settled in the desert of Nevada. I write M/M contemporary romance, subgenres: sweet low angst, age-gap, cowboys, mysteries, and military/mercenary to name a few. I am a firm believer in "Love is Love" regardless of how it presents itself, and I'm a staunch ally of the LGBTQIA+ community.

    I have a loving, supportive family, and I feel blessed by the universe and thankful every day for all I have been given. I'm old enough to know how to have fun, but too old to care what others think about my definition of a good time. In my heart and soul, I believe I hit the cosmic jackpot. Cheers!

DON'T MISS OUT...

On The Rocks
(Forbidden Romance)

Whiskey Dreams

Ima-GIN-ation

Absinthe Minded

The Men of Memphis Blues
(Sports Romance)

Kim & Skip (Prequel)

Cash & Cary

Dori & Sonny

May/December Hearts Collection
(Age Gap Romance)

A Wise Heart

Heart of Stone

Weighting...
(Cowboy Romance)

Weighting For Love

Weighting For Laughter

Weighting For A Lifetime

Weighting... Complete Series Boxset

Elves After Dark & Dawn

(Urban Fantasy / Holiday Romance)

My Jingle Bell Heart (Christmas)

Georgie's Eggcellent Adventure (Easter)

Standalone Books

The Secrets We Whisper To The Bees

(Crime & Mystery)

Sinners' Redemption

(Priest & Ex-con Forbidden Romance)

Unbreak Him

(Dark Romance)

Holiday Gamble

(Christmas Romance)

Printed in Great Britain
by Amazon